The Trials of Nellie Belle

The Trials of Nellie Belle

a novel

SYDNEY AVEY

Torchflame Books
An imprint of Light Messages
Durham, NC

Copyright © 2018 Sydney Avey
The Trials of Nellie Belle
Sydney Avey
sydneyavey@gmail.com

Published 2018, by Torchflame Books
an Imprint of Light Messages
www.lightmessages.com
Durham, NC 27713 USA
SAN: 920-9298

Paperback ISBN: 978-1-61153-248-7
E-book ISBN: 978-1-61153-247-0
Library of Congress Control Number: 2017941368

For my family, with gratitude and compassion
for those who went before us,
with wonder and awe at the present generations,
and with hope that our stories, inspirational and cautionary,
will nurture generations to come.

Acknowledgements

*H*eartfelt thanks to family members down through the generations who have supported (knowingly and unknowingly) the telling of this story: to my great grandmother, Nellie Belle Scott, for writing and preserving the short stories that made their way into my book; to my grandmother, Opal Nellie Wolff, and my mother, Shirley Jane Matheson, for passing down to me Nellie's writing and Leone's scrapbook; to my cousins, Dorothy Meyer and Nancy Bishop, who spent an afternoon listening to me tell my story and gave me their blessing to write this book; to my sister, Cheryl von Drehle, my daughter, April Avey, and my good friend, Arnette Cratty, for their feedback and encouragement; and to Joel Avey for helping me maintain balance between work and rest.

No published book is the author's product alone. Thanks to development editor Marcy Weydemuller, copy editor Katie Vorreiter , and publisher Wally Turnbull, for their diligence, gifts, and talents. Also to author Jane Kirkpatrick for suggesting that "the quiet one" in my story might have a larger role to play.

Finally, to my church family at Groveland Evangelical Free Church for their prayers, and my communities in California and Arizona for their support.

1

A Progressive Woman

Spokane, 1906

*T*ry as she might to convince herself that her daughter's death was not her doing, Nellie could not help but feel that her price for freedom had been Mabel. She smoothed a hand over the faded quilt spread on the grass, stretched her legs out in front of her, and reached her fingers into the damp weeds sprouting on the knoll that marked the young woman's grave.

"John sent flowers," She told her sister.

"That was nice." Jessie reached over and touched the gold locket nestled against Nellie's breastbone. Nellie slipped her hands behind her neck and undid the clasp. She opened the pendant and let it rest in the palm of her ringless left hand. The two women sat shoulder to shoulder, scrutinizing the photo inside, the familiar face so full of the promise of things to come that never would.

Nellie allowed her sister to wrap dry fingers, roughened by housework, around her own well-tended hands. She winced when Jessie squeezed a little too hard. She knew what Jessie would say. Selfishly, she wanted the comfort of her sister's forgiveness and blessing.

Nellie hadn't always been interested in what Jessie had to say. Growing up in a three-room sod farmhouse, squeezed between two older brothers and this afterthought of a sister, she often stuffed her ears. Sounds that she did respond to tended to be solitary in nature—

the clop of her paint pony's hooves as she raced him across the north-central plain; the ding of a bell as the Kansas Pacific chugged through the crossing and departed. Her ears were tuned to the sounds of freedom. But as the sisters grew older, Nellie came to value Jessie's opinion more. After all, Jessie was the first to welcome Nellie and her husband John to the West and the last to criticize when Nellie left John.

Nellie had waited to make her escape until their son Johnny was seventeen. Twenty-year-old Mabel and ten-year-old Opal would accompany her on a summer trip to Spokane. Johnny would stay behind and work with his father in the building trade.

"Johnny and I will be just fine, Nellie Belle." John had stepped forward and placed his hand under her elbow to steady her as she boarded the northwest-bound train. "Don't you worry none about us."

Johnny had handed luggage up to his sisters and flashed the same rakish smile his father always employed to charm the female members of his family. *Dear boy.*

Today, Nellie held back her tears as she had done five years ago when she blew her son a kiss good-bye, caught her husband's eye, and raised her hand in farewell. Etched in memory were their hearty waves as the train pulled back from the station, their jaunty steps as they walked away, their arms wrapped around each other's shoulders.

Jessie took the necklace from Nellie, pinched the heavy locket shut, and handed it back. "I think you should go. It would help you get past this terrible grief."

"What about Opal?"

"She can come stay with us if she wants to."

Nellie tugged up a ragweed rosette, shook dirt from its root ball, and added it to a neat row of weeds she absentmindedly plucked. "She's a funny one, Jessie. She says she hates to be alone in the hotel when I'm working, yet she wants to go New York and audition for the stage."

Jessie shielded her eyes from the high noon sun and searched Nellie's face. "She's a bit young for that, don't you think?"

"She's almost sixteen. A dancer's life is short. I think she should give it a try."

Jessie's eyebrow shot up.

"I know what you're thinking. But I raised Opal differently than I raised Mabel. Opal is city-wise. She's the quiet one, but her spirit is strong."

"And Mabel?"

"My Mabel was a good girl. A sweet girl. Trusting, too trusting."

Jessie frowned. "What do you mean?"

Nellie poked her finger into a dirt hole to dislodge a beetle that had just lost its cover. "I mean, she was naive. In her world, all people wanted the best for each other. All flowing water was clean …"

A small shudder twitched her shoulders and threatened to rupture the place in her soul where grief lay tightly lidded. She bid tears not to form.

"Mabel lived as though she were immune to threats," Nellie said.

"And so did we all when we were children."

"But she was not a child. She was twenty when she died. No amount of cautioning held any sway with her."

"We none of us knew. Even the doctor didn't know."

It had been on a hot day at a family picnic that Mabel had walked down to the creek, cupped her hands, and lapped the cool water. A few days later, she developed a fever. When her fever spiked, the doctor assured Nellie it was a good sign. Her body was fighting an infection, he said. But after three weeks of no improvement, Mabel descended into delirium and died. The infection she had been fighting was typhoid. The doctor had missed the signs.

Jessie ran her fingers through her untamed curls; an old-fashioned do for the day. "Funny, I don't remember you being the cautious type either."

Nellie snorted. "Given that I am contemplating taking assignments from the court that will have me traipsing all over the Northwest, I suppose you are right."

"You have worked hard for this. Working your way up in the steno pool, getting your court reporter's certificate—I'm so proud of you."

Nellie sighed. "It is the only thing I have to be proud of. I made a mess of my marriage. I have not been all that good a mother ..."

Jessie placed her fingers against her sister's lips. "Shush." Then she stood and held out her hand to help Nellie to her feet. Standing side by side, they circled each other's waists and gave one last moment of silent attention to the flower-laden grave of Mabel Leone Scott.

Just as Nellie fit her key into the lock of the hotel room she rented for herself and Opal, the door flew open.

"Where have you been?" Fifteen-year-old Opal stood in dark relief against the window light that filled the room. Nellie need not see her daughter's face to know her expression. Concern and aggravation tolled in the young girl's voice.

Nellie pushed her way past Opal into the living space they shared, not homey but comfortable enough. At least the rooms the Ridpath rented out to mostly single professionals were clean and new.

"You should have come with me, Opal." Before the small, slim girl could answer, Nellie dropped into one of the upholstered wing chairs that backed up to a pair of tidy twin-sized beds. She reached across a small table to pat the empty seat of the other chair. "Sit down; I have something I need to talk to you about."

Opal took measured steps in the opposite direction. She retrieved her sewing basket from a writing desk piled high with books and papers, unopened mail, and take-out menus. Opal set the basket on the small table and pulled out a dance costume she was decorating with ribbon trim. Without a word, she folded herself into the chair next to her mother and bent her head to her task.

Nellie looked down at her hands. She picked at the dirt crusted beneath the unpolished nail of her index finger. A quick scrub with a nailbrush would take care of it. How she wished she could as easily wash away the unsightliness of regret. Would she live to regret this new decision? For better or worse, she had set her foot on this path a long time ago. She would see it through.

"I have been offered an opportunity by the Spokane Superior Court to accompany the judge when he is required to travel and, on occasion, to go out by myself to record witness statements."

Opal kept her head down. She brushed a wave of dark hair out of her eyes and poked her needle through the red ribbon trim she was attaching to a black tarantella skirt. Her small fingers plied the needle tip in and out through the ribbon, picking up three more stitches.

"Opal, did you hear me?"

"I heard you."

"Well?"

Opal raised her dark eyes briefly and then returned to her stitching. "You won't mind, then, if I go to New York for audition season."

Nellie took in a quick breath. "You don't want to finish high school first?"

Opal set aside her project and launched into a sales pitch Nellie had heard before. The great stages were on the East Coast. Competition was fierce. Younger dancers had an edge.

"But fifteen is too young, Opal. Sixteen, maybe."

"Promise you will let me go to New York when I'm sixteen, and I promise to live here quiet as a mouse and finish the school term. No one will even know you aren't here."

Nellie relaxed. "I won't be gone all the time, and when I'm away, Jessie has offered to let you stay at her house." She looked at Opal and raised a questioning eyebrow.

"You know I can't do that. How would I get to my dance classes?"

A picture floated before Nellie, tiny Opal on a grassy hill whirling about with a beribboned tambourine. Where did that talent come from? Nellie's own feet refused to obey when Opal tried to teach her the box step, and John would have sooner eaten a beetle than attempt a two-step. Light on her feet, quick to learn, what Opal lacked in stature she made up for in flawless technique, or so the ballet mistress said. But what most impressed Nellie about her daughter was her patience with the children in their building.

Opal had stenciled flyers and drummed up business giving dancing lessons to the girls and boys who lived in the hotel. If Opal punched her ticket in New York, she could make a legitimate living as a teacher.

If only I had been able to begin a career so young. But to wish that would be to wish away her children, and that she would never do. Although she would never say it out loud, she knew she would not stand in Opal's way.

"All right, then. If you want to stay here, there are people you can go to if you need anything."

"I'm sure I won't need a thing, Mother. I've been pretty much on my own ever since you went to work."

Nellie let that go. She got to her feet and busied herself putting away the small stack of work blouses Opal had ironed and folded. "It will be good to know that you are here keeping house for us."

Opal pressed her lips together and gave a low grunt. "The hotel maids do all the cleaning. Most nights, I pick up dinner from a restaurant. I'd hardly call that housekeeping."

Nellie smiled brightly. "It may not be housekeeping, but I'd call it homemaking. You are the one who keeps us together, body and soul."

Opal put a knot where the ribbon trim met a seam and bit off the thread. "I will take credit for keeping us in clean clothes. Since we have stopped attending church, I'm not so sure about the state of our souls."

Nellie's shoulders slumped. How easy it had been to attend church when she and John sat like bookends, three children between them, performing their religious duties. After watching Mabel get sick, slip into a coma and die, all because no one recognized the symptoms in time, Nellie had not cared to sort out who to blame, the doctor, herself, or God.

Tell the truth. You didn't have the nerve to show your face in church after you left John. Nellie bit her lips.

"I'm sorry, Mother. I shouldn't have said that. I'm just confused, that's all. If God is not our comfort in time of need, then what's the point?"

"I'm not the person to ask. You will have to figure that out for yourself." Nellie pushed the dresser drawer shut a little harder than she intended. Softening her voice, she continued, "I certainly won't stand in your way if you want to go to church. I just don't feel comfortable. Someone always wants to know about my husband. It's nobody's business."

Opal shrugged. She stuffed her sewing back into the basket and jumped to her feet. "Let's celebrate your new job. Let's go across the street for some spit-roasted turkey at the Silver Grill."

A month after their celebration dinner, Nellie fastened the strap on her train bag and slipped an arm into her heavy tweed motor coat. Opal followed her to the front door.

"How long will you be gone?"

Nellie cupped her hand under Opal's chin. "Such a long face." She moved her daughter's face side to side. "But a clean one." She tapped her on the nose. "I should be back in two or three weeks. Walk me to the train station?"

Dawn light greeted them as their feet hit the pavement outside the hotel. The streets began filling with men and women on their way to work. Motorcars pulled up to curbs and took their places in a stationary parade that would line the streets all day. Nellie and Opal began the three-block walk to the station. The closer they came to the moment Nellie would board the Northern Pacific passenger train, the more Opal began to object.

"I've never been left on my own for so long."

Nellie kept walking. "We talked about this, Opal." She did not turn to look at her daughter's face. "You said you'd be fine, and you will. I raised you to be independent. You are almost grown, and besides, I will only be gone a few days."

Opal slowed her pace. "What if …" A distant rumble on the tracks prompted a flurry of activity. A clanging bell charged the air with excitement. The stately train pulled into view. Brakes screeched and hissed; trainmen, porters, and passengers spilled from the train; Opal's apprehensions were all but lost in the scamper and noise.

Nellie found her car and hefted her train bag up onto the first step. She turned to look at Opal. She threw out an arm and the girl came running. Nellie drew her in for a quick hug and leaned over to brush her lips across Opal's ear.

"This will be good practice for you before you go to New York," she whispered in a gravelly voice. "Jessie has promised check on you."

Passengers lined up behind Nellie and began to push. Nellie released Opal and climbed aboard. On the landing, she turned and shouted over the din, "Telephone Jessie if you need anything." She handed her bag to the porter, blew Opal a kiss, and entered the coach. Once inside, she found a seat by a window and drew the curtain across the pane. A large, matronly woman sitting on the aisle looked to be the type to discourage idle conversation. Good.

Nellie welcomed the long hours of solitude ahead of her. She peeked through the side of the curtain and watched Opal stand by the tracks until the last passenger boarded. When Opal finally turned to go, Nellie leaned her elbow on the windowsill, rested her head against the palm of her hand, and closed her eyes. *This is good for Opal. She'll be fine. God, let her be fine.*

Lulled by the rhythmic jostling of the train, Nellie drifted in and out of sleep. She was awakened by the conductor who asked for her ticket.

"All the way to Butte, Montana." He positioned his punch over her ticket and pronounced Butte with two syllables as he punched a hole in her destination. A chatty sort, he followed up with commentary. "Butte, Montana. A mine of opportunity for some." He twisted the tip of his handlebar mustache. "A pit of toil and trouble for some others." He winked at her and walked down the aisle.

I'll make mine opportunity. Nellie chuckled to herself and settled back into her seat. Hours passed, and her peace was interrupted only when stops and starts jolted her awake. Whenever the train picked up speed and cantered through mountain passes, she pulled back the window curtain and peered out. Sheer joy spread through her being. If there was a fountain of youth, this was it.

I am forty-four years old today. I have never been on my own. Not for one moment! Nellie reached into the satchel that held personal items and the tools of her trade. She pulled out a special treat tied up in a red and white checkered napkin. Almost reverently, she unwrapped the indulgence she had purchased for just this occasion. It lay glistening on the napkin in her lap; a devil's food cupcake smeared with thick buttercream frosting and topped with chocolate sprinkles. She had purchased two bakery cupcakes, leaving one behind for Opal to discover.

The first bite was the sweetest. Mama used to say that you can't have your cake and eat it too. *Then best to enjoy what you have while you have it. That's what I say.*

Nellie let the sweetness melt on her tongue, gathered every crumb from every cranny in the napkin folds, and dabbed the corners of her mouth with the napkin. When she finished, she looked up into the unsmiling eyes of the large woman sitting across from her.

"Was that good?"

Sourpuss. "Delicious." Nellie turned her head toward the window and began to dream. What enjoyment life might hold for a progressive woman, gainfully employed in respectable work, able to travel through life on her own.

2

The Miner's Wife

Montana, 1906

*T*en hours by train and a streetcar ride later, Nellie stood on the curb facing the Butte Hotel at the dinner hour. Downtown Butte was just as Judge Webster described. Electric streetcar tracks crisscrossed the boulevards. Horse and carriage rigs jockeyed with motor cars, clip-clopping past new hotels and restaurants—all this to serve the booming copper mining industry.

Exhaustion and hunger competed for her attention. Falling into bed fully clothed tempted her, but a short walk, a nourishing meal, and a bath would serve her better.

In her hotel room, Nellie splashed water on her face. "You can do this," she lectured her tired reflection in the mirror. A swish of rose-pink lipstick and a smile put the sparkle back in her eyes. A brisk walk in the mild evening breeze to nearby Mikado Dining Hall restored her confidence.

The Nesbitt sisters owned and operated the fashionable restaurant. As instructed, Nellie asked to see Annie Nesbitt.

"I am Mrs. Nellie Scott from Spokane. Judge Webster sends you his greetings."

"And more business, how delightful. I have the perfect table for you." Annie signaled her sister. "Katie, please take Mrs. Scott to the section reserved for our guests who wish to eat a quiet dinner undisturbed."

Nellie followed her hostess to the back of the dining hall where single diners relaxed over dinner plates, reading newspapers or jotting in notebooks. The only other woman dining alone kept her eyes on her plate as they passed. When Nellie was seated two tables away, the woman looked up and caught her attention with the merest smile and an almost imperceptible nod. Then she returned her eyes to her meal.

Nellie took note and trained her eyes on the menu and plates of food put before her. Between courses, she busied herself with her expense ledger. Three dollars a night for her hotel room, fifty cents for dinner; Butte was expensive.

When Katie brought Nellie the dinner check, she nodded in the direction of the single woman who was just finishing her coffee. "Mrs. Nora Hanley would like to know if you would care to walk back to the Butte Hotel with her."

"Wh... how did she ...?"

Katie laughed. "That's where most women who are traveling alone stay. Our streets are safe, but we encourage women to walk together at night."

Katie escorted Nellie to Mrs. Hanley's table, and after brief introductions and pleasantries, the two women strolled back to the hotel. Time limited their conversation to a polite exchange about what assignments brought them to Butte. Mrs. Hanley talked about her work as an organizer for the Women's Protective Union. Nellie wanted to know more about that.

In one evening, a whole new world opened to Nellie. Maybe it was time she joined a trade association. She determined she would put in her membership application to the National Shorthand Reporters Association as soon as she returned to Spokane.

The next morning, Nellie hired a horse and carriage to transport her to a small town outside Butte that housed miners and their families. The workers were predominately Irish, but Nellie read in a newspaper editorial that *no smoking* signs in the mines were written in sixteen different languages. Although knowledge of mining practices was not a job requirement, she had prepared herself for this assignment by reading everything she could about life in the mines.

Despite the enactment of laws to improve and monitor mine safety, fatal mining accidents were on the rise. Her assignment was to record an Irish miner's eye-witness account of an explosion that killed six in a mining accident. Mr. McGregory's testimony was part of an investigation into the practice of using unskilled immigrants to perform dangerous tasks.

Stepping down from the carriage, Nellie set her foot on the uneven surface of the rough road and wished she had invested in boots with thicker soles instead of such a fancy coat. She paid her fare and began her walk past a busy new housing construction zone. At the end of the road stood McGregory's ramshackle dwelling, one among many destined for replacement as soon as its occupants could afford to move.

Nellie approached the miner's shack, turning her head to take in the houses that shouldered each other on both sides. Children's toys lay scattered in the vegetable rows scratched out of dirt patches in front of each house, but not this one. She squared her shoulders, removed a glove, and rapped on the front door. Quickly, she pulled her hand back and examined the skinned knuckle of one finger that caught on a splinter in the wood. A small scrape, really, but it produced a sharp sting that put her whole body on alert.

She was sucking on her knuckle when the door inched open soundlessly, and the moon face of a female shone against the darkness inside. *The missus has taken care to oil the hinges on the heavy door,* Nellie thought. The door opened just wide enough for the woman to come into full view. A tidy person blinked in the daylight.

"Oh. Are you …?" The woman clasped her hands together and searched for words.

"I'm Mrs. Scott." Nellie stepped over the threshold and extended her gloved hand. "I've been sent by the court to—"

"Oh. Oh." The woman stepped back and smoothed her hands over an apron more stylish than serviceable. "My husband received a letter telling him to expect a representative from the court today, but I didn't think … well, I didn't think, did I?" She laughed and took Nellie's hand in both of hers. "I'm Mrs. McGregory. I'm so pleased to make your acquaintance. Come in."

Mrs. McGregory took Nellie's coat and led her through the tiny parlor to a dining alcove. "May I offer you a cup of tea while we wait for Mr. McGregory to return from an errand?"

Nellie nodded, and her hostess busied herself lighting a burner under a copper teakettle and setting out two shabby teacups and saucers. Under these circumstances, one would expect the miner's wife to be worn out as well, but that was not the case. Despite her pale complexion, the woman possessed a natural beauty that no amount of squalor could diminish: lustrous auburn hair, large green eyes framed with long lashes, ample curves admirably displayed on a well-proportioned frame. Tall women had every advantage. Nellie, always conscious of her tendency to gain weight, hoped not to be offered teacakes.

"I can't imagine what is keeping my husband." Mrs. McGregory whisked the teakettle from the burner. "I read the letter to him. I made sure he understood the importance of his deposition to the government's case against the mine."

Nellie traced a finger along a wrinkle in the stiff cloth that topped the small dining table. A crisp crocheted doily attempted to conceal a patch of yellowed fabric. Too much starch.

Mrs. McGregory poured the amber-colored tea at precisely the moment Nellie's nose detected the scent of sulfur drifting through the open window. Hoping to dispel the odor of rotten eggs, Nellie drew the cup of steaming tea to her lips and breathed in the vapor. The mineral content overwhelmed any fragrance that the lemon balm tea leaves floating in rusty water offered. Nellie set the cup back on its chipped saucer and gazed around the walls.

The walls, absent the usual framed needlework or family portraits, featured fashion plates cut from *The Delineator* and *Fashionable Dress* magazines. Faded images of graceful women in feathered hats and ruffled skirts served as windows on a world the miner's wife had likely never seen and more likely never would.

Mrs. McGregory sat with her hands in her lap, worrying the thin gold band on her finger. She followed Nellie's gaze around the walls. "I am teaching myself fashion design." She cast her eyes downward. "It is my desire to throw myself into work that will help me forget my great tragedy." Her voice trembled. Raising a hand to the tatted lace trim attached to the plain collar of her dress, her delicate fingers played with the fine stitchery. "You see, my husband and I lost our only child, a boy I loved more than life itself.

For the next hour, Mrs. McGregory confided the grim details—a spooked horse, an innocent toddler, the collision of hoof and head. Nellie slipped her hand into the pocket of her black wool skirt. Her fingers searched for the delicately perfumed embroidered linen handkerchief she kept with her at all times. She pulled it out and dabbed the rosewater-scented finery to her upper lip, hoping to catch the thin trickle that either the sulfur smell or the sad story had coaxed from her nose.

Nellie looked around the room for a clock. Finding none, she reached into the folds of her skirt for the timepiece she kept on her chatelaine. What was keeping Mr. McGregory? Absently she asked her hostess what kind of work she hoped to find.

Mrs. McGregory perked up. "I wish to open a dressmaking shop." She chattered on.

What makes her think she could do such a thing? A prick of conscience brought to Nellie's mind the prairie girl she had been in her youth. She reprimanded herself sternly. *Of course, this miner's wife could achieve her dream. She could take in sewing, build a clientele, hang a shingle above the cottage door*, but Nellie had no time to pursue this thought.

The front door swung open and through a cloud of dust stomped Mr. McGregory. Mrs. McGregory's face turned white, and her hand flew to her throat, but Nellie laid her hand on the woman's knee and then rose to her feet.

The miner swayed on his feet and blinked at Nellie. "Who're you?" He narrowed his eyes at her.

Nellie stepped forward and put out her hand. "I am Mrs. Scott. You and I have an appointment to talk about the incident that has deprived you of work—a temporary condition, we sincerely hope."

It took a minute for Nellie's words to penetrate the whiskey fog that clouded the miner's vision. His face reddened. His right hand began to rise to shake hers, but he jerked it back before it made contact. Digging into his pocket, he brought up a handkerchief and placed it against his pant leg. He rubbed his palm clean, returned the hanky to his pocket, and only then did he give Nellie's hand a perfunctory shake.

"I'm pleased to meet you, ma'am."

"Come sit down at the table with me, Mr. McGregory. Perhaps your wife would be so kind as to bring us both a glass of water." Nellie returned to the table, pulled out a chair, and invited the miner to sit.

He looked behind him. His wife had moved silently to close the door and now stood leaning against it, her arms folded across her chest. "Get us some water," he told her in a toneless voice. He coughed and took a seat, put his right elbow on the table, and leaned over it so close that Nellie had to fight to keep from wrinkling her nose at the smell of alcohol and sweat.

How often had John come home from an "errand" in this condition? With less excuse than this poor man. Nellie composed her face into a stern but kindly expression.

"Mr. McGregory, I have a set of questions that an attorney has prepared. Your testimony will help us understand the conditions in the mine that may have led to the deaths of six of your fellow miners."

"It were the explosion what killed 'em."

That was the longest string of words the miner put together during the next hour. Nellie's questions met with stares and grunts, one- or two-word answers, head shaking, and eye shifting. It occurred to her that a court of justice two states away might be blind to the devil's bargain miners had to make between their livelihood and their safety. If he spoke against the mine operations, what might happen to him? She set aside her list of questions and began to probe on her own.

After another hour of questioning, Nellie uncovered the source of the miner's discomfort. Workers who spoke out went on a list of troublemakers. They were the first to lose their jobs in a slump. She put her notebook away and leaned back in her chair.

"Do you miss Ireland, Mr. McGregory?"

A light she had not seen before cleared his rheumy eyes. His native brogue began to play like a fiddle in the lower register.

Gently she interjected a question or two here and there between the narratives of his youth. She asked about the lads who arrived weekly to take jobs in the mines. What skills did they have? What training did they receive? What jobs were they given? Memories of the old country and affection for his countrymen brought McGregory's guard down, and he did what all good Irishmen do when they are in their cups. He told stories. On the record? Nellie wasn't certain, but sure enough, she'd wrestled the truth out of her reluctant witness. The greenest of the new arrivals were offered the jobs that more experienced miners refused to do.

Anxious to get back to her hotel room and write up the stories the miner told, she thanked him for his time. "Now, Mr. McGregory, you take care of that wound so it will heal properly. I will write up my report for the court."

The miner looked at the stump below his left elbow. He lifted teary eyes to Nellie's face. "I are never going back in the mine, are I, missus?"

Oh dear. Now Nellie needed a drink. She turned to the miner's wife, who had been silent for the last two hours.

"Thank you so much for your hospitality and the refreshing cup of tea."

The woman rose to accompany Nellie to the door. Nellie slipped into her coat, and just before she stepped outside into the street, she took Mrs. McGregory's hand. She lowered her voice. "You would be wise to seek work. I wish you much success in whatever enterprise you choose to pursue." She squeezed the woman's icy fingers. "I hope someday to see a shingle out for Mrs. McGregory's Dress Shop."

How did women with refined taste and obvious talent get themselves into such a pickle? Nellie's head ached. Her skin itched. Had she been right to give Mrs. McGregory advice that was certain to have disruptive consequences? Men like Mr. McGregory did not like their women to work. She removed the jumble of clothes she had tossed into her valise and began to fold and stack each item back in her bag.

We all make mistakes. How far back would she have to go to face *her* first mistake? Of course, her hasty marriage was not her first mistake, but perhaps it was time to stop laying all the blame at John's feet. The success of her budding career might depend on understanding her part in that failure.

3

Marriage and Escape

Kansas, 1879

Nellie stood before the preacher and married her father's ranch foreman in a small Presbyterian church ceremony in McPherson. She was seventeen. He was twenty-nine. A rough and tumble sort, it was Canadian-born John Henry Scott who talked Nellie's father into expanding the farm operation to include cattle shortly after he hired on. A wheat boom had restored what the locust had destroyed, and a season of prosperity had allowed the Carter family to build a modest ranch house. The mustachioed young man moved into the sod homestead the Carters vacated and into her father's high esteem.

John was a new generation of ranch boss. He was younger than the men her father usually hired to manage the ranch, but rough and weathered in the way of men who spent most of their time outdoors. To his credit, he spoke well, and he always cleaned up before coming inside the main house. When he looked at Nellie, though, his brown eyes twinkled under wild eyebrows in ways that unsettled her stomach and made her heart race. She liked that he never called her "little lady" when he tipped his hat, but she didn't know what to make of the saucy winks he gave her when her mother wasn't looking. Certainly he could not be attempting to charm her the way her rubber-faced brothers hoped to win attention when they pulled faces at the girls at church. John was her father's employee. And he was old. The very idea! What were her parents thinking when they pressed her to accept John's proposal of marriage?

Nellie's parents had no way of knowing about the deep wound she nursed over the loss of her first love the year before her wedding. Jessie had kept her confidence. Although Nellie had banished the wealthy Easterner from her hopes and dreams, his parting words were never far from her thoughts.

As he handed her a gift, the smile on his lips had stolen her breath. Feeling his eyes upon her, she had lifted the shiny object from the velvet box.

"It's a solid silver dipping pen," he said.

A friendly hand dropped down on her shoulder. She stared at the weighty object through tears she willed herself not to spill.

"You write so well; I thought it would be the perfect token of my gratitude."

Gratitude? That's it?

Perhaps she had agreed to marry John to bury the shame of that moment. She was a girl who would take what she could get. That included praise. She never forgot Eustace's genuine praise of her abilities. The new journal she had started began on a cautious note of hope, but all too soon its pages were crowded with bitterness and disappointment.

Dear Diary,

Although John is old, he is not unattractive. He recommends himself well to Father because he is an excellent ranch manager. Evidently, Father believes he can keep John in his employ if he indentures his eldest daughter to him in marriage. No one seems to care what I want.

I want to leave this locust-infested land! I want to see some of the world I only read about in books. I want to travel and have adventures, if not in the East, then in the West. John is well traveled. He came here from Canada; why should he not want to go west where there are real opportunities?

I am determined to be a good wife to John and help him make something of himself.

Nellie had taken the twinkle in John's eye for a smitten heart. His careful manners made her feel safe. His furtive kisses thrilled her. Only after the wedding did she discover that the gleam she mistook for true affection was, in fact, a cockiness born of hard times, hard work, and hard living.

> Dear Diary,
>
> As Mother instructed, I am a dutiful wife in bed. I always allow John to have his way. He certainly seems to enjoy what we do, but if there is pleasure in it for me, I don't know how to find it.
>
> That his parents came from Canada for our wedding and are still with us does not help the situation! When John reaches for me, all I can think about is Rebecca and Jobe sleeping on the other side of our thin bedroom wall. I try not to make a sound, but John is not so cautious. The only saving grace is that he is quick. Afterward, he sleeps like the dead. I lay awake for hours, wiping away tears that trickle from my eyes and plug up my ears.
>
> What did I expect? I thought I might find some deep comfort for the uneasiness in my body in the arms of my husband. Perhaps one day, if we ever have time alone.

John's parents never did return to Canada. Shortly after Mabel's birth, Nellie cornered her husband out behind the barn where he was supervising a delivery of limestone.

"I can't live like this, John."

"Nellie, can't you see I'm busy?" John checked an inventory list while the farmhands unloaded pallets of boulders and slabs.

"You are always busy." The pallet hit the ground with a *thwack* and raised dust that stung her eyes. She stomped her foot and shouted above the din. "I have to talk to you now."

"Not now, Nellie. Wait until I make sure this order is complete." He waved her away as if she were a pesky fly.

Nellie marched past the soddy where they lived, down to the pasture where she could sit in the shade underneath the eastern cottonwood tree. She removed her straw hat and set it on the grass, then lifted her hair and let a small passing breeze cool the back of her neck.

From the house, Mabel's wailing was all but lost in the wind that blew through the tall grass. She should be napping. Undoubtedly, Rebecca would pick the baby up if she kept hollering.

Nellie put her hands to her ears and laid her head on her bent knees. Marriage was not the escape she had hoped and prayed for. She was still her parents' daughter, and now she was her husband's wife, her baby's mother, and her in-laws' servant. Not fair. Rebecca and Jobe helped out, but they had old ways of doing things that drove her mad. Take soap: you could buy it cheap these days, but Rebecca insisted on making her own. That was work and mess on top of the work and mess Nellie already had keeping her house and baby clean and her husband and the hired help fed.

The breeze stilled, and the air around Nellie closed in. She raised her head and opened her eyes. There was John, squatting down in front of her. He touched her cheek with his rough, calloused hand.

"Nellie, I know this is tough on you, but you know what I'm doing up there?" He nodded in the direction of the barn. "That delivery is material for a new limestone house I'm going to build for us."

Nellie stared at her husband. Hot tears sprang to her eyes. "You are building a house?" She wiped the tears from the corners of her eyes with the palms of her hands. "And you didn't tell me?"

John smiled the way he used to when he was courting her, but she knew better now. He had given no thought to her desires, had no idea what she wanted—not then, not now. She shook her head violently.

"I don't want to stay here."

John rose to his feet and offered her his hand. "Come back up to the house, then. I'll knock off early, and we'll talk."

She slapped his hand away and leaped to her feet. "John! I don't mean I don't want to stay here under this tree; I don't want to stay here on the farm. I don't want to stay here, in …" She spat the word. "Kansas!"

He took off the flat-brimmed nut-brown hat she had bought him as a wedding present, looked up into the tree, and ran a hand through his hair. Facing her, he placed the hat over his heart and bowed his head. "Nellie, I'm sorry I didn't talk to you first. But you know, you'll feel better when you have your own house. You will." Then he walked up the gentle slope toward the soddy.

Nellie took several deep breaths. The afternoon sun passed from behind the tree to the open sky and glared down on the back of her neck. Was John right? Would having her own place make a difference? She tried to imagine herself the mistress of a house like her mother's, but her mind offered no picture.

From the paddock at the other end of the pasture, she heard her pony squeal, a noise he made when someone approached him too aggressively. She tried to return her thoughts to the home John proposed to build for her. *I don't want a house of my own. I want freedom.* So clear as to almost be audible, this thought shook her from her heated stupor. She reached down and picked up her hat, set it on her head to relieve the discomfort at the back of her neck, and went to see about her pony.

Eight years passed and the family grew. One late afternoon, Mabel played with her younger brother Johnny in the house while Nellie rested in her rocker on the porch that wrapped around the house John had built for her. She was pregnant again.

To blot out awareness of the pain in her lower back, Nellie closed her eyes and paid attention to the catch in the rhythm of the rockers as they moved across the uneven floor joists. The groan and squeal reminded her of the onset of labor pains that would begin any day now. She didn't want to think about that. She opened her eyes and looked across the pasture to the empty paddock where her pony used to exercise. John had offered to buy her another horse after Patches died, but she said no—they had enough mouths to feed. She didn't want to think about that either.

For as far as she could see, dead grass, deserted outbuildings, and dusty farm equipment moldered in the sun. Their neighbors were moving off debt-ridden farms into small towns springing up nearby.

Nellie's head began to nod. She was slipping into a familiar dream when a crash inside the house brought her to her feet. In the kitchen, broken glass littered the counter and Mabel stood in a puddle of milk, crying. No blood, thank the Lord.

"I'm sorry, Momma, I was trying to get dinner started for you, but Johnny grabbed for a slice of cheese and knocked over the milk before I could cream the potatoes." Mabel grabbed a dishrag and dropped down to wipe up the mess. "I'm not very good at this." She glared at Johnny, who was hiding under the kitchen table.

A sharp pain in the small of her back alerted Nellie that she had best settle things quickly. "It's okay, sweetheart," she told her oldest. "Your father won't be home for dinner tonight, so let's just have some cheese toast and finish up the corn soup."

"*Ewww*." Johnny pulled a face. "It's got cabbage in it. I hate cabbage." He scooted out from under the table and ran outside.

After the children had been fed and put to bed, Nellie returned to her porch rocker. In her hand rested the silver pen she usually kept wrapped in its turquoise-colored satiny gift paper and buried in her letterbox. She loved feeling the weight of it resting in her palm, loved rolling her treasure gently between her fingers and the palm of her hand. She opened the journal that lay propped on her large belly and began to write.

Dear Diary,

While John stays out nights carousing with what few farmhands we have left, I sit here in this deserted wasteland and wonder what is to become of us? Rebecca dead and Jobe off courting a widow woman—in Michigan of all places. The old coot! My poor brother, Louis, lost to us from influenza before he was twenty. Frank and Jessie, married and gone. Even mother and father have moved to town. What am I to do with myself?

Mother comes to visit and play with the children, but she never stays long. She has made a remarkable transition from farm wife to townswoman. How I envy her.

Never would I have imagined that John and I would be the last holdouts. I must get him to see the folly of fighting the times.

When John stumbled home later that evening, Nellie handed him a mug of coffee and raised the subject again. His answer was the same.

"We can weather this, Nellie. I ain't leaving this land. It's all we got." He looked at her swollen belly and shook his head. "Things will turn around. They always do."

Nellie shivered and pulled a knit shawl tight across her shoulders. She lowered herself into a chair and tried to ignore the rolling twinges in her abdomen. "We have no indication that will happen anytime soon, John. We've not had cattle to run since the Great Die-Up. We can't sell our crops. We can't even sell our land. Let's just go. Now, before winter sets in."

John stood at the window, peering out into the darkness of a starless night. He raised the mug to his lips and drank the murky brew down to the dregs. "That's bitter, woman." He set the cup down on the windowsill." What did you do to it?"

"I double-brewed it."

"You used twice the amount of coffee?

"I reused the grounds from this morning."

John grimaced. "You trying to poison me?"

"I'm trying to sober you up and talk some sense into you, John. We could do better if we left this farm."

He continued to stare into the darkness. "I don't know."

Nellie pushed herself up out of her chair and duck-walked over to her husband. She touched his arm, and when he turned to face her, she ran her hand gently across his furrowed brow.

"John, this will be an adventure." With effort, she raised up onto the tips of her toes as far as she could carrying the weight of their child, kissed him lightly, and smiled. "You used to be so adventurous. Don't you remember?"

John put his arms around her shoulders and held her in an awkward embrace. He whispered in her ear whiskey-soaked words that turned her stomach but brightened her hopes. "Adventurous enough to father three children on you, Nellie Belle. I suppose if you want to raise them in a town, we might think about taking ourselves a little trip out West to see what all the fuss is about."

Nellie took a sharp, inward breath and waited for her husband to release her. The light in the room was nearly gone, the temperature dropping. Cold air slipped in through gaps in the doors and windows, and groans and squeaks from the cast-iron radiator signaled bedtime. John stepped away and searched her face for a reaction.

Passing her hand over her ear, chilled now with the dampness of his breath, she tried not to sound like a little girl who had just been promised a trip to the circus. "Out West?"

"Sure. I got a brother in Los Angeles who wrote me. He's got something going there. Says he can fix me up with work if I want."

"Why didn't you tell me?"

John frowned. "Because this is my decision, Nellie."

Nellie hugged herself, not from the cold but excitement. *California! Land of opportunity. I can't wait to see the ocean!* At just that moment, a warm rush of water gushed from between her legs.

"John, it's time."

He frowned at her. "I say when it's time."

She laughed and then gasped as a contraction started. "Not in this instance."

John sent one of the farmhands for the midwife, and a baby girl was born early the next morning. They named her Opal.

In the months that followed, letters from John's brother Samuel were full of assurances that work was plentiful for skilled laborers and tradespeople. Surely trade labor would be a step up from farm labor, but Nellie kept a tight lip on any suggestion that John should consider what skills might be required out West and set his mind to learning a new trade. He did not take kindly to advice she offered unless he asked for it. He didn't ask. Neither did he seem in any hurry to make the move to which they'd agreed.

One day, Nellie found a letter l on John's desk informing him that a construction job was open. *You better move quickly on this one,* Samuel had written. He had found them a house to rent in East Los Angeles.

Nellie read the letter through carefully, looking for a hint that Samuel had any idea about the housing needs of a growing family. She found no such sensibility, only ramblings about a happy reunion of the clannish Scott brothers. It had not occurred to Nellie that a new opportunity for their family to prosper was not as strong a draw for John as a chance to be with his brothers again.

If she and John were indeed to have a fresh start, she needed to make her feelings clear to her husband. She waited until the older children left for school and baby Opal was down for a nap. When John came into the kitchen from the morning's chores, she handed him a cup of coffee. He raised the mug to his nose and sniffed cautiously.

"It's a fresh cup." She laughed. "Single brew." She poured a cup for herself and sat down at the table. "John, when we move, I want us to choose our own neighborhood. This time, I want to choose the house." She held up the letter she had found on his desk and tried to muster a smile that communicated a confidence in him she didn't have. "And wouldn't *you* like a say in what kind of employment you accept?"

"Accept?" John sputtered and set his mug down so hard that hot coffee splashed onto the tablecloth and ate through the starch, spreading into an ugly brown stain. He grabbed the letter from her hand, balled it up in his fist, and threw it on the floor. Then he loomed over her, jabbing his finger inches from her face.

"Nellie, let's get one thing straight. The Scott brothers have always looked after each other. Anything Samuel has set up for us we will accept and be grateful that I don't have to do all the legwork myself."

Nellie's arms stiffened at her sides. She willed herself to say no more, but her will did not serve her well this day. She stood up and backed away so she wouldn't have to talk to the buttons on his chest. "Listen to me, John. We have an opportunity to improve our station in life. You don't have to be a farmer. You don't have to be any kind of laborer. You are a smart man. You're good with numbers. You can get a better job."

"A better job?" He held his rough, calloused hands up to her face. Splaying out his fingers with their dirt-encrusted nails, he dropped his hands for her inspection. "Dirt offends you?"

He rotated his palms and stared into them. Then he raised cold, angry eyes to her face. "I work with my hands. These are my tools. They put food on your table and clothes on your back. Don't you ever tell me what kind of work I should do."

Nellie opened her mouth to reply, but a quick run through her reservoir of retorts came up dry.

The anger in John's eyes melted into defeat. "I done right by you, Nellie Belle, just like I told your father I would. Remember, this move was not my idea. If it wasn't for Samuel, I would not be making this move at all."

Quietly, Nellie ended the conversation. "May I remind you that you are not making this move alone? You have a family that depends on you. We are all making this move together." And she said no more.

4

A Gypsy Life

Idaho, 1907

*J*udge Webster had been pleased with Nellie's report. "It seems that, in addition to filing your reports on time, you have a knack for wheedling information out of people," he told his protégé. He encouraged Nellie to go ahead and volunteer to accompany him whenever he was scheduled to fill the bench in one of the provisional courthouses. She could look forward to assignments in small Washington, Oregon, and California coastal towns where court convened only once a year and also in newly constructed halls of justice whose growing cities could not staff their legal departments fast enough.

Nellie was finally free to do as she wished. Her daughter had moved to New York. After recovering from her disappointment that she couldn't dance her way around the strict height requirement for ballerinas, Opal discovered that vaudeville companies had no such limits. Vaudeville tapped into an audience for character dancing— the folk and national dances of the European immigrants who were hungry for cheap entertainment. This lower form of classical dance might command lower box office receipts, but it was high in demand on stages in New York, Toronto, and Chicago. Vaudeville opened her arms, and Opal stepped in.

Nellie spent long hours recording testimony in court, transcribing her notes into court reports, and keeping company with judges and attorneys who debriefed court cases in the evenings over glasses of sherry, brandy, or port. On the road more than she was at home in Spokane, Nellie wrote weekly to Opal.

My dear girl,

The Pacific Northwest coastline is breathtakingly beautiful. So different from the warmer waters of Southern California, where people splash in shallow tides to rid themselves of the itch and stickiness of life under a relentlessly cheerful hot sun. (It is a false safety, as all those sunburns can attest.)

I far prefer the bracing sting of brisk, salt sea air, and the deafening roar of huge waves breaking against the rocky bluffs. It is a sound as incomprehensible as the voice of God. Even the fog lifts my mood. It keeps me from looking too far ahead.

I am not a churchgoer these days, but when I stand on a cliff overlooking the ocean, I always say a prayer for you. I have no picture of what your life is like now. Half the time, I'm not even sure where you are. Many of your letters get returned before one with a new post office box number finally reaches me. I know you have left New York—with a dance troupe? For an audition? The address I have for you now is Toronto, but you mentioned Chicago in your last letter. No new address though, so I hope this reaches you.

I am not complaining! This is your time, and I would not have it otherwise. But I do worry. There is something about you being the other side of the Rocky Mountains that makes me feel like you've gone to the moon.

While you are dancing and going to the theater, I am working long hours in the courts. I'm thinking about giving up our room at the Ridpath and looking for a cheaper headquarters for the two of us.

Ever,

Your mother

Many weeks passed before Nellie received a telegram from Opal.

MOTHER,

BOOKED AT CHICAGO AUDITORIUM DANCING CHINESE
CHARACTER POLKA MAZURKA VIENNESE WALTZ COSTUMES
LOVELY PARTNERS LOVELIER NEW ADDRESS SOON.

OPAL

Partners. Men. Nellie had never stopped to consider the consequences of her young and attractive daughter being on her own. Had she prepared Opal for what might happen when she worked so closely with men? Producers, directors, male dance partners, stagehands? She supposed someone looked out for the interests of the young female dancers, but she had to admit to herself that she did not know.

Her situation was so different than her daughter's. She employed her age, experience, and professional demeanor to keep men in their place and her reputation intact. Despite Opal's insistence and Nellie's best intentions, should she have kept her daughter by her side a little longer?

To keep her worries about Opal at bay, Nellie threw herself into work. Young U.S. Senator William Borah was scheduled to deliver a political speech in Boise, Idaho. The powerful politician had been charged with attempting to defraud the people. So far, he had managed to evade trial over a questionable purchase of timberland he made as attorney for a lumber company. Nellie's assignment was to record every word the senator said in his speech.

She arrived in town late in the afternoon. On her way to the square where the senator was to deliver his speech, she strolled by the dress shops and was taken with a display of dainty handkerchiefs in one particular store window. Opal's birthday was coming up. Nellie had time. She entered the shop.

It was like stepping into a fashion magazine. Nellie had never been to Paris, but this must resemble a Parisian dress shop. In the center of the room stood an elegant display rack of handmade blouses in three slightly different styles, all cream color, all size small. Her doe-eyed daughter would look lovely in one of the blouses. How long would it take to have one made in Opal's extra-small size?

A careful arrangement of lingerie on a low table in the corner distracted her. Undergarments that peeked shyly from beneath more substantial dressing gowns warranted investigation. And the dresses; Nellie loved the cuffed blouson sleeves that left the forearms bare. The skirts fell to ballet length and featured rows of ribbon trim near the hem. Skirts seemed to be getting shorter these days.

While Nellie fingered covered buttons and admired the quality of the stitching, the proprietor of the shop glided soundlessly over to stand next to her.

"Do you like what you see?"

Nellie jumped. "They are lovely." Because she made it a practice to always look at the person to whom she was speaking, she raised her eyes. It was Mrs. McGregory!

Slimmer now and fashionably dressed, Mrs. McGregory's formerly pale cheeks were high with color. She gushed over her delight in encountering Nellie once again. As she chattered, she ushered Nellie around her dressmaking shop.

"Every article of clothing is handmade. My clientele are ladies who are willing to order and wait for something perfectly tailored to fit them."

When Nellie's eyes traveled to the shopkeeper's left hand and lit upon the thin gold band that still adorned her ring finger, Mrs. McGregory reddened and brought her hand to her throat.

"Oh, Mrs. Scott, I truly do not know what to do. My husband pleads for my return. He promises he will reform his whiskey-drinking ways. I know I have my duties as his wife, but ..." She left off speech and swept her hand around the room. Embroidered blouses with perfectly formed pleats at mutton sleeve shoulders; gored skirts with smooth French seams; these were the products of her hopes and dreams.

How had she managed this? Nellie pursed her lips. Certainly not without some help. Years of working in the courts had taught Nellie that women who challenged the standards of propriety usually had accomplices.

"My dear, I am not the person to advise you about that." Nellie consulted her watch fob and clicked her tongue. Turning her attention to the tray of embroidered handkerchiefs, she selected a cream-colored square embellished with delicate, grassy-green and crystal-white lilies of the valley. "However, I would very much like to purchase this lovely piece of your work."

Back on the street, Nellie bustled to the town square where a crowd was gathering. She should not have stayed so long at Mrs. McGregory's dress shop. It would be a struggle now to find a place close enough to hear the senator's words but far enough away to be out of his field of vision. She needed a place where she would not draw attention to herself while she scribbled in her stenographer's notebook.

A group of newspaper reporters gathered off to the side of the podium that the recently elected senator people called the Lion of Idaho would step up to shortly. Would she stand out if she joined them? She would be the only woman in their midst. Even so, she would be less likely to attract attention for jotting on a steno pad.

When the senator appeared, a cheer went up from the crowd. Nellie chose that moment to take her place alongside the newsmen and open her notebook. Just as she touched her pencil to her tongue to moisten the lead so it would move faster across the paper, she felt warm breath in her ear.

"You got a press pass, madam?"

Nellie took a quick breath and held it. She was prepared for this. Slipping an identification card from between the pages of her notebook, she held it up.

The breather whistled. "Officer of the court. That might work."

Nellie looked over her shoulder at him. "You had better start taking notes if you want to get your story." She used her no-nonsense mother voice. Then she glued her eyes to the senator's profile and started up her pencil.

"I'd rather get your story. Catch you at the reception?"

Without a look, Nellie gave her head a quick nod, and the newsman straightened up and did not bother her further.

An accomplished speaker, the senator spoke ardently on his favorite subjects: the evils of monopolies and the virtues of local self-government. Nellie had no time to reflect on the logic of his thoughts; she just recorded them. At the exact moment the senator finished fielding the last question, she snapped her notebook closed and stepped away. The crowd that pushed forward to be part of the glad-handing provided her cover. She made her way back to her hotel room, sorry to miss the public reception but convinced of the wisdom of her decision. In her experience, news reporters were a cocky lot, admirable when setting words to the page, but glib with women.

Sometimes Nellie wondered if she had been too hasty in leaving her twenty-year marriage. The protection John provided, while it chafed, freed her from the lecherous intentions of men who cared not if a woman came to ruin. Might there have been another way to satisfy her longing to experience more of life?

Alone in her hotel room, she contemplated the senator's words as she transcribed her notes. Whoever was attempting to build a case against the senator would find nothing of use in his very impressive public speech. This man who had represented big lumber interests now staked his political career on championing the sanctity and self-reliance of the common man. She knew from reading the papers that Borah took criticism for inconsistency. He didn't mind. He would quote the poet Emerson: "A foolish consistency is the hobgoblin of little minds." If true, then a woman's right to change her mind was not an amusing foible, it was a formidable indication of good character.

Nellie packed up her writing tools and prepared for bed. Sinking into the soft mattress, she pulled the sheets up under her chin and reviewed the day's events. What a surprise to find the miner's wife now the mistress of a dress shop. Mistress was most likely an apt description. How else could an impoverished woman become a business proprietor? An uncharitable thought, she admonished herself. *I am as inconsistent as the senator.* Wouldn't people find her own rising fortunes surprising? *In today's world, if a woman has vision, the will to work hard, and the sense to be beholden to no one, she can do well for herself.*

Nellie set the alarm on her Lady Liberty travel clock to 5:00 a.m. and turned out the light. In the morning, she would catch the train back to Spokane. Fourteen years ago, her first cross-country train trip had been new and thrilling. Now it was routine but still exciting. Back then, she could not have imagined hopping on and off trains, dining in restaurants, and sleeping alone in hotel rooms. She had almost forgotten what it was like to put everyone else's needs and wants ahead of her own.

Had enough time passed that she could visit the shadowy recesses of the past without nameless regret? Every time she tried to feel her way back, she was drawn instead to the light of her discoveries—the unimaginable beauty of the West and the vast potential of the human soul to invent the future. Fourteen years ago, her first glimpse of the West wiped the flat plains from her interior landscape, but not before her eyes were opened by an event that historian Hubert Bancroft dubbed inspirational to Americans and a revelation to the world. It was at the World's Columbian Exposition that she caught the spirit of a new era. So taken had she been by what she had seen, she had committed to memory the historian's description of a fair that "showed the power and progress of a nation where all are free to strive for the highest rewards that energy and talent can win."

5

Riding the Rails

Chicago, 1893

Samuel had continued to press John for a commitment to work with him in Los Angeles, but Nellie remained silent. Baby Opal was walking by the time Nellie saw her opportunity.

It took an economic catastrophe to convince John that his future as a cowboy in Kansas had dried up. The economy languished under a lingering cloud of deflation, a legacy from the Civil War. Shaky railroad financing led to bank failures, and panic ensued. Meanwhile, in Los Angeles, Irishman Edward Doheny sharpened a eucalyptus log and punctured an oil reservoir, sparking a migration.

Samuel's frequent letters described opportunities not to be missed, and finally, the family started packing. One Sunday after church, Nellie spread a picnic lunch out under the old cottonwood. While the children trampled paths in the tall grass and the bobolinks song bubbled in the blue sky overhead, Nellie suggested that they combine the move with a vacation. John surprised her by agreeing to the plan. They could take the Great Northern Railway excursion train along the northern route, Nellie proposed. That way, they could visit the World's Fair in Chicago and see Jessie on the way out to the coast.

"That will be mighty expensive." John adopted the same look he reserved for salesmen trying to sell him seed.

"Well, we can't go by covered wagon, John." Nellie had learned that gentle teasing made stronger inroads with John than did ultimatums. "People don't do that anymore. They all ride the train."

"How we going to pay for that?"

"We'll sell off everything here. We'll make a fresh start in California." Nellie pulled a railroad map from her basket and spread it out on the grass.

"Look here." Nellie traced her finger along the route she had memorized. "After a few days in Chicago, we get back on the train. Next stop is Minneapolis; then we see Jessie in Spokane, then we ride the rails over to Seattle, on down to Portland and San Francisco. And look here"—she put her finger in a little notch along the western coast of California—"we connect in San Francisco with the Southern Pacific Railroad for the trip south."

The corner of John's mouth ticked up and a sparkle Nellie hadn't seen for many months lit his eyes. When was the last time she had managed to tap into his sense of adventure? That, and the possibility of bragging to his brothers about visiting the Columbian Exposition, the four hundredth anniversary of Christopher Columbus's discovery of the New World, must have done the trick. He took the map from her hand and slipped it into his shirt pocket. "You see to getting yourself and children ready for the trip, and I'll take care of the arrangements."

A few weeks later, three children in tow, Nellie and her mother traveled to Topeka to shop for the long journey that lay ahead. They settled the children on the train seat across from them with a hamper filled with hard-boiled eggs, tomato toast, and jars of honeyed tea.

Amanda sighed deeply. "It was just a few years ago that a train from Edmonton, Canada pulled into the station and collected so many of our neighbors who decided to return home."

"I remember. That was a sight."

"Did you know they had whole cars for their household goods? Some of them who came here twenty years ago with nothing returned home with everything they had acquired during the good times. Others sold it all. They didn't want to be tempted to return. That's what they said."

John and Mabel, nine and twelve, vied for the window seat while baby Opal slept in her grandmother's arms.

"We will leave with little more than the clothes on our backs." Nellie folded her gloved hands in her lap.

Amanda shifted the sleeping baby and said nothing.

"A few trunks of clothing, that's all."

"You don't want to take the basics you will need to set up your new household?"

Nellie shook her head firmly. "I do think it's best to travel light. We'll be four weeks on an excursion train, and we have no idea what we are facing at the end of the journey. There is no telling how we will live, or what we will need."

"Oh well." Amanda looked down at the sleeping baby. She traced Opal's soft cheek with her finger. "You've not traveled before, but your husband has. I'm sure he will take care of everything."

Nellie stretched her shoulders, turned her head, and allowed the blur of vast stretches of recently introduced Kansas Sunflower corn to lull her as fields of bright leafy stalks whizzed by.

Amanda touched her hand. "Is this really what you want?"

Nellie turned back to face her mother. How much of what was in her heart could she tell her mother? "What I want is to live a life where my husband doesn't take care of everything."

"What do you mean?"

"All my life other people have made decisions for me—who I marry; where I live; what I can and cannot do with my life."

Amanda's face froze. "We never said you had to marry John."

I've gone too far. Nellie looked across the aisle. Two sets of eyes met hers. She tapped the corner of her lip. "You both have crumbs all over your mouths. Use your napkins." She looked back at her mother and lowered her voice. "Not in so many words. I can't talk about this right now."

"Well, we need to talk about it sometime. Moving across the country isn't going to solve a marital problem if that's your intention." Opal squirmed in Amanda's lap and raised her head. Amanda stroked the child's dark hair, moist from sleep and matted against her cheeks.

Nellie handed her mother a cup of juice to offer Opal. "Mother—"

Amanda cut her off with a stern look. "Word of advice. These are the hardest years of your life, raising children and struggling to keep a roof over your head. I understand that John needs to go where the jobs are but don't expect that anything will be different for you. You raise your children. You do what you can to support your husband, and if you have any energy left over, you thank God for your good health and volunteer your services in church and community. Your life doesn't have to be boring."

"That's the answer? Whip up another batch of cookies for the bake sale?"

"Don't be impertinent. Yes, by all means, there is the life of the mind. You can find time to read. And if cooking and sewing bore you, volunteer at the library."

The train slowed and blew a long whistle, a signal that they were approaching Topeka, but Nellie kept going. "What if I'd rather run the library, and get paid for my services?"

Without moving her lips, Amanda spoke through her teeth in low tones. "Then you shouldn't have gotten married and had children. No one held a gun to your head." She turned her attention to Opal and tickled the tot into a fit of giggles.

Once off the train, conversation dissipated in the din and clatter around them. Amanda weaved through the crowd, Opal on her hip. Mabel and Johnny tripped along after her, and Nellie straggled behind, lost in thought. Why had she let her mother drag her into such an unprofitable conversation? *I'm unfit as a wife, and a mother.* It wasn't that she wanted to earn a paycheck. Any money she brought in would do nothing to ease the tension between her and John. No: what she wanted was to use her mind to higher purposes than converting measurements in recipes. John had no use for a wife with a mind of her own. But her mother was right. She had made her bed.

Nellie raised her head just as her little brood turned the corner into the train station waiting room. She scurried to catch up, got past the older children, and reached out to tug at Amanda's sleeve.

"Look over here." She pointed out the Harvey House, known for excellent service and delicious meals. Panoramic windows glistened, drawing attention to the Harvey Girls bustling about inside, bibbed white aprons gleaming against their black dresses. "Let's treat ourselves before we shop."

Amanda handed Opal over to Nellie and reached for the hands of her other two grandchildren. "Let's do that."

―⸎―

Whatever discomfort the Scott family of five suffered on the long trip west would dim in the light of Nellie's memories. Where did John get the money to pay for a room at lake-front Leland Hotel in Chicago? Surely such a luxury could not have been covered by the money they made selling the farm equipment and household furnishings, but she decided not question him about expenses.

Thoughts about her parents' decision not to sell the land in case Frank or she and John ever wished to return vanished as soon as they pulled into Grand Central Station. More people milled about under the arched ceilings of the train shed than she had ever seen in one place. And the spectacular view from their hotel window? The prospect of reaching the fairgrounds by boat? Those benefits were well worth the five dollars they had to pay for one small room.

Since Opal was free, two dollars got them into the fair, and another dollar and fifty cents bought John and the two older children a twenty-minute ride on the Ferris wheel. While baby Opal struggled for freedom in Nellie's arms, Mabel and Johnny took their seats in fancy twisted-wire chairs. John stood next to them in the glass-paneled car.

Soundless but for a soft clink of chain, the monstrous wheel began to turn. Nellie had glimpsed the children's wide eyes and huge grins before the mammoth car rose so high in the air she could no longer make out faces. Brave, adventurous children. They would love California, she was sure.

The family spent hours at the exhibits. John called Nellie's attention to the household appliance displays that included a prototype of an electric dishwasher.

"Lookee here, Nellie Belle. This machine will make your job easier. We'll have to get us one of those."

"Hmm," was all she had to say. Other women gathered around the exhibit, oohing and aahing over Josephine Cochrane's invention. The wealthy matron, the story went, tired of having her expensive china slip through her servants' soapy hands and break. So she built the first automatic dishwasher, an engineering marvel.

Good and well if kitchen maid is your job, but I would rather be Mrs. Cochrane. I want to be out in the world using my mind, not stuck in the kitchen operating a dishwasher.

They moved on to the Midway Plaisance, where they listened to gypsy music and ate Hungarian sausage at the Orpheum. Consumer goods vied with cultural exhibits for the crowd's attention. They feasted their eyes and spent their imaginations and the contents of John's money clip on as many experiences as they could cram into a day.

John and the two older children loved the gewgaws and gadgets. Nellie and Opal preferred the music and dancing. Both older children received a commemorative coin as a souvenir and a few cents to purchase a new invention called a picture postcard. Nellie bought Opal a toy tambourine with ribbons and set the toddler down on a grassy hill to exercise her legs. Toward the end of the second day, John passed around a box of Cracker Jacks. Then, hot, tired, and sticky-fingered, they trooped back to the train and began the long journey west.

If the fair opened Nellie's eyes to the change new inventions might bring into their lives, crossing the Continental Divide opened her heart. No entertainment invented could surpass the thrill when the train wended its way through Homestake Pass in the Rocky Mountains and crossed the Great Divide. Granite peaks rose in the distance. Legions of junipers, pines, and aspens stood in attendance. Water danced the tarantella in rushing rivers. The panorama before her eyes cracked open a small hard seed in her soul that sprouted and opened to the sky. *From this moment, I will not be put in my place. Not if it means giving up seeing and learning and trying new things.*

Nellie's reunion with Jessie at the Great Northern Depot in Spokane brought her to tears, not so much because of the distance that had separated them for so long as the happy look of self-possession she saw on her little sister's face.

In the elegant clock-towered train station, Nellie set Opal down on her feet, and Jessie allowed her two-year-old daughter to slide down from her perch on her mother's hip. The little girls stared at each other. Jessie put a hand of encouragement at her daughter's back and pushed her gently forward.

"Opal, this is your cousin, Nellie Marguerite."

Nellie smiled down at Opal's inquiring eyes. "My namesake." She kissed her sister's cheek and laughed. "I hope these two will get along better than we did when we were girls."

John corralled the older children and offered to find lunch for them so Nellie and Jessie could visit before the family had to board the train again. Jessie produced some snacks for the toddlers, and the sisters settled themselves on a bench.

Jessie took Nellie's hand. "Oh, how I wish you were moving to Spokane so our children could grow up together."

"I wish so too." Nellie shook her head slowly.

"Spokane has come back from the fire. It will come back from the panic. There will be work in the mines and the lumber camps." Jessie squeezed Nellie's hand. "What has Los Angeles got that we don't have here in Spokane?"

"I'm sure I couldn't say." Nellie looked out the window to the comings and goings alongside the river. Then she faced her sister and blurted out her concern. "John's brothers are going to be living on top of us. We have had such a good time on this trip, but my concerns will be of no consequence once he has his brothers around him."

Jessie's face fell. "Oh, I am sorry. I didn't know that."

"I didn't know either. I knew Samuel was there. I didn't know about the others until it was too late. No matter, I will find a way." Just then, little Nellie pushed herself up to her feet and began a determined, if shaky, run for the door. Opal scrambled to her feet and followed. Like two inebriates, the little girls weaved through groups of travelers until they were apprehended. They giggled at the game and tried to pull away. When they could not secure release, they engaged in a howling duet that turned heads.

A scowling John came striding through the crowd with his charges in line behind him; their smeared faces showed evidence that they had found a place that served their new favorite food, hamburgers with mustard and ketchup. "Good heavens, Nellie. Can't you keep these girls under control?"

Jessie shot Nellie a look of sympathy. On the tracks outside, the train engines hissed and sighed. It was time to go.

41

6

Loosening the Reins

Los Angeles, 1894

*T*he house Samuel had arranged for the family to rent turned out to be a tiny cabin in an orange grove at the end of a long dirt road. The grove had once been part of a large ranch whose orchards had been purchased and parceled into lots to be sold. The citrus industry was slowly moving to the Central Valley, leaving a grid of irrigation systems that would turn the scenic floodplain into subdivisions of small farms and sprawling neighborhoods.

Nellie sat on the front porch steps, her children gathered around her. She looked out across the road dotted with yucca, and up into the empty hills. In the dirt yard, the men stood in a tight gathering, smoking cigarettes and belching comfortably after a meal of chili con carne.

Samuel stretched out his hand and pointed to a two story house with a barn in the distance. He swept his arm around in the direction of a smaller house, whose entrance off the road was marked by palm trees. "In time, this will all fill in with houses."

His brother Charlie pushed his hat back and wiped his forehead. "The American Dream; every house sitting in the middle of a garden with an orange tree in the backyard."

Brother Jimmy looked over to where the children played jacks on the porch step and trained his eyes on the back of Johnny's head. When the boy looked up, his uncle waved him over. Johnny dropped his handful of jacks and slipped into the circle between his uncle and his father. Jimmy tousled the boy's unkempt hair and added his piece to the conversation. "Have you ever tasted an avocado? They grow 'em down by San Diego. Man, they are tasty. The Mexicans, they smash 'em up with lime juice, onions and tomatoes, salt, other stuff I don't know—*muy bueno*." He kissed his fingertips.

My Johnny looks more like his father every day. Nellie called for her boy. "It's time to go in now, Johnny. You have homework to finish."

"Finished it." Johnny did not turn around. He moved closer to his father, who put an arm around his son's shoulder and pulled him off balance. John let go just as quickly, causing the boy to stumble. Johnny righted himself and laughed. The two of them reminded Nellie of the mule deer she had seen in the lower elevations of the San Gabriel Forest. In the spring, young bucks sparred with each other, testing their strength. She doubted that Johnny had finished his homework, but without John's support, there wasn't much she could do.

The sun beamed low in the grove now. Mabel had gone into the cabin to sit at the table and finish her homework. Nellie led Opal back inside, prepared her for bed, and tucked her into a small cot wedged between the wall and the double bed where Nellie and John slept. The only good thing about this arrangement was that there weren't likely to be any more children. John was too tired anyway. Forty-three and in his prime, nevertheless long hours swinging a hammer wore him out. After work, he was more likely to replenish his spirits from a bottle of whiskey in the company of his crew or his brothers than he was to come home to Nellie.

Evenings after the children were in bed she sat on the porch step hugging her knees and looking up and down the empty road. In all this open space, how could she feel so confined? It helped when she lifted her head to trace the endless sweep of the star-studded Milky Way across the night sky. She marveled that the galaxy seemed to have no beginning and no end. Tonight was so quiet that if she ceased listening to her complaining heart, she would hear the owl begin her hunt.

Nellie strained her ears to hear the soft hoot. She was rewarded instead with the joyful yip of a lone coyote in the distance. Soon the pup would be joined by others. She felt a tightness in her groin. *When was the last time I felt whooping, hollering joy?* Tendrils of her hair swished across her cheeks in the night breeze, triggering a memory of the days when she raced her pony across the plains, her loose hair flying. She reached behind her head and undid the pins that fastened her hair, shook it out, let it fall. Another memory shook loose of one night back in Kansas when the children had their own bedrooms. John had been full of hope for their future. Under the covers, he reached for her and all their differences melted away. One timeless moment of slow-dancing what was usually a rushed affair. That night, a guttural sound rose in Nellie that John had never heard before, not from a lady. As close to a whoop and a holler as she supposed she would ever get. It embarrassed them both. It never happened again.

Nellie re-pinned her hair. Far off, the lone coyote set off a chorus of noisy celebrants. What did they celebrate? Freedom to roam and howl and hunt for food, she imagined.

John had promised her that once he built up some savings, they would buy a lot and he would build her a house. She dropped her head into her hands and rubbed her temples. No! No, no, no. It wasn't the cabin that cramped. If he built her a mansion, like the Queen Annes in Lincoln Heights, she would still feel … what? Soul. Crushing. Boredom. Only sweet moments with her children kept her from despair. That, and the thought that they wouldn't be children forever. When her job was done, she would still be young.

Nellie released the breath she had been holding. She gave herself to the vast expanse of stars overhead and the symphony of revelers satisfying their hunger in the moonlight. But for the loosening of the reins on her horse, and following the sensations John raised in her that one time, when had she ever felt free? There were times. Listening to Dvorak's *New World Symphony* at the World's Fair took her out of herself. Cresting the top of the Rockies, the sight of nature's panorama dwarfed and enlarged her at the same time. Thrilling. Longing would kill her if she didn't find a way to satisfy whatever primal urge compelled her to pace her cage and chew at the lock, instead of her foot.

You don't have to chew your foot off to be free. Watch. Bide your time. Your turn will come.

It was the approaching turn of the century that turned up the heat on Nellie's plans. They had not argued. Nothing had changed. John continued to work long days at various construction sites and wile away his evenings telling stories at the local tavern or swapping tales with his brothers around the dinner table at one of their homes. Weekends, he took Johnny fishing. He spoke politely to Nellie and did not ask her any questions about how she filled her time.

For her part, Nellie kept a clean house and a full larder. The meals she prepared for her children were nutritious but unimaginative. She mended their clothing, corrected their homework, and dreamed about the day she could slip away, conscience free.

John had made it clear that he would not allow her to work for a salary, but nothing prevented her from volunteering to teach poor young women the Graham method of shorthand so they could get jobs.

Nellie smiled to herself as she recalled the day she pulled a copy of Andrew Graham's shorthand primer from a moldy box of books. Easterners had sent religious and educational books earmarked for the children of families whose fortunes had withered when locust stripped the wheat stalks bare. While her brothers fought over a copy of *The Youth's Companion*, she secreted away the tattered manual full of odd squiggles.

That winter, she assigned herself exercises from the book. She sweet-talked her brothers into reading aloud from *The Old Farmer's Almanac* so she could practice transcribing from speech. By her thirteenth birthday, she was proficient enough to accompany her mother to her historical society meetings in Topeka to record the speaker's comments so Amanda could write them up for the local town newspaper.

Back then Nellie did not consider her wizardry with a pencil much more than a parlor trick to amuse her mother's friends. Now the world was opening up to young women with secretarial skills who were unencumbered. Approaching her late thirties with Opal still in grade school, Nellie could not count herself young or unencumbered, but her experience teaching night school opened her eyes. She earned the praise of her students and the night school administration for her diligence and quick mind. She gave no hint that she had never employed her skills in the workforce. As the young women warmed to her wit and encouragement, the hope that simmered low in her heart flared. Seeking no advice, saying no prayers, she set Monday, January 1, 1900, as the day she would board a train for the Northwest and begin a new life.

7

The Sheriff's Report

Silver Beach, Oregon, 1908

Had it been only eight years since she made good on her promise to herself? It felt like a lifetime. Nellie's discoveries had surprised her. Boredom was an element of any life's work. Just when her children became interesting to her, they left. She missed them every day. And John was doing surprisingly well for himself.

This day the train headed to Portland, where she would connect with transport over to Silver Beach. There, the very attractive Sheriff McFarland waited for her. He had some explaining to do. A fish and game expert on the government payroll had gone missing, and the governor's office was not satisfied with the reports.

Nellie reviewed the scanty information she been given and jotted down a list of questions she intended to ask the sheriff. The bump and rumble of the train wheels on the tracks made working difficult, so she stuffed her papers back into her legal briefcase and reached for a small bag that held her few personal items; mirror, comb, lipstick, address book, pencil stub, and keys. And John's letter. She smoothed the paper over her knees and stared at the familiar script. Small, neat, looping letters marched across the page in perfect formation. Try as she might, her handwriting would never approach that of her former husband.

John had met a woman with a young daughter. In his letter, he did not mention that Leota was twenty-five years his junior. That she had to hear from Opal, who heard it from Johnny.

The old coot, John was just like his father, Jobe. At least John had let some time go by before setting a snare for a young woman. That wasn't fair. Jobe was likely looking for a nursemaid after Rebecca died. John still looked robust, handsome and cocky as ever. Most likely the young woman had set her cap for a working man who could provide for her and her child.

Nellie searched her heart for pangs of jealousy and satisfied herself that she felt none. Well, she might have a few reservations about the child. That another young girl would likely receive the attention Opal had missed from her father put Nellie out of sorts. *And whose fault is that?* The nagging voice of reason piped up. She silenced the self-accusation. No need to dredge up old reproaches.

The thrill she felt when she matched wits with her professional colleagues more than compensated for her occasional misgiving about her status as a divorced woman. Tiring though it was to be always on guard for the sake of her reputation, she was not as lonely now as she had been in her marriage.

If John and Leota did marry, as the letter suggested they would, she hoped the young mother and her daughter would exert a civilizing influence on her son and his father. Johnny was falling into the ways of his father that Nellie had most disliked. He was the same dirt-under-the-nails drover. Even though the two of them no longer ran cattle, their free-range ways bonded them in a joyous boys' club. They were impervious to the finer things in life.

Truth be told, not all cowboys put her off. While Nellie indulged her newly acquired taste for the dining-car coffee that sloshed in her thermos cup, her thoughts turned again to Sheriff Mack McFarland. They had worked together before, and very pleasantly. Places in her body she thought she had tamed long ago sprang alive at the very thought of the lanky lawman, who was known as an independent sort who used his own judgment. Why he was still a bachelor, she could not imagine. He was catnip; not a ladies man, but a man who truly enjoyed female company.

A sudden twinge in her lower back crowded out more pleasant thoughts. She'd best get up and walk through the cars to ease the stiffness long hours of travel imposed.

By the time Nellie reached Mack's office late in the day, her limbs were trembling. The combined weight of the briefcase she carried, her heavy black skirt, and the stiff motor coat that had yet to soften even after two year's wear weighed her down. Her toes, tingling in their tight boots, threatened to lose all feeling, and her fingers, armored in leather gloves, were nonetheless stiff with cold.

The solid wood door to the sheriff's office resisted her push, but she saw that Sheriff McFarland had spotted her through the window. He crossed the room in two steps and pulled the door open. Once inside, Nellie peeled off her gloves and beelined for the wood stove. The snap, crackle, and glow in the belly of the iron beast warmed her bones. Or was it the smile that spread across the sheriff's face?

"Good to see you again, Mrs. Scott." He clapped her on the shoulder and sat back down at his desk. While Nellie defrosted, Mack rolled a pair of bullets around on his desktop and peered at them through a magnifying glass he held to his eye. "Look here."

Nellie hung her coat on the coat rack. She walked over and stood behind him, training her eyes on his hand as he examined the surface of each slug.

"Do they tell you anything, Mack?"

"All I want to know." He craned his neck and swiveled his head around to look up at her. "But I can't arrest a dead man."

Nellie walked around to the front of the desk. She pulled up a chair and sat down opposite Mack. He laid the magnifying glass aside and leaned back, keeping his finger on the bullets, rolling them back and forth on the ink-stained desk pockmarked with deep scratches. "The Carnagan case is closed as far as I'm concerned, so you might as well go ahead and file your report for the governor."

Nellie laughed. "I've got to put something more in the report than what the governor has already read in the newspapers. He wants to know what happened to his fishing industry expert." Nellie let her bald request hang in the air for a moment. The clock ticked. The sheriff rubbed his stubbled chin. Outside the window, dusk turned to darkness and the street lights came on. "Say, when did you get electric street lights?" Nellie asked.

"The town fought it, but the town council converted to electric a few months ago." Mack shifted his gaze from Nellie's face to the window. She pulled her steno pad and a pencil out of her heavy case and sat up straight in her chair.

"The DA told me you knew the girl who was murdered."

"Sure I knew her. I've known Mary Marsh ever since she was a baby. Her mother keeps the Marsh House here at Silver Beach. But I imagine you already know that."

Nellie didn't acknowledge that she had already checked into the Marsh House and had a disappointing conversation with tight-lipped Mrs. Marsh. "And Charles Hudson?"

"Your government expert?" Yeah, I saw him a few times. He came out early one spring to look into some trouble with the fish. Flores Creek was full of dead fish. It created quite a stink." Mack smirked and looked at Nellie to see if she caught his joke.

"Funny." She repressed a smile.

"No, really." Mack tried to look serious. "Dead fish littered the creek bank for miles."

Nellie wrinkled her nose dutifully. Her pencil remained poised at the top of her notepad. "So, what was Hudson like?"

Mack leaned back in his chair and delivered the deliciously slow grin he was famous for, the one that let Nellie know she was in for a fish tale. She met his teasing eyes with a direct gaze that told Mack it better be a good story.

"Hudson was a standoffish sort. A real cold fish, you might say." Nellie winced, and Mack chuckled. "He did a little investigation and was getting ready to slip out of town when Mary Marsh came home from college. One look at Mary and he unpacked his bags and stayed the summer."

"So, not that standoffish." Nellie ran her pencil across the paper in quick movements.

Mack laughed and shook his head. "Mary had a sweetheart, Glen Carnagan. Hudson knew about that. Mary told Hudson she was going to marry Carnagan as soon as they'd saved up a little money. It made no difference to Hudson. He was one of those quiet fellows with cold gray eyes and a determination to have what he wanted."

"And he wanted Miss Mary. How did Carnagan handle this state of affairs?"

Mack's blue eyes twinkled. "There was no *affair*, Mrs. Scott."

"May I suppose, though, that little Mary practiced her Cleopatra arts on our handsome stranger?" Nellie rose from her chair and came around the desk to stand behind the sheriff. She bent over his shoulder to take another look at the shiny brass bullets.

Mack swiveled his chair around and pushed back to where he could get a good look at her. "Well, she was pretty, if that's what you mean." His eyes traveled from Nellie's face to the buttons on her blouse to her waist. Nellie took a small step backward and waited. Mack dug into his pocket and retrieved his pipe. Waving the pipe stem in the air, he continued his story.

"Anyway, the three of them were at the Marsh House, fishing and tramping the woods all summer. Hudson and Carnagan seemed to be pals. But along in August, Hudson got word that his father had died, so he went back to New York. Before he left, he told Mrs. Marsh he was coming back for Mary."

"But Mary married Carnagan." Nellie reached across the desk for her notebook. She flipped through it, checking her facts.

"The very next month."

Mack stood up, reached for a stained coffee mug sitting on a stack of papers on his desk, and headed for the coffee pot on the stove. As he moved about in close quarters, smells of tobacco, leather, and pine wood displaced the warm air around Nellie. There was a time when John had smelled of the earth and roused the same unsettling feelings she felt now. When had that stopped? In Los Angeles, when he came home every night smelling of tar and sweat, cigarettes and cheap whiskey. Her involuntary shudder at the sudden emergence of the country girl she had once been caught Mack's attention.

"Want some?" Mack put his nose close to the mouth of the pot, inhaled deeply, and clicked his tongue. "It boiled awhile ago, but it's still nice and hot. Do you good on a day like this, Mrs. Scott."

Nellie shook her head. "No thank you, Sheriff. I hold myself to one cup a day, and I had my ration on the train."

"You sure?" He held the pot up.

"One more and I'd be awake all night."

He was silent.

"Truly. A good night's sleep will do me better."

"Hmm." He poured the hot liquid into his mug and raised it to his lips. "That would do us all good."

What would it feel like, to have those warm lips tasting of coffee pressed to hers? Nellie's cheeks grew warm. If she didn't take control, she would not get what she was after. She walked around to her side of the desk and sat down. Tapping her pencil on the desk and nodding in the direction of his empty chair, she suggested that they resume the interview.

"What happened next?"

Mack walked past his chair to the window and stood to look out. "They spent their honeymoon on Carnagan's claim up in the mountains." His warm breath formed a mist on the cold glass. He gestured with his mug toward the Cascades, where the outline of the snow-capped peaks was visible in the light of a full moon, just now rising due east.

"It was just about this time last year. Fall equinox." Mack seemed to be talking to the mountains. He fell silent once more. Logs that had burned to ash settled in the iron stove, and it creaked as it began to cool. Mack set his cup down on the desk and walked back to the stove.

"It's pretty up there in the fall, so they decided to stay all winter. That was foolish." He unlatched the heavy door. "No one stays up there in the winter but trappers." He added a few sticks of wood to the ash. "You can't get in or out after the snow starts." He poked and stirred the ash until sparks flew and the kindling flamed. Then he shut and latched the door.

Nellie took a cue and did a little poking of her own. "Did Hudson return?"

"I'm getting ahead of my story."

Nellie took a long, deep breath. One thing she had learned, a key to good standing in the legal community was the ability to hold an audience captive for as long as possible. Mack was a member in good standing.

"Mrs. Marsh sent Hudson a wedding announcement and invited him to join them all in the spring. Hudson wired his congratulations, and that's the last they heard of him."

Mack sat down and looked up at the clock. He rolled his chair forward, set his elbows on the desk, and leaned over them. "The young couple got their supplies and their phone in, and they settled down. Mary phoned her mother every day. They seemed well and happy. Carnagan set his traps, but the snow came early. A big storm hit on November sixteenth. That's the day I got word that somebody had been killed at the Carnagan cabin."

Mack took a long draw on his coffee and made a face. "Gets bitter when it gets cold." He eyed her mischievously over the rim of his mug.

Nellie avoided his gaze, focusing on the broad expanse of sienna-toned skin that stretched across his prominent cheekbones. Nez Perce? Paiute? Where did the blue eyes come from? *My goodness.* Just as she was wondering how to get back on track, he set his mug aside, reached for his Dunhill Shell pipe, and picked up his story.

"It took the county coroner and me two weeks to get up there. Hardest trip I ever made." He rubbed his thumb against the pebbled surface of the Algerian briar bowl and stood up again. Lighting the contents of the pipe with all the ritual of a baseball pitcher alerting the catcher to his intentions, he paced the floor, puffing his pipe.

"I'm glad to see you are enjoying my Christmas gift."

"Nice stuff," Mack nodded. He puffed until he had a good draw going. Then he began to describe what he'd seen.

"We found Carnagan up there in the cabin, crazy as a loon. He'd been alone all that time with his wife's body."

Nellie's eyes widened. She became so engrossed in the grisly story that her pencil stopped moving while scenes of the crime played out in her head like a silent D.W. Griffith film.

"He told us he'd gone out the morning of the sixteenth to check his traps. When he came back that afternoon, he found Mary lying dead on the floor, shot through the heart."

The sheriff sat down again and folded his arms on the desk. He let his pipe smolder. He shook his head slowly and looked up at the ceiling. Nellie couldn't be sure, but she thought his eyes glistened.

"There was no struggle." He was silent for a moment. "She hadn't been … touched." He returned his eyes to Nellie's. "Nothing had been taken." He shook his head again. "The dog had been shot too."

"Oh, my stars. Mack, this is the worst story I have ever heard. Who would do such a thing? Surely you don't think—"

Mack held up his hand. He tapped the ash out of his pipe and laid it on top of the humidor filled with his Elephant Butts tobacco, a noxious novelty that allowed gentlemen who preferred cigars to pack cigar butts into a pipe when lighting up a stogie might offend.

"I didn't find any footprints. The snow likely covered any tracks. I did find these two casings though." He pulled the spent cartridges out of his pocket and placed them next to the bullets on the desk. "Look here."

Nellie took the magnifying glass he offered and peered at the array of brass and lead.

"See the lines on bullets and the casings?"

She squinted. "Oh yes. I see."

"Those rough etchings tell me the killer used a rifle with a barrel that had been had re-bored by hand."

"What does that mean?"

"Okay, now this is where you want to make careful notes."

Nellie put down the magnifying glass and picked up her notebook. Finally. Something new she could use in her report.

"The barrel of any rifle can be hand re-bored to a larger caliber, but the work is not smooth like a machined bore. The cartridges will bear marks every time."

"Okay, that's interesting, but I don't see what …"

Mack pulled his handsome eyebrows together in a frown. Nellie returned her attention to the evidence and then back to the storyteller.

"We buried Mary right beside the cabin, and then had to stay there until we could get Carnagan in shape to get him out. He was a wreck." He shook his head, and Nellie nodded her sympathy.

"Two trappers who lived ten miles away came up one night. They hadn't heard of the murder, but they had found a badly mutilated body. They thought it might be Carnagan. It took them two days to travel up to the cabin to see if that boy had gone missing. We followed them back to where they'd set their traps, and sure enough, we found a dead man. You know what else we found?"

"The murder weapon?"

"A hand-re-bored rifle and some cartridges."

Mack gave a sideways glance in Nellie's direction while he busied himself sweeping the evidence back into his desk drawer.

"Did you identify the body?"

"We did not. Like I said, animals had gotten to whoever was foolish enough to be out in that weather."

Nellie raised her eyebrows and waited.

"The man had been dressed well, but not for the mountains. We found a compass and a wad of cash in his coat pocket. He was wearing a fur coat that had a New York label, but lots of those around." Mack rolled back his chair, shoved the disarray of papers and pencils in front of him into the drawer, and shut and locked it. Then he stood up and leaned back against the desk, arms folded across his chest. "There was no other identification. No real indication it was your missing guy. Those are the facts."

Nellie nodded slowly. "And if that wasn't Hudson's body you found, where would you suggest we look for him?" She closed her notebook.

"Oh, there's no telling." Mack grabbed his pipe and the keys to his office. He helped Nellie into her coat and guided her toward the door. "If you were to check the passenger lists on the ships that sailed to Europe about that time, you might find a Charles Hudson listed as a passenger. He was an independent sort, after all. Want to get some dinner?"

How tidy. Stepping into the street, Nellie breathed the cold evening air. The breeze that swept up from the beach below the Marsh House tasted of salt. Behind her, the lock turned in the door, and Mack fell into step by her side, adjusting his Stetson against the gusts of air that were gaining strength. They walked together in silence.

Had justice been served? Perhaps so. Another lesson learned. Sometimes discretion was the better part of a full accounting for the truth. She would write her report, just the facts, and lay the issue of the government's expert to rest.

8

Hopes and Dreams

*I*t was the rare occasion that Nellie allowed herself to accept an invitation to dine alone with an attractive man, but she had forged a friendship with Mack that, despite the amusing flirtation, she knew how to handle. Once inside the Flying Coffee Pot, Mack headed in the direction of an empty table for two in a dimly lit back corner of the small dining room. Before he could claim the table, Nellie caught the eye of the waitress and nodded in the direction of a front-window table set for four. The waitress glanced at Mack.

"Whatever the lady wants." Mack grinned and followed Nellie to the table of her choice. He seated her, set his hat on the empty chair next to Nellie, and sat down opposite her.

"The Flying Coffee Pot, an odd name for a restaurant."

"Might be a nod to their quick coffee service," Mack spoke from behind the menu he was studying, "or"—he lowered the menu and raised his eyebrows—"it might refer to one of our local ghosts."

"Oh, I think I've heard that story. Some phantom malingerer throws the carafes on the floor at night?"

"That's the story." He closed his menu and slapped it down on the table. "Now it's my turn to ask the questions. What's *your* story?"

No one had ever asked her to explain herself. "How far back do you want me to go?"

The waitress set cups of coffee in front of them and took their order. The coffee smelled so delicious that Nellie broke her one-cup rule. Her first sip of the fresh, strong brew flipped a switch in her senses. Did they come suddenly awake or take leave of her altogether? What brought her out west, Mack wanted to know. That was a story she had never told anyone. A haunted coffee shop seemed as good a place as any to exorcise the restless spirit that had possessed her from such a young age.

"I suppose it began with a book ..."

———⎯∞⎯———

Kansas, 1876

The pastor of the Presbyterian church the family attended made the announcement. The town fathers called for the return of a book that had been donated by mistake.

"The book is a special edition of *The Man Without a Country* by Edward Everett Hale," the pastor said, drawing out each syllable as if he were illustrating a significant point in a homily. Nellie stopped doodling on her offering envelope and sat up straight. Might there be a reward? He made no mention of that. Instead, he segued cleverly into a sermon on the sin of carelessness.

Nellie was still thinking about the lost book when the pastor stopped in the pews to chat with Mr. and Mrs. Carter. He dropped his hand down atop Nellie's head, and let it rest there. His palm lay heavy on her hair, neatly parted in the center and hanging in damp braids that absorbed the chill of cold sunlight shining through the high, leaded glass windows.

I'm glad I washed my hair this morning. Nellie sat perfectly still, feeling the weight of his words in the large hand that commissioned her into service.

"We are asking all the children to keep an eye out, Mrs. Carter. If Nellie should happen to find the book, there might be a little reward."

Nellie raised her chin and searched his pale, wintery face with her round dark eyes. "What is the story about?"

"What does that matter?" A man of great height even when he wasn't standing in the pulpit, he looked down as if seeing her for the first time. "It's about a man who renounces his country and has to spend the rest of his life on a sailing ship with no news of home. But that's of no consequence; what is important is that this particular book had a patriotic verse penned on the flyleaf, with the name and address of the young man who lost the book written below. That is what you want to look for."

Nellie drew herself up and thrust her chin a smidgen higher. "How did the young man let such a gift land in the donation pile?"

The Reverend removed his hand from Nellie's head as one would withdraw from a source of heat reaching an uncomfortable temperature. "As I said in my sermon, he was careless, as many rich people are. You weren't listening." He waggled his finger at her. "He did not guard a treasured gift from his grandfather." His eyebrows knit together in accusation. "There is a lesson for you in that." Then he laughed.

"I'm not rich." Nellie tossed her braids with the backs of her hands and smoothed her bangs. "Just the same, I am sorry for his loss." These were words she often heard people say when they wished to end a conversation. They had the desired effect. The pastor reached his arm out over her head to shake the hand of another parishioner.

"I will keep an eye out," Nellie assured him. Her words were absorbed by the damp, slightly acrid smelling shirt fabric that clung to his armpit.

And if I find it, maybe I will turn it in for the reward, but not before I read it.

Early the following winter young Nellie was leading her horse through Indian grass in the chalky hills, searching for a stray lamb, when the sweet strains of "Lead, Kindly Light" reached her ears. So unusual was the sound of a human voice on the barren plain she often roamed, she turned her horse to follow the music.

Coming upon a sod house so near the color of the ground it was indistinguishable as a habitat, she discovered a large family of children. They invited her inside. Nellie's eyes had to adjust to the darkness before she could identify which child sang the hymn so sweetly.

A little girl sitting on a ragged pallet in the corner turned her face in the direction of Nellie's voice. A waxy veneer coated the pupils of the child's eyes. The film reflected the thin winter light that streamed through the open door in the way moonbeams bounce off a shallow pool of water. Blind from birth, Nellie discovered, the girl had never been taught to walk for fear she might wander off. The other children explained that their sister occupied herself singing hymns they taught her.

The child's name was Helen. This particular hymn came from a hymnal they had found in a box of donated books.

"How does she know the tune?" Nellie asked the other children. She looked around the room to see if she could spot the box.

"My daddy plays the fiddle." Helen spoke up in a voice so clear and musical it startled Nellie.

She is blind, not deaf and dumb, Nellie chided herself. She kneeled down beside Helen. "You are a church-going family then?" Perhaps they knew about the search for the missing book.

"Oh no. We have no clothes for church, but Daddy knows a few church tunes from when he was a boy. I can sing most any hymn to the music my daddy knows how to play."

"Where is your mother?" Nellie asked the children.

"Our mother died with the last baby," Helen said.

"I am sorry for your loss." As the words marched from Nellie's mouth, her face began to burn. *Brave, motherless children.* At this point, her mother would be planning donations of hand-me-downs and food baskets, whereas she was absorbed in the challenge of getting her hands on their box of books. Only because she had promised the pastor, she told herself.

"Well, you have a very pretty voice, Helen." Nellie patted the girl's hand and turned to the other children. "May I see the books you were given?"

In the way of children who only ever had one thing to call their own, they proudly showed off their stack of books. At the bottom of the pile, Nellie found the little book that had made its way from a rich man's library to a poor child's heart.

The child who laid claim to that particular book reluctantly gave Nellie permission to return the book. Nellie promised the children a reward.

She kept the book for a month, read it twice, and then asked the pastor about the reward.

"Reward?" He glowered at her. "The reward is knowing you have gladdened the heart of a young man who has lost a treasure."

"But you said …"

"I made no promises, young lady. Should that young man decide a reward is in order, a donation to the deacon fund would be appropriate, wouldn't you think?" He raised his eyebrows and smiled broadly at Nellie, showing his teeth. "Have you, by chance, found the book in question?"

"No."

"No?" He was standing very close, his big face leaning down over her, his pockmarked jowls hanging loose, like sunflowers heavy with seed.

"No sir, I was just curious." She looked up into his face, eyes wide and lips pressed into a whimsical smile. Giving her shoulders the merest shrug, she turned and skipped away.

Nellie used her egg money to mail the book back to its owner. Before she wrapped the slim volume, she slipped a note between its pages.

Dear Sir:

I read your book with the greatest interest. I hope you don't mind. I thought about what I would miss most if I had to live on a boat in the ocean for the rest of my life. I would miss my horse (of course!), but mostly I think I would miss my family.

Yours truly,

Nellie Belle Carter

In time, she received correspondence from one Eustace William Carver. In a lovely script on monogrammed stationery, the young man acknowledged Nellie's supreme effort to restore the treasured centerpiece of his grandfather's legacy.

My dear Nellie,

Words cannot express my gratitude for your perseverance against the odds of discovering the whereabouts of the book my grandfather intended for me to have. How I regret my carelessness in not safeguarding the precious volume against thoughtless members of my staff, who scooped it up with less esteemed works and sent it to Kansas to relieve the misery of those who are famished for spiritual and intellectual food, as well as meaner sustenance.

I shall one day travel to meet you. I was much taken with your description of the blind child with the lovely voice. I should very much like to meet her. Keep a gentle eye on her for me, will you?

Your servant,

Eustace

Folded inside the note was a crisp ten-dollar bill. Nellie hid the note and the money in a letter box she had just received for her fourteenth birthday from her aunt who lived out west.

Eustace began to fill her thoughts. He took on the character of a shining diamond among the rough men who worked the family farm. Every word of his letter fired latent desire within her. *Perseverance against the odds*--she looked the word up in the dictionary. It meant *steady persistence in spite of difficulties*. Nellie's mother often called her a tenacious sort, especially when she set herself against her brothers. Perhaps her mother meant it as a compliment.

By his own account, Eustace was a man with a grateful heart: a gentleman with compassion for the less fortunate, a squire with means and education. In her estimate, he was a prince with the wherewithal to rescue her from a life of farm labor. She thrilled to delightful sensations as she imagined their meeting.

In her dreams, he would step down from a private train car and catch sight of her standing apart from the others waiting for arrivals. He would approach, take her hand in his, and murmur, "Nellie, you are even more lovely than I pictured."

Their courtship would be short; the wedding a discreet perfection of white satin, flowers, and violins. Eustace would whisk her away to the East. She pictured a future where he would teach her how to manage a staff. She, in turn, would educate him about the needs of the poor. Together they would exceed her mother in good deeds and charitable works.

A week after she received the letter, she rode her horse out to the sod house and gave the ten-dollar bill to the children.

—◦◦◦—

Nellie's impassioned correspondence with Eustace over the two years that followed was nothing compared to her excitement when she learned that he would be making a visit to her family's farm. She re-read all his letters, looking for his responses to her many declarations of regard for him. She concluded that he must be a formal sort, the kind who would express emotion only when the circumstances were right. That would be up to her, of course.

"A good thing we have the new house," Nellie told her little sister Jessie. "Wherever would a gentleman like Eustace stay if Mother and Father had not had the good sense to get us out of that dirt hovel at the first opportunity?"

"Will you take him to see Helen?" Jessie sat on the floor of the bedroom they shared.

"I suppose I will have to." Nellie pulled down the corners of her mouth. "I don't understand his interest in her. It's maudlin."

"What does that mean?" Jessie danced her rag doll on the floor.

"It means to go all mushy, Jessie. Helen can walk now, for heaven's sake. He doesn't have to feel sorry for her."

"But she still can't see, can she? I feel sorry for her."

"Pshaw! You've never even met her." Nellie stood in front of the mirror that hung over her sister's bird's-eye maple dresser.

"I have too."

Nellie narrowed her eyes. "You have not." She continued looking in the mirror as Jessie stood up, letting the doll slip from her hand to the floor.

The little girl stood on tiptoe to peer over Nellie's shoulder. She began to imitate her sister's movements, lifting her light hair off her neck, arranging it this way and that.

"I saw her in church last Sunday when you stayed home. Remember? You said you had a cold."

"I've *never* seen her in church."

"She was wearing a pretty dress, one of your old dresses, I think."

Nellie whirled around. "What? How?"

Jessie shrugged. "Mother donated it to the Ladies Aid Society, I guess."

Nellie frowned. "Why didn't she save my dress for you, like she always does?"

"I don't know. Maybe she thought girls like Helen would go to church if they had a dress to wear."

So now I have to see my old clothes walking around on strangers, Nellie thought. "Well, good for her." She gave her sister a quick, small smile and pinched her cheek, a touch somewhere between fondness and irritation.

Jessie rubbed the side of her face and made round, innocent eyes at Nellie. "The pastor called her up in front."

Nellie froze. "What did she say? Did he say anything about a book?"

"A book? No, he asked her to sing a song."

"Oh, of course. Helen has a beautiful voice. I'm sorry I wasn't there to hear her sing." Then Nellie turned back toward the mirror. She piled folds of her dark hair on top of her head. "Jessie, do you think this makes me look older?"

The little girl cocked her head and wrapped her bottom lip over her top lip. "No, not really. Well, maybe. My teacher wears her hair up."

Nellie let her long, dark locks drop back down on her shoulders. "Well, I certainly don't want to look like somebody's teacher."

"What do you want to look like?"

"Like a lady."

Silver Beach

The waitress removed Nellie's barely touched dish and stacked it on top of Mack's clean plate. She set small bowls of spumoni in front of Mack and Nellie and splashed more coffee in their cups.

"A long, boring story, forgive me." Ravenous now, Nellie spooned some of the pink, green, and white frozen custard laden with pistachios, chocolate bits, and cherries into her dry mouth.

"Not at all." Mack scooped dessert into his mouth in two bites. You were a saucy little thing. But we are just getting to the good part. I want to hear about Eustace. Was he your first love?"

The restaurant had emptied. The waitress circled the room, blowing out candles and lowering blinds. She laid the bill in front of Mack. Nellie reached for it. "Let me have that." She gave Mack a sweet, complicit smile. "We will let the court pay."

Mack let her pick up the tab. "I'm not going to hear the rest of this story, am I." He stood up and reached for his hat.

"Not this visit, I'm afraid. You may escort me back to the Marsh House, and we will say our good-byes at the door."

On the bottom porch leading to the veranda that hugged the Marsh House, Mack took a step back and surveyed Nellie. The full moon rising behind him cast a light over his shoulder that shone kindly on her face. "You are, you know."

"What?"

"A real lady."

Although she had never witnessed the process, this must be what a maple tree felt when sunlight hit it after a crushing winter, and the sap began to flow. She might burst with the pressure of holding back. She stood still for a moment and then extended her hand. "I enjoyed your company at dinner this evening, Mack."

He took her hand in his firm grasp, pulled her slightly to him, and leaned in to brush her cheek lightly with his lips—soft lips still warm with coffee and smelling of sweet cream. Then he stood tall, straightened the Stetson that had been knocked slightly askew, and took a step backward. "Good night, Mrs. Scott. I look forward to working with you again." He pivoted and strode back up the road to town, whistling "Cuddle Up a Little Closer" into the wind.

Nellie stood for a moment and watched him go. *Nothing subtle about you, is there Mack?* It would take her awhile to get to sleep tonight.

9

Whistles and Bells

Portland, 1910

Nellie did not like to think of herself as a grandmother. If only it had been Johnny who had settled down, married, and presented her with a granddaughter. But it was Opal.

Nine months ago, Nellie had received a letter postmarked New York from Opal saying she had married Jack Barry, a fellow dancer on the vaudeville circuit. They were expecting a baby, she wrote. The sequence of those events was not at all clear.

With both mother and daughter traveling, communication was difficult at best. Nellie had been in Portland for several months. She was on contract as a court reporter while the burgeoning city's administration tried to build up staff to handle the heavy caseload. It was Jessie who got the call. Opal had given birth to Mabel Leone Barry in Chicago, where the young couple had rented an apartment. The baby's father, however, had returned to New York to fulfill his contract. The tour was supposed to finish in Chicago.

"Opal told me he plans to join her after the season," Jessie told Nellie in a phone call. The phone line was quiet. "Nellie, are you there?"

"Why didn't she call me?" Nellie asked in a small voice.

"She said she couldn't find your latest number."

"It's not like her to lose track of things. Besides, you could have given her my number."

Again there was silence on the line. Then Jessie spoke. "She's had a lot on her mind, and you are often hard to reach."

It was probably true. Opal was not one to retaliate against what she might have perceived as disregard. For the first time, Nellie wondered if she should have traveled to be by her daughter's side when she heard of her pregnancy. Word had not reached Nellie until the baby was near due. Too late for regrets.

"In Chicago? Is that where they plan to live?" Nellie asked.

"I don't know. Opal didn't say." Jessie had nothing else to tell Nellie. After their goodbyes, Nellie went for a walk to clear her head. Tourists crowded Portland's city streets, drawn by invitations to attend the increasingly popular Rose Festival. They brought an energy with them that usually infused Nellie with a sense of well-being, but not today.

Now that Opal was a mother with family responsibilities, her dance career was surely over. Nellie trudged along, head down, shoulders drooping, weaving in and out of the onslaught of people. How would the little family make it on a seasonal paycheck? Would the baby's father give up the stage to settle down and take care of his family? Surely Opal did not expect Nellie to give up her career and move to Chicago to help out. Nellie's body tensed. The ranks of the National Shorthand Reporters Association were 580 professionals and growing, and she was contemplating a position on the organization's governing board. Now was most certainly not the time for her to toss in her pencil. The different scenarios simply did not want thinking about right now. *Don't borrow trouble,* she told herself. *It will all sort itself out.*

The more time Nellie spent near the Oregon coast, the stronger her affinity for the coastal climate grew; so much so that she began to feel this was where she belonged.

Young people were flocking to Portland, a progressive city that was growing and changing. No longer young, Nellie banked on her experience and ability to remain employable to afford her freedom to enjoy the promise of the new century. Teddy Roosevelt was out stumping for a square deal. She had every hope that would include women in the workforce.

On a sunny spring Saturday, Nellie sat in a restaurant doodling on a paper pad while she waited to be served. This particular day, strangers crowded the streets and spilled into local eateries, so Nellie wasn't surprised when her waiter sought permission to seat a lady at her table.

"Why, most assuredly." Nellie nodded toward the chair opposite hers and smiled at the stranger. "We must all extend our hospitality to our guests on every possible occasion."

"Thank you for your willingness to share your table." A matronly woman squeezed herself into the tiny space and sighed heavily. "But I hardly consider myself to be a guest."

"Oh, not so." Nellie set down the menu she had been studying and began a study of the woman seated across from her. "The entire world has been invited to the Festival of Roses. I shall consider you one of our guests. You saw the parade today, I assume?"

"Beautiful beyond description." The stranger spoke in the modulated tones of someone who is used to public speaking. "This is my first trip to the coast. I've no language at my command to express my admiration for your beautiful city. I am a convert. We intend to make your city our future home."

We? The question got lost in a discussion of menu options and the bustle of service. When they finished their meal of Chinook salmon and roasted potatoes, Nellie's guest glanced at the clock.

"Oh my, it's getting late. The shops will close soon. By any chance could you give me the address of a reliable jeweler? My watch needs adjusting to your western time."

Nellie scribbled the address of her old friend Mr. Reeves on the back of her card, handed it to her companion, and they said their good-byes.

A few mornings later, Nellie ambled through the shopping district on her way to the courthouse. Her thoughts were on the long day ahead when Mr. Reeves accosted her from the doorway of his shop.

"Good morning, young lady. I want to thank you for the customer you directed to my door the other day." He beckoned her inside. "I have something I want to show you that I know you will admire."

Perking up, Nellie followed Mr. Reeves into the jewelry store. He walked behind the counter and retrieved a black felt square, which he smoothed out on the countertop. With a bony-fingered flourish, he set a small object on top of the cloth.

"This is her purchase for a very dear friend of hers. I have just finished the engraving."

Nellie leaned in close to inspect a beautiful gold pocket knife.

"I was just starting to wrap this for the post." Mr. Reeves placed a finger on the knife and rotated it so she could see his handiwork.

At the sight of his clipped, rosy nails, Nellie slipped her hands into the pockets of her skirt. She kept her hands so busy with work that her cuticles were ragged and her nails were chipped. She bent closer to read the name engraved on the handle in a signature font: *Ray Tanner.*

Mr. Reeves lowered his chin and jumped his bushy eyebrows up at her, a clear invitation for an appreciative comment.

"It's lovely." Nellie straightened up. "Is there an occasion for this thoughtful gift?"

"It is a birthday present for the gentleman, I'm told." Mr. Reeves winked and smiled at Nellie. "Your friend expected her gentleman to be here on his birthday, but business delayed him. From the little conversation I had with her, I imagine that when he arrives—Mr. Reeves placed the tips of his long, slender fingers together and pronounced his expectation in a singsong voice—wedding bells will ring."

"Is that so?" Nellie turned her attention to a display case and pointed to a small manicure gift set. "I'll take that."

"Lovely. Would you like that gift-wrapped?"

"No thank you. It's a gift for me."

———

Several weeks passed before Nellie had another occasion to dine with her new friend, whose name, she had learned, was Lucy. After dinner, the two women walked over to the Ellwood Apartments, where her companion kept rooms. Lucy had discovered Nellie's ability to type information neatly and accurately. She begged for Nellie's help to complete an employment application on the typewriter Lucy had yet to master. Nellie learned more of her story as she typed.

Name: Lucille A. Hanson
Age: 51 years
Residence: Portland Oregon, formerly a resident of
Burton, Kansas.
Experience: 20 years, elementary school teacher.

"I have no intention of resuming my former occupation."
Lucy settled into an easy chair in the stuffy room. "I want to keep
working, though."

"Oh absolutely. You should." Nellie sat on a straight chair at
a small writing table. She rolled the barrel of the typewriter up so she
could examine the page.

"But after a woman has followed one profession for twenty
years, it is almost impossible to engage in another line of work
successfully, don't you think?" Lucy gave Nellie the look of an overfed
dog hoping for a treat.

"I have known several women who have begun new
endeavors later in life. I'm thinking of a Mrs. McGregory."

"Even if a woman has been provident during her wage
earning years and has no need to seek other employment, life would
be a long, dreary stretch without an occupation, don't you agree?"

Before Nellie could open her mouth to reply, Lucy launched
into a long tale of how she had renewed her contract faithfully
each year, had seen the day coming when a younger woman would
supplant her, had known she would be compelled to give way to the
rising generation. Lucy moved from her chair to stand at the window.
The dusk slowly shadowed her face. Nellie went to stand behind her
slump-shouldered friend.

"It is the law of nature." Nellie clasped her hands together
under her chin and looked out. Across the street, a light switched on
in a large, front-facing window. A man and a woman entered their
dining room, the man first, his hands full of dishes and cutlery. He
began placing them on the table. The woman followed close behind,
adjusting a plate, refolding a napkin, moving a spoon to the right side
of the knife. Light from a crystal chandelier illumined a silver tea set
holding court with china tea cups in the corner of the room. Who
used these relics anymore, now that instant coffee and tea bags made
clean up so much easier? Times were changing.

Nellie shook her head slowly. "It is a situation we all must face, Lucy; the old giving way to the new. I think it is just and right."

Lucy circled Nellie's waist with her arm, and they turned from the window and walked toward the door. Lingering in the doorway, the dispirited woman changed the subject abruptly and began to talk about what marriage might mean to her—love, a home, companionship to the end. Her face lit up when she acknowledged her prolonged absence from Ray had, indeed, made her heart grow fonder.

Nellie turned to face Lucy. "You've not mentioned this before. An old friend whom you have admired for years? A friendship that has flamed into romance?"

"Oh no! I have only known him a short time since my last term expired. Rather quickly, we found ourselves to be a most congenial couple." A flush rose to Lucy's cheeks. She chattered on, speculating that Ray wished to marry for a home, acknowledging that it was his idea to move west.

"It all came about so suddenly." Lucy began to talk faster. "I sold everything I had, gave Ray power of attorney to settle my affairs, and here I am."

Nellie's hand went to her throat, and she gave a little gasp.

"Oh I know what you're thinking; a plain woman like me, a handsome businessman like Ray." Lucy lowered her chin and looked at Nellie over her wire-rimmed glasses. "He only wants to relieve me of all worry and financial responsibility. After so many years of being on my own, it is such a relief to have a man like Ray take charge of my affairs."

Down the hallway, the elevator bell rang. Nellie leaned in to peck Lucy's cheek goodbye, but the woman grabbed the sleeve of her coat and kept talking.

"My Ray is settling his affairs also, but it has taken him longer than he expected. He is driving across country right now in my little roadster. He arranged the purchase for me, courtesy of his connection to a large automobile firm in Kansas City."

The elevator door shut and shuddered its way down to the lobby. When Lucy grabbed her hand, Nellie's insides shuddered as well.

"Thinking of him on the road alone, well I just pray my life would end quickly if something were to happen to him." Lucy spoke in a stage whisper. Then she gave herself a little shake and brightened. "I would like to write a story and let the whole world know that romance is not dead and that life is lovelier than the most imaginative fiction. You could help me with that." Lucy laughed and gave Nellie's hand a little shake, then released it. "I know you understand."

The elevator bell dinged again, and Nellie nodded her head. "Oh yes, I understand." She turned away as politely as she could and scurried for the elevator. Once inside, she jabbed the button to close the doors and then hit the lobby button before leaning against the elevator wall. *I understand only too well.*

A few days later Nellie entered the courtroom to relieve Tom O'Brien, a reporter in Department No. 7. Tom's reputation as a moralist was much in evidence that morning. The judge had just sentenced a prisoner, who was being led back to jail. As Nellie approached the reporter's table, Tom nodded in the direction of the convicted.

"The court just gave him the limit." Tom began to load pieces of evidence into a cardboard box.

Nellie set her note-taking implements on the table. "Why is the Judge in such a bad mood?"

"That guy? He got what was coming to him."

Nellie scanned the room. Jurors were filing out the door in groups of twos and threes, discussing the case. The attorneys were making lunch plans, and Judge Wolverton had retired to chambers.

"Wolverton has a special dislike for men who prey on older women."

Nellie bristled. "Older women? Older women are wiser, I would hope, and better able to recognize a charlatan." But as she said those words, she thought of Lucy.

"Young or old, they all fall for that Chesterfield gallantry." Tom laughed wickedly. "Just look at the denomination of the check he cashed on Mrs. Crawley's account."

Nellie counted so many added zeroes that she doubted a check of that amount could ever be cashed. When she expressed her disbelief, Tom pointed out that the plaintiff had a line of credit established at the bank that would bring the rosy blush to a millionaire's cheek.

"Mrs. Crawley had a case in court last winter, didn't she?" Nellie leafed through her memory of lawsuits and brought up a seventy-five-year-old woman full of dignity, pride, and parsimony.

"She is well known by the courts for challenging her creditors and collecting her debts. How she hitched up with a fancy man, I just can't figure."

Fancy man. The back of her neck began to prickle.

"Tom, where did this man come from?"

"Blew in from the East, Kansas City I think, a month or so ago. Lived like a prince at the Ambassador, sported around in a swell roadster and kept lots to drink and lots of pretty girls around. How he managed to get acquainted with old Mrs. Crawley though, I can't figure. And why he couldn't resist a heist before blowing town with her money? Boy oh boy, when he got picked up for theft she blew the whistle on him."

Nellie cupped her elbow with her right hand and tapped her cheek with her left finger. "You know, Tom, it takes two to tango. These men wouldn't so likely go down the garden path if women didn't fall so easily for their charms."

"That is a funny way to look at it, Mrs. Scott. You make a good point, but it isn't relevant in this case." Tom held up a stack of exhibits. "For all his charming ways, in the end, he was just a lowdown sneak thief."

"And this is the take?" Nellie reached for the exhibits Tom was marking for the theft case that would follow the check fraud conviction. She leafed through them quickly, shook her head, and handed them back to Tom. She turned her attention to arranging her pads and pencils on the stenographer's desk.

"In a couple of years, they say we'll have stenotype machines." Tom stuffed his papers into his portfolio. He continued to stand by the desk.

"That will be a welcome change."

At the side of the courtroom, the bailiff pushed open the heavy doors and ushered in the afternoon's jurors. "I was thinking about the holler the defendant put up over one of the exhibits. Claimed it was a birthday gift and had sentimental value. Can you imagine?"

Nellie remained focused on her task. "Even criminals show sentiment, Tom; they are human after all."

"Beautiful little knife ..."

Nellie's cheeks began to burn. She looked up. "Was it a gold knife?"

"Yes." Tom zipped his portfolio and tucked it under his arm. "That's unusual, don't you think?"

"Was it engraved?"

Tom did not have time to answer. The bailiff called court back into session. Tom lifted the box of evidence from the desk and made a hasty exit.

Nellie did not register the subject matter of the case she reported that day. She took her shorthand notes automatically until court adjourned. Her nervous tension was somewhat relieved that evening by the vacant chair at her table in the restaurant where Lucy often joined her.

On Saturday, Nellie lounged in her room until late, reading the morning paper. After perusing the stock reports and the society column, she scanned the casualty report. The third listing caused her to bolt upright in her chair and clap her hand over her mouth. She reread the item: *An unidentified woman was killed instantly by the northbound bus at the intersection of 74th and Oak streets.* That was the vicinity in which her friend lived; Nellie sucked in her breath and let it out slowly. *Oh, poor soul, her prayer has been answered.*

Just then, the phone rang. "Mrs. Scott, your services are required at the Ellwood Apartments." She didn't recognize the voice, full of proper authority. The man did not identify himself, but she was used to such calls.

Nellie got dressed and made her way to the apartments. In the hushed atmosphere of the lobby, a clergyman with a melancholy face stepped forward to greet her in hushed tones.

"She is in here." He pulled open the heavy drapes to an alcove off the lobby just enough to allow Nellie, head bowed in respect, to follow him into the dimly lit room. She had never been called to identify a body.

How did they think to call me? I suppose they found my card in her room. But it's been days since the accident. And it makes no sense that her body would be laid out in her apartment building! With all the cross-examination going on in her head, it took awhile for the scene to register in Nellie's brain when she finally looked up.

Under a bower of roses, Lucy stood in a shimmering white wedding gown, a distinguished looking gentleman at her side.

"We wanted you as a witness to our marriage." A bright smile lit up Lucy's face. Then the two elderly lovers turned to face the clergyman and joined their lives together.

10

Passion and Pain

Spokane, 1916

The joy on Lucy's face and the respect in the ardent gentleman's eyes remained with Nellie for the rest of her life. In the years ahead, she learned to reserve judgment. But as she gypsied up and down the Pacific coast, recording court proceedings and collecting stories, she could not help notice the trouble people brought on themselves for want of prudence and a proper sense of purpose. She began to question her ambitions.

"I spent the first half of my life praying for the wrong thing," she told Jessie during a visit. "I prayed for a life that would engage my imagination and allow me to use my mind. I was wrong to do that."

"How were you wrong?" Jessie stood at the sink, washing up the lunch dishes.

Nellie recited a favorite quote from memory: "It is for us to pray not for tasks equal to our powers, but for powers equal to our tasks, to go forward with a great desire forever beating at the door of our hearts as we travel toward our distant goal."

"Helen Keller." Jessie finished drying the china soup tureen and set it back on the sideboard.

"Yes. Miss Keller rallies against all preparations for war. She urges women to be heroes in an army of construction. As much as I enjoy my job, I can't pretend I am working for any great cause. Due process keeps society orderly. It changes nothing."

"Are you saying that you are as dissatisfied with your career as you were with your marriage?

"No, I am just wondering. Instead of all the grumbling I did, what if I had prayed for the power to perform my mundane tasks with good grace? Might I have been granted a higher calling?" Nellie removed the unused dishtowel from where it hung draped over her arm, refolded it, and set it aside.

"Perhaps." Jessie pulled the plug on the sink and wiped away the moisture that glistened on her forehead. She eyed the clean towel. "Then again, it's never too late to start."

Noise and laughter erupted from the back bedroom. The sound advanced like the tremors of a California earthquake. Walls shook, and the floor resounded with the thud of small feet. Leading the pack, Leone burst into the kitchen and threw her arms around her grandmother's waist.

Four years before, Opal had returned to Spokane with her child barely out of diapers. Before the dance troupe arrived in Chicago, Jack had abandoned the tour and traveled to California where there was an opportunity to make some quick money in Oroville. He wrote Opal, suggesting she give up their apartment and go back to Spokane to wait for him.

Desperate and lonely, Opal managed to get a telephone call through to her mother. "What could be in Oroville that interests Jack so much?" Opal asked Nellie.

"Gold, gambling, and a growing olive industry are all I know. Come home, and we'll figure it out." Nellie sent her a train ticket.

They rented a small house in Spokane near Jessie, and Nellie helped Opal find clerical work. She bit her tongue and bridled her ambition, telling herself that it was just for a season.

It took Nellie only a few inquiries among her colleagues to discover that Jack was a gambler. But Opal could not acknowledge that Jack might not be ready to settle down, that family life with a drifter might not be in the cards. Gentle Opal would not confront her husband. She would wait.

Nellie had little hope that Opal's letter campaign would lure Jack back to her side, but if anything could do the trick, perhaps it might have been the photograph a friend took of Opal and Leone. In the portrait, Opal shined in a stylish black dress that showed off her tiny waist. She sat on a small stool alongside her waif, who was dressed in a frilly white frock and seated on a tricycle. In the photo, Opal gazed at her child with a look of pure love. Leone looked straight at the camera, a small smile on her lips.

Three years ago, it had been that photo that Nellie spotted lying on top of a pile of mail when she returned home from work. Hadn't Opal sent it to Jack? She heard noise in the hallway. Could Jack be …? A door shut. Nellie flipped the photo over and read the words penciled on the back. *If only you saw her, you would never want to leave us.* Down the hall, behind the closed door, someone sobbed. Nellie walked down the hall and tapped on the door.

"Opal?"

The bed creaked, and the door opened. Tear-stained Opal, holding Leone in her arms, stepped aside, and Nellie walked into the room.

"What has happened?"

Opal held out an envelope clutched in her free hand. Stamped in red across the Oroville address were official words, *Return to Sender, Addressee Deceased.*

Leone wriggled in her mother's arms, and Opal set her down. When Nellie wrapped her arms around her daughter, the little girl began to wail. Opal pulled Leone into the folds of her skirt and rubbed her back.

"He never saw her. She will never know her father. What will I tell her?"

Nellie procured the death certificate. It wasn't a weak character that killed Jack Barry; it was a weak constitution. At age twenty-five, he succumbed not to a gentleman's disagreement or a barroom fight, but to pneumonia. A harsh winter, the virulent flu, and a compromised immune system put him in his grave.

The ensuing three years, Nellie had tried to be patient with her grieving daughter, but she had grown frustrated with Opal, who was sad and tired all the time. Hadn't Nellie felt the same way after Mabel died? Yes, but in her experience, it was best not to sit too long with the loss. She must find a way to help Opal move forward.

Now six-year-old Leone hugged Nellie's waist and raised her arms to her grandmother. Nellie placed her hands on the girl's shoulders and pushed her arms gently to her sides.

"You are too big for me to pick up, Leone. You would break my back."

Leone grinned and skipped off. Nellie called after her. "Get your coat. We need to get home so I can pack my bag."

"Off again?" Jessie gave the counter a final swipe.

"Los Angeles."

"How long this time?"

"Three or four weeks, I imagine. I am taking a little time off to look in on Johnny and meet his wife and son."

"Oh good. I'll be interested to hear if marriage has tamed that rascal son of yours."

Before she left, Nellie slipped some money into an envelope and handed it to Opal with the suggestion that she employ a neighbor to watch Leone one evening and go out with her co-workers.

"Go see Douglas Fairbanks in *Habit of Happiness*," she suggested. "That should cheer you up." Her words sounded hollow, but maybe small doses of happiness could inoculate Opal against the chronic sorrow that threatened to overwhelm her. She prayed it would be so.

11

Displays of Grief

Los Angeles, 1916

*B*eing on her own usually lifted Nellie's spirits, but after a long
day transcribing a lengthy cross-examination that yielded
nothing significant, she was tired and sore. She limped through the
downtown Los Angeles shopping district toward her hotel. Her toes
throbbed in her tight shoes and her neck chafed under the starched
white collar attached to her navy cotton-serge day dress.

At the end of a day like this one, the prospect of dining alone
made her a little teary. On occasion, she would accept an invitation
from a judge or attorney to dine at his club, but only if the evening
held promise to produce enjoyable conversation. No such invitation
had been extended.

The week before, Nellie had ridden the streetcar out to East
Los Angeles to visit Johnny and meet his wife and their son—her
grandson, she had to remind herself. A beautiful boy, but she would
not be there to watch him grow up the way she likely would for her
granddaughter. That's how it was with sons.

This thought did nothing to coax Nellie from her dark
mood. She was a block from her hotel when a floral fragrance with
a lemony-peachy float pulled her from her malaise. The energizing
scent lingered in the wake of a slender woman passing by on the
street.

How lovely to be young and able to treat yourself to a little
time in a parfumerie. The woman who now walked ahead of Nellie
was all peaches and cream, from her blush-colored tea dress with

its alabaster-satin-beribboned waistline to her delicately heeled shoes. Where was the sprite headed? To the Palm Court, to meet a gentleman? Back home, where a nanny waited to hand over a curly-headed tot? Nellie laughed at herself. How easy to imagine a dream life. Like a new perfume that warms on the skin, thrills the senses, and dissipates, so it was with dreams. After you wear them for awhile, you hardly notice.

Back in her hotel room, Nellie sat down at a small writing table and reached for words to describe her new daughter-in-law in a letter to Jessie.

> Dearest Jessie,
>
> How shall I describe the new Mrs. Scott? Her name suits her. She is a formal sort, very ladylike. That Johnny would choose jewel-like Pearl for such a rough setting surprises me. I am even more surprised that the latest Mrs. Scott accepted him, but they seem very much in love.
>
> I sometimes wonder what my life would have been if I had considered my choices more carefully. At one time, married life seemed like freedom. I did not realize then that I would be chained to home and hearth, while my husband roamed freely.
>
> I can only hope that Pearl will turn out to be a better homemaker than I was and that Johnny will be more appreciative of her unique talents than his father was of mine. Of course, I've yet to discover what those talents are, but every woman has them. I can say this, she is soft-spoken, and there is a natural sweetness about her that puts one at ease. That's a talent, don't you think?
>
> It was a joy to meet my new grandson, another, John! They call him Jackie. He is adorable.
>
> Ever,
>
> Nellie

Nellie continued to arrange her schedule to remain in Spokane as much as possible. A year passed, and the United States finally declared war on Germany. An upshot for Nellie, Opal, and Leone was that female households were now the norm. Women planted victory gardens and went to work filling the jobs men left behind. A sense of sisterhood pervaded neighborhoods and workplaces.

Nellie happened to be back in Los Angeles when she received some sad news. One day while she worked with other officers of the court filling in for members of the legal community who had marched into battle, her supervisor pulled her away from her desk to take a telephone call. The caller identified herself as Leota. The young woman had to talk awhile before Nellie put together that the bearer of bad news was her former husband's new wife.

Leota and Pearl had taken three-year-old Jackie shopping for his birthday. Leota relayed what had happened in a somber, halting monotone. Nellie had to strain to catch it all. The gist of it was that as a special treat, Pearl bought the boy a balloon. She wound the string lightly around his wrist and cautioned him to keep a tight hold of it. What happened next played out in Nellie's mind like a silent film. So mesmerized was the child by the bright red balloon bobbing in the air, he let go of the string. A breeze tugged the balloon, the string unraveled from its loose tether, and the balloon floated off. With a yowl, young Jackie pulled away from his mother and dashed into the street to retrieve his prize. He was hit by a motor car and killed instantly.

Several days after the funeral Nellie found herself sitting in the circle of her ex-husband's new family. Although she was hesitant to intrude on their grief, she accepted an invitation to her son's new Spanish bungalow. The visit required more courage than she had anticipated.

Pearl never left her bedroom. The men quickly excused themselves to the backyard, and Johnny followed. Through the window, Nellie watched them adjust their hats, wipe their brows, smoke cigarettes down to the nub, and stub the butts out in the palms of their hands. Furtively, they looked over their shoulders toward the window before swigging the communal flask that passed hand to hand.

When Nellie pulled her attention away from the men, a pattern of smudges on the window above the slipcovered sofa came into focus. Pearl was an excellent housekeeper. How did those smudges get there? Fingerprints. Oh God, tiny fingerprints formed parentheses around a nose print. Directly below, she thought she could make out the outline of little lips. Her imagination filled in the hunched shoulders, the blond curls on the back of a child's head as he stood on the sofa and pressed his face to the window. For an instant, Nellie thought the specter of the boy was in the room. A last farewell. She pinched the inside of her arm, and the wraith vanished.

Nellie desperately wanted to get up, get a towel, and wipe the evidence away to spare Pearl renewed anguish. Instead of sitting here murmuring about nothing, shouldn't these women be making plans for how to help the grieving mother dispose of reminders of her loss?

After Mabel had died, Nellie had been quick to get rid of her things. All that remained of her eldest daughter were the childish possessions of a young girl barely out of her teens, one who left no legacy of womanhood. And now, this war. How many other young lives would be cut short? How many women would lose themselves in sorrow while their men drowned their grief in drink? A woman who lost a husband was a widow. A child who lost parents was an orphan. What was a mother who lost a child?

It was selfish she knew, but she was grateful that her only son had passed his thirtieth birthday by the time the Selective Service Act became law. Perhaps Johnny and Pearl would have more children.

In the tiny stucco house, the bedroom door remained closed. In the living room, the women continued to prattle. Was it her place to organize them in a campaign to coax Pearl from her tomb back into the land of the living? No. She had no place here. Nellie made her excuses and let herself out the front door to catch the trolley back to her hotel.

Perhaps she should have gone around to the backyard to say goodbye to Johnny. She hesitated at the end of the walkway.

"Nellie?"

John's voice sounded in her ears. She turned to see him round the corner of the house and lope toward her.

"You're leaving?"

"Yes, I ...,"

"Okay, well, could we talk for a minute?"

He planted himself in front of her and hung his head, tapping the palms of his hands against his thighs.

"What's on your mind, John?"

He raised his head, and she saw something she had seen only once before. His eyes glistened with tears.

"He was a sweet boy. I can't believe he's gone." John pulled a handkerchief out of his back pocket and blew his nose. "First our Mabel, and now our Jackie." He shook his head slowly. "The sins of the father, I guess."

"What are you saying?"

"I should have been able to keep us all together."

"You think this was God's judgment?" Nellie put her hands on her hips. "Accidents. These were accidents. No one is to blame." She reached out, grasped John's shoulder, and held him at arm's length. "You think I haven't said the same thing to myself?" When her voice broke, John pulled her into his chest, and they both sobbed.

Nellie was the first to back away. Wiping the tears from her cheeks, she glanced toward the curtained front windows. "Goodness, I hope no one saw that."

John shrugged. "Pay no mind to that, Nellie. If we can't mourn our children together, what was it all for?"

John stood tall and resumed his habit of beating his hands in rhythm against his legs. "How are Opal and her little girl?"

"They are getting by. Opal appreciates the money you send."

John slid his hands into his pockets. "I do what I can."

Silence like an old friend took up a familiar place between them. If she had any overtures left to make, now was the time. "I don't know if I've told you: I like Leota very much. For one so young, she appears quite capable."

John laughed. "I seem to be drawn to capable women, don't I?"

"What I mean to say is that she is capable in ways I am not. She handles family matters well."

"I suppose she does."

Before the conversation could go any further, the front door opened. Visitors engaged in extended leave-taking spilled onto the porch. Nellie used the distraction to scoot away.

On the trolley, she reviewed her encounter with John. To know that he thought of her as capable in any sense gave her comfort. She would write Johnny and Pearl a long letter of sympathy and encouragement. Well chosen, heartfelt words were of much more value than inadequate postures of grief. She would find the right words. Expressing herself on paper—of that, she was more than capable.

⁂

When Nellie returned to Spokane, she described the goings-on to Jessie, omitting the part about her encounter with John. When she got to the part about her desire to help by packing up all remembrances, her sister looked troubled.

"Don't you ever feel like you might have been hasty in getting rid of every reminder of Mabel?"

"Why dredge up such sorrow?"

"Perhaps sorrow is the path we have to walk to preserve the memory of someone we love." Jessie excused herself and left the room, returning several minutes later holding Mabel's treasure box, her scrapbook, and her bisque doll. When she laid the keepsakes in Nellie's lap, tears left unshed washed down Nellie's cheeks.

"How?"

"I know we agreed that I would dispose of everything that belonged to Mabel, but I feared there might come a day when you regretted that decision. I kept a few things back."

Nellie picked up the doll. She ran a finger across its round glass eyes—brilliantly blue, clear and unseeing—eyes that fixed on the unknown. A familiar pain thrust itself deeply into her chest, a quick cut that took her breath away but did not stop her heart. When she was able to catch her breath again, she felt peace settle into her inner being and begin to do its healing work. Perhaps Pearl knew best. Maybe the only way to grieve was to be allowed to feel the pain.

12

Madame Cyrette's Jewels

Los Angeles, 1918

*W*ork took Nellie back to Los Angeles more often than she anticipated. Was it short staff and long hours that frazzled her nerves, or was she in a temper because what had once been a joy was now routine? Walking back to her hotel at the end of a particularly grueling day, she spotted a bevy of beautifully dressed ladies of leisure gathered in a circle on the walkway ahead. Laughter spilled from their midst. She supposed she would have to step into the street to get around them.

If any one of these aimless women had to earn her keep, she wouldn't have the energy to flit about the street like a songbird announcing her discovery of juicy berries. Nellie's tongue was beginning to stick to the roof of her mouth. She looked across the street to see if she might escape to a cafe and refresh herself with a glass of iced berry tea. She was stepping into the crosswalk when one of the songbirds called out her name.

Bright sun shone behind the figure of a tall woman. Nellie could not make out her features. The woman broke from the flock and glided toward Nellie, her silhouette shimmering in the heat. Nellie did not register the face until she was close enough to take in the pointy-toed Italian-heeled satin shoes peeking out from under the hem of a frothy frock and the delicate gold chain studded with precious stones that rested on lovely collar bones. The miner's wife!

Mrs. McGregory took up Nellie's hands in her own and greeted her effusively. As she spoke, Nellie detected a slight accent she did not recall hearing before. Not Irish. No, it was French. Mrs. McGregory volunteered answers to questions Nellie would have asked, given a chance. At the same time, she kept a sharp eye on her companions. Los Angeles was now her home, she offered. Life had treated her well. She'd been lucky.

The tittering throng broke apart and began picking their way closer. Mrs. McGregory leaned in and whispered in Nellie's ear. "Please. No one here knows me by my old name. I am known as Madame Cyrette." She squeezed Nellie's hand. "Madame Cyrette. Please remember." Pressing a calling card into Nellie's hand, she extracted the promise of a visit to her apartment. "I live in a fashionable section of the city: you'll see." As she turned to go, a breeze lifted the hem of her billowy skirt. She fairly floated in the direction of her friends, stopping once to turn back briefly and call out to Nellie, *"J'ai beaucoup à vous raconter!"*

Nellie stood alone on the sidewalk betting that, indeed, Madam would have much to tell her. Forget the cafe across the street. She marched herself over to West Seventh, took the lift to the twelfth floor, and entered the elegant new Mary Louise Tea Room.

Shoppers seated all around her were tucking into Thursday's special, chicken dinners. A waitress costumed in a svelte black dress and a spotless white apron secured at the waist by an ample bow set a plate in front of her. The breast of chicken glistened on white china. Buttered English peas, glazed carrot coins, and a scoop of mashed potato smothered in chicken gravy circled the piece of roasted poultry. Nellie spread a linen napkin across her lap, took a few sips of her mineral water, and savored the aroma in the steam rising from her plate. When was the last time dinner had been an occasion? The holidays with Opal and Leone, she supposed. She placed a forkful of moist chicken in her mouth.

What was the occasion that brought her to the tea room on a Thursday? Loneliness and boredom: conditions not of circumstances but of the soul, she was coming to realize. The miner's wife looked to be neither lonely nor bored. How did Madame Cyrette manage to migrate from a shack in Montana, to a shop in Idaho, to a life of leisure in Southern California? Nellie had to know.

It turned out that Madame Cyrette's view of a fashionable neighborhood was Venice of America. Developed a decade before by Abbott Kinney, the area struggled to live up to Kinney's vision of an art and cultural center. Ornate Venetian style buildings vied with an amusement pier that featured lowbrow entertainment, and the Philistines were winning the competition. No matter, when Nellie stepped out of a lift and onto lush green carpet in a hallway smelling of fresh beeswax, she concluded that Madame Cyrette likely never set foot on the pier.

The warm glow from the mahogany wood wainscot played well with the rich cream-colored wallpaper adorned with sketches of French courtiers frolicking in the woods. Nellie found her way to a tall door encased in ornately carved trim. She tapped a brass door knocker. A maid opened the door and stepped aside, allowing Nellie to enter. Nellie spoke a few words of greeting and offered her card to the expressionless young woman, who glanced at it quickly and beckoned Nellie to follow her.

Without a word, the maid ushered Nellie into a tastefully appointed room, where the exquisitely robed lady had arranged herself on a velveteen divan, prepared to serve tea against a decor that was a symphony of rich brown hues.

Nellie chose a tapestry-patterned Louis XV armchair to settle into and murmured thanks to the silent domestic who served her lavender tea and slightly stale lemon shortbread cookies.

"Thank you, Maria, you may leave us now. Go do the shopping, why don't you." As soon as she heard the front door close, Mrs. McGregory launched into the story of her transformation into Madame Cyrette.

"When the lease was up on my little shop, the landlord and I were unable to come to a new agreement. I felt it would be uncharitable of me not to give my husband a second chance, so I returned to Montana. Good people had contributed to a fund for injured miners, and it appeared that we might be able to purchase a new house. It seemed that he had pulled himself out of his alcoholic abyss, but to my sorrow, his sobriety proved short-lived." Her eyes filled. Teardrops formed on her long, dark lashes. They glittered in the morning sunlight that streamed in through the window. She drew a handkerchief from the pocket of her Chinese kimono and touched the corner of her eye, drawing the moisture without removing the Vaseline that made her lashes shine.

"Mrs. Scott, I've left him for good to his boisterous friends, his whiskey, and his coarse ways. I did the right thing, wouldn't you say?"

The crumpled face of the damaged man floated before Nellie. "I … suppose." Her voice trailed off. The older she got, the less she liked being asked to rubber-stamp the actions of others.

Madame lifted her teacup to her lips in such a way that Nellie could not help but notice the large diamond ring that now replaced the thin gold band. "I moved to San Francisco to learn dress design and then I moved here, where I have found great success."

"Evidently." Nellie smiled. "How did you manage that?"

Madame's face froze and then defrosted as quickly as Nellie imagined she had dispelled thoughts of her suffering husband. "I had a benefactor, shall we say, and leave it at that?"

Steps in the hall alerted them that the maid had returned from her errands. When she entered the room with a fresh teapot, Nellie declined and began to rise from her chair, but her hostess implored her to stay.

"It's not often I have the company of another woman who understands the rigor it takes to do what we have done, Mrs. Scott."

Nellie raised her eyebrow. "And what is that?"

"We have achieved independence and career success, wouldn't you say? Of course, the hard work is over and done for me." She shooed the maid out of the room. Reaching into her lavish robe, she pulled forth a money belt from its hiding place around her waist. She emptied the contents onto a heavy gold charger that sat on the low table beside the silver tea set. Sparkling gems, clear and white, spilled into the dish. Next, she retrieved from deep within her bosom a chamois-skin bag she wore, filled with sapphire stones.

"I keep these darlings close to my skin, my dear Mrs. Scott." She flushed with pleasure. "I love them more than anything in the world."

A tap at the door drew the maid from the kitchen. Madame Cyrette scooped up her darlings and sent them back into hiding just as Maria brought her mistress an embossed card and set it down on a silver card tray in plain view. *Mr. Arthur Clarke, Realtor*, the card read. Madam dismissed Maria with a nod and then turned to Nellie. Touching her bosom with one hand, she raised the other hand to her mouth and placed the tip of her forefinger to her lips. *Shhh shush.* Was there more to this subterfuge than the story madam was telling?

"Ah, Madame Cyrette, so good to"— a good-looking young man swept into the room with the proprietary air of a tomcat—"see you." The warmth drained from his eyes when he spotted Nellie. Recovering quickly, he caught up madam's hand and pressed his lips to her fingers. When he raised his eyes to appraise Nellie, she tucked her hands under her skirt and gave him a curt nod.

The maid returned with refreshments for the new guest. She locked eyes with the young man. Then she drew up a chair for him next to her mistress. Mr. Clarke took the seat, crossing his legs in the way of men who feel at home in their surroundings. Nellie, who guessed this was not the benefactor, watched as he worked himself into a fever over the wonderful values in real estate and the fortunes women were making. Her hostess hung on every word, placing her hand over her heart now and then. Whether it was a gesture of wonderment at the gentleman's wisdom or an unconscious check on the safety of the little bag nestled between her breasts, Nellie did not know.

After Mr. Clarke had excused himself, Madame Cyrette confessed what Nellie already knew. She had never revealed the details of her former life to her new friends. The discordance between the miner's wife Nellie had met several years ago, and the redolent Jezebel who now sat before her made Nellie's head hurt. Again, she made signs of leaving, but Madame Cyrette leaned across the tea table and laid her hand on Nellie's arm. "Arthur is such a wonderful companion. He takes me to dinners at the San Gabriel Mission. We go for walks on the beach and dances at the Ambassador Hotel." She continued to restrain Nellie. "He drives a little red roadster, and we tour the streets where the movie stars have their beautiful homes."

Nellie's impatience grew. She extricated herself from the grip her hostess had on her arm and made her excuses, more firmly this time. The maid was quickly on hand with Nellie's coat.

As she made her way back to her utilitarian hotel room, where court reports in need of transcription piled up on the writing desk that doubled as a bedside table, she puzzled over the twists and turns life takes. In truth, Mrs. McGregory had risen from circumstances meaner than any she had experienced, yet Nellie saw no life of leisure ahead for herself. Would she be happy in Madame Cyrette's present situation? She shuddered at the thought and resolved never again to allow curiosity to tempt her to play the voyeur.

In the months that followed, Nellie often thought about Venice of America's doyenne. When had the comfort from sorrow the woman sought in dreams of a better of life and the diversion of creative work turned into a steely-eyed love of money? Nellie searched her own heart for traces of avarice and burned with shame when she recalled arguments with John over bettering their circumstances. *It wasn't about money*, she told her heart. It must not have been about independence or career success either. She had a good measure of both, and still, she was dissatisfied. What, then?

Nellie chanced to be at the court reporter's table on the day Jack McGregory made an appearance to petition the court. Nellie did not recognize the miner until he began to tell his story in a boozy Irish brogue. Careful to keep her fingers moving on her stenotype machine, she looked up at the petitioner. His hair was combed, his clothes were clean, and he was missing a hand.

"You have come to town to identify the body of your wife, Marianne McGregory, also known as Madame Cyrette?" The judge spoke kindly.

The miner stood before the judge and removed his hat. "Yes, sir. It were she."

"And you wish to take her back and bury her in Montana, even though she was not living with you as your wife?"

The miner dropped his head and shuffled his feet a bit. "Yes, sir. She were the mother of my only child. I don't want her put in a pauper's grave. She should lie beside her child."

The judge set his elbows on the bench and rested his chin on his folded hands. "The lady in question was hardly a pauper, but it is true. Due to the circumstances of her death, and the fact that her fortune has not been recovered, it is likely she is headed for potters field."

The judge handed a file to the bailiff. "I am referring to Exhibit A." He looked at Nellie. "Please prepare this newspaper article to be entered into the testimony."

The bailiff handed the file to Nellie.

"Mr. McGregory, I am going to grant your petition. You are a man of honor, and I am pleased to make your acquaintance. I don't see many honorable men in my courtroom. My condolences on the loss of the mother of your child."

Nellie thought about going forward to offer her condolences as well, and then she thought better of it. She did not want to answer any questions concerning what she knew about Madame Cyrette. Let him remember her as he chose.

When the judge adjourned the court session for the day, Nellie gathered her things and retired to a corner of a small courthouse office where she could transcribe her notes. She set up her desk and reread the newspaper clipping in the evidence folder.

Body Identified, Maid, Local Realtor Sought

VENICE, CA--The mutilated, stripped body of a middle-aged woman found on a lonely stretch of arroyo outside the city last week has been identified as Mrs. Jack McGregory, formerly of Copper Butte, Montana. Known locally as Madame Cyrette, the former shopkeeper lived in elegant rooms in a Venice of America apartment that was reported to have been looted of all valuables.

A maid who was in the employ of Mrs. McGregory has also been reported missing. Police have an APB out for Maria Hernandez as well as Mrs. McGregory's close companion, local Realtor Arthur Clarke, who disappeared about the same time as Miss Hernandez.

The miner buried his wife on the bleak, black hillside of Copper Butte, alongside the baby boy she "loved more than life." Her surrogate "darlings" were never recovered. The Realtor and the maid were never found.

13

Love's Broken Dreams

*N*ellie often pondered the miner's wife's fate—Mrs. McGregory, grieving mother and put-upon wife; Mrs. McGregory, aspiring fashion designer and failed shopkeeper; Madame Cyrette, self-invented socialite undone by a scheming flatterer. At what point had her life taken a turn that sent her hurtling to the grave? Life is like working the mines, Nellie wrote in her journal. *We labor in the dark, never knowing how close we may have come to tapping gold or triggering disaster. Only God knows.*

"Only God knows," her mother used to say when Nellie asked questions Amanda did not care to answer. Surely to dream about employing one's talent to rise above a bad situation was not unworthy of God's blessing. But if broken dreams are not God's way of derailing us from the tracks to hell, might they be His way to test our mettle for the journey ahead? Nellie shook that thought from her head. Before she could acknowledge that she did not believe in such an interfering God, her thoughts jumped the rails. It came to her that it was not fashion design Mrs. McGregory had failed at, it was love.

A deep sadness wrapped soft fingers around her heart. She had always supposed that her dreams were born of a hunger similar to Mrs. McGregory's, not for bodily sustenance, but for nourishment that satisfied a curious mind and fed an adventurous soul. In truth, she was living that dream, but at its core, it was cold comfort. When had she stopped believing in love? She knew exactly when.

92

Kansas, 1878

When Nellie was sixteen, Eustace made good on his promise to visit Kansas. The elegant young man arrived by train with no entourage or fanfare. Nellie accompanied her father and oldest brother to the train stop, putting a calculated distance between herself and the two men as they stood waiting beside the tracks.

At the sound of the distant whistle, her heart beat wildly against the steel stays of her corset. Clanging and clattering filled her ears. She didn't hear her brother's admonishment to stand back from the tracks. Everything on the ground receded from her awareness until the train came into view. The tug of a stranger's fingers on the sleeve of her dress caused her step back, throwing her off balance.

The train pulled into the station and settled on the tracks like an overlarge person sinking into a chair, weary from exertion. Nellie raised herself on tiptoe so she could see above the heads of those who crowded in front of her. Disembarking passengers were greeted with handshakes or embraces.

Did she get the date wrong? Did he miss the train? Nellie stared at the recessed doorway. There he was! A slight gentleman carrying one piece of luggage stepped lightly from the train and made straight for the men. He introduced himself and shook hands, first with her father and then her brother. Nellie waited quietly, shifting from one foot to the other while the men exchanged pleasantries. She strained her ears to catch his words. Surely he was aware of her presence. Finally, her father pointed in her direction, and Eustace turned to stare blankly into the small group of people who were rapidly dispersing around her.

Dressed in her Sunday best, Nellie pulled herself up to her full height of five foot two inches, raised her chin ever so slightly, and composed her lips in a practiced smile—warm but not too wide, welcoming but not immodest. The young man's face lit up. He bounded over to her and chucked her under the chin!

"You must be Nellie." He flashed his perfect white teeth in a grin appropriate for artless children or cute puppies.

How dare he! Even John didn't treat her like a child. Nellie took a step back and extended her hand. "I am very pleased to make your acquaintance, Mr. Carver."

The young man bowed his head, brought his lips together, and brushed them lightly over the back of her hand. He raised apologetic eyes to hers. "Please, call me Eustace."

"And you may call me Nellie." She allowed her hand to rest briefly in his before pulling away.

Back at the ranch, Nellie's father quickly exhausted the topics of conversation he was prepared to discuss with gentry and excused himself to attend to fence repair. Her mother settled their guest in the spare room and then left it to Nellie to entertain the gentleman in the parlor. *Buck up, buttercup, he'll come around*, Nellie told herself, and she began her campaign to win his affection.

While her mother worked her garden in the mornings and devoted herself to a women's club literacy project during the afternoons, Nellie and Eustace sat on the front porch watching the road, talking about the suffrage movement—he was for it—and the demise of the thirty-cent coin—he was against it. When the heat of the day drove them inside, they read to each other and played cards.

On the third day of his visit, Eustace reached into his pocket. "I almost forgot, Nellie; I have something for you." He handed her an elongated velvet box.

Good things come in small packages, her mother often told her. Her head buzzed with delicious anticipation. Of course, it wasn't a ring, but in her imagination, she could feel his gentle hands fix the clasp of a promise necklace around her neck. She lifted opened the box.

It took every ounce of will she had to hold back the tears that wanted to come. In her chest, a burning ball of lead settled where once her heart had beaten. Widening her eyes, she forced a smile. "I love"—she rolled the slim tool between her fingers and the palm of her hand, feeling the weight and smoothness of it—"the pen. Thank you, Eustace."

That night, Nellie unpinned the hair she had so carefully arranged on top of her head. The next morning, she drew her hair back in a braid, looped it low on her neck, and fastened it in place.

At breakfast, she asked her mother to purchase a bottle of India ink when she went to town.

Nellie began to observe Eustace, making notes in her journal about amusing mistakes he made trying to adapt himself to his new surroundings. Dressed in a Norfolk suit more appropriate to a round of golf, he asked John about hunting conditions in Kansas.

"I am most interested in a recently relocated herd of elk I have read about," he told the ranch foreman, who gave a surly grunt in reply but saddled a horse for Eustace nevertheless. Eustace proved to be an excellent horseman. They didn't find elk, but at the interloper's insistence, John took him to visit Helen. After that, Eustace did not require so much of Nellie's company.

Nellie set her thoughts to paper.

Dear Diary,

Eustace is the most elegant man I can imagine. As hard as I have tried, he fails to notice that I have the wit and winsomeness a man of his stature requires in a companion. He spends all his time with a girl who has not eyes to see what manner of man stands before her. I will give him credit for his compassion for poor Helen. If I were a good Christian, I would have to confess a querulous spirit over his attentions to the mite. It is not in my nature to be so grouchy, but there it is.

It was not until many months after Eustace returned to the East that Nellie learned the young man had set himself the task of making a new life possible for Helen. It was all the buzz at church. He had enrolled her in a school for the blind near his home and sent her a train ticket.

How was it possible? What did Eustace see in a sightless girl that prompted him to offer her a new life, where the most he had been moved to confer upon Nellie was a fountain pen? Her wound was deep, the pain like a poisoned arrow, personal and penetrating. Never—never, she vowed—would she allow herself to be hurt like that again. The callous young man had stolen her innocence without touching her body.

Nellie trailed her parents as they left the Sunday morning service. Her father pumped the pastor's hand and congratulated him on his sermon. Her mother managed to scoot past, but Nellie was not so fortunate. Trapped behind her father who had stopped to lecture the pastor on a fine point missed in his retelling of the Prodigal Son, she tried to get around them both. She lost her balance and stumbled directly into the big man's path. The pastor reached out and took her elbow to help her regain her balance. Turning his attention toward her, he kept hold of her elbow and addressed her so all could hear. "No good deed goes unrewarded, does it, my girl?"

Nellie straightened and tugged her elbow from his grasp.

"I was surprised to learn that you located the book we spoke of and took it upon yourself to facilitate its return without allowing us the pleasure of congratulating you on your good deed." He buttered his rebuke and served it to her with flourish.

"Oh. No need." She lowered her eyes.

"Such modesty." His booming voice held an edge that belied the sentiment. "You must be so pleased that our Helen has a bright future, thanks to your charitable action."

Nellie raised her eyes to his. "Praise God, from whom all blessings flow. Isn't that right, Pastor?" And she took herself off after her mother.

The day Helen boarded the train to travel East, Nellie once again mourned her lost hope in her diary.

Dear Diary,

As I have no disability with which to attract the attention of a benefactor, I shall have to consider my parent's wishes that I marry John. I have cried all the tears I have. This is God's punishment, I suppose, for my wanting to rise above my station and for being so churlish about Helen.

The truth is, I miss Eustace terribly. He is the first man I could ever really talk to. He spoke to my secret self and made me smile inside. I will miss him every day for the rest of my life.

I am not enough of a romantic to spend my days dreaming that Eustace will one day return, the way Mr. Darcy came back for Elizabeth. I must be practical and look ahead. From this day forward, I will place no faith in the love of a man.

14

Dismissed Without Prejudice

Portland, 1919

A year had passed since Madame Cyrette was laid to rest. Mother and baby son whose earthly lives had intersected briefly now lay side by side in companionable silence on a hill, an incomprehensible act of love performed by a broken man. What prompted such a man to love a woman who had spurned him?

Used to be, Nellie could puzzle things out with Jessie. Now Jessie was gone, moved to Utah because her husband got an itch to try his hand at a new job. Nellie couldn't fault him for that, but it raised an issue.

Before her sister left, Nellie took her to lunch and blurted out over a dish of Neapolitan, "Jessie, where will we be buried?"

"What? Why would you ask me that? You aren't planning to die because I'm leaving, are you?"

Nellie laughed and shook her head.

"Because that would be flattering, but quite unlike you." Jessie circled her small dessert dish with her spoon, collecting the remaining vestiges of hot fudge from her sundae into a tiny last bite.

Nellie pushed away her half-eaten ice cream. "It's just that we are all so scattered. Our parents are buried in Kansas. Mabel is buried here in Spokane. It's a serious question."

"Do we have to decide right now?" Jessie spoke through a mouthful of vanilla wafer.

"I suppose not. It's just that I wonder. When we are all gone, who will tell our stories?"

Now that Jessie was less accessible, the inland northwest began to lose its charm. There was nothing to keep Nellie in Spokane, except Mabel's grave. She would not abandon Opal and Leone, but a change of scene might do all of them some good. Nellie began to choose assignments that took her to Portland, extending her visits to include sightseeing and house hunting.

Portland revived Nellie's spirits. She welcomed the noise of new construction in this city that was widening its streets to accommodate the bustling traffic. Mobility characterized the City of Roses. Young people moving in, large office buildings going up, streetcars running back and forth, all served to make the city livable, workable, and enjoyable. The temperate weather compared favorably to Spokane's hotter summers and colder, drier winters. Winter dampness softened her skin. Rain nourished a profusion of flowers the like she'd never seen.

Over the years, Nellie had saved a nest egg. To her surprise, she now found herself desirous of a nest. Real estate agents who showed her charming craftsman cottages pointed out that fussy Victorians were no longer in vogue.

"Notice the lower ceilings and open living spaces, Mrs. Scott. From the kitchen, you can see into the living room and out to the backyard."

"In the last several years I've not spent much time in the kitchen."

The agent took the cue. She pointed out the modern appliances that made food preparation and cleanup easy. Nellie eyed the kitchen nook. Quite adequate for the three of them. Surely it would not be difficult to talk Opal into coming with her. She had already raised the subject, suggesting that a fresh start in a city full of hopeful young people might renew Opal's energy and give her the strength she needed to guide Leone in the proper direction.

Opal certainly had her hands full. She juggled temporary clerical jobs, taught dance classes, and tried to keep her headstrong daughter out of trouble. The nine-year-old was prone to leave her homework and her chores and wander off with older girls Opal didn't know. Pretty and popular, Leone used her knowledge of the latest dance steps to make friends far and wide.

On her last trip home, Nellie followed Opal into Leone's bedroom, where they found the girl's wet, sandy bathing costume dumped on the floor. Leone came out of the bathroom wrapped in a bath towel and stood in the hallway.

"Why are you two poking around in my room?" Her cheeks were high with color. Sunburn.

"Where have you been?" Opal held the soggy evidence of yet another misadventure up in front of her daughter.

"Swimming in the river." Leone took the costume from her mother's hand. "I was just about to wash this out."

"The Spokane River?"

Leone shrugged. "I guess."

"That river is dangerous, Leone. Did you swallow any water?"

"Not on purpose. Anyway, the river is perfectly safe, Mother."

Nellie stepped in and placed a hand on her granddaughter's shoulder, pulling the girl around to face her.

"Don't be impertinent. Go do your washing, and then get dinner started." Nellie gave Leone a little push in the direction of the kitchen. Then she turned to Opal.

"This is the very reason why we should move to Portland. You are losing control of her. A fresh start with a new group of friends is what she needs."

Opal stood in front of her mother as if she were standing on a stage. Spine erect, feet in third position, waiting for the dance master to call the familiar steps.

"I have students here. What would I do in Portland?"

"We will buy a house. We will rent a space where you can have your own dance studio. Portland is full of new theaters. There will be many opportunities for you."

Opal tilted her head and rubbed the back of her neck.

"I will help you with Leone."

"What if she is beyond help?"

"At nine years old? Don't be ridiculous. If she continues to misbehave, we will send her to Catholic school and let the nuns deal with her. She'll be fine."

The matter was settled.

They found a bungalow in Marshfield, farther outside Portland than they had hoped, but closer to the coast. Nellie loaned money to Opal to open her own studio: the Barry School of Dancing. At first, she taught children's classes on Fridays and Saturdays, schooling tykes in ballet technique and the aesthetics of expression in a variety of dance forms. Opal offered instruction in the latest ballroom dance steps to adults by appointment. So popular was dance as a form of physical education and social grace that it wasn't long before she had a full schedule of classes.

Opal employed Leone teaching the barre and floor exercises in the three and four-year-old classes. That kept her busy and out of trouble. Leone lapped up adoration from the toddlers in the baby classes. She thrived on the admiration of their parents, who never failed to remark on her rare combination of technical proficiency and expressive movement.

Now that her daughter and granddaughter were settled and happy, Nellie sought occasions to spend more time in Portland. She allowed her restless feet to carry her all over that city. Among a number of acquaintances she visited, she checked in often with her distant cousin Ned and his much younger wife Nadine. Their congeniality, despite their age difference, intrigued Nellie. After frequent visits to Portland fairs and festivals, the pair had fallen in love with the city's cottage-style bungalows and made Portland their permanent home. Nellie rode the trolley out to their Rose City Park neighborhood to visit. On this occasion, she discovered Nadine alone in the bedroom, sobbing into a flowery chintz bed pillow.

"What is the trouble?" Nellie put her arms around Nadine.

"Ned is breaking my heart." Sitting up, the young woman wiped furious tears from her eyes. "It's this blonde toe dancer they are featuring at the Revue. Ned is there every night."

"That's nothing to cry about, Nadine." Nellie straightened up. "Dress yourself up and go with him."

Nadine sat up and snuffled into her soggy tissue. "Well I did go the first three evenings, but he sits in the bald-headed row and makes himself so conspicuous that I refuse to go anymore."

Nellie snickered. Such behavior had once ignited her own outrage. She wished she had had someone to sit her down and talk some sense into her. She took Nadine by the shoulders and sat her up straight."

"You know how Ned loves dance."

Nadine dropped her head and stared at her knees. Nellie lifted the girl's dimpled chin with her finger and looked directly into her tear-filled blue eyes. "No doubt this girl is an artist and very beautiful."

Nadine wiped her eyes and composed herself. "Oh, she is very artistic, I'll give her that. She is a dazzle from top to toe. As far as Ned is concerned, her top starts about six inches below her chin and ..." Nadine gestured, making it clear that her rival was well-endowed.

"*Ooohhh*, I get the picture." Nellie waggled her eyebrows, pulling a laugh from her cousin's injured wife.

"While I despise her, I will admit she is a beauty." Nadine stood up, restored the pillow to its proper place, and began to pace back and forth in front of Nellie. "Ned raves over her; he says she is the most luscious bit of femininity he ever saw." She bent over to collect her trail of pink tissues from the floor and tossed them into a trash basket hand painted with blush-colored cottage roses.

My goodness, thought Nellie, *she coordinates the color of her tissues with her trash can.* Could it be Ned's young wife saw drift where there was only *draguer*? In the French way, men often dallied where they felt no obligation to remain. Still ...

"While Ned's observations may be true, his remarks to you are unkind." Nellie circled her arm around Nadine's shoulder and walked her to the kitchen. "But you are taking this too seriously. Ned can't be led astray simply by watching a girl dance."

"He has never even looked at another woman since we've been married." Nadine spilled a fresh flow of tears into the flower vase she was preparing to receive the daisy bouquet Nellie had brought her.

"We have been so happy." She shook her head and jammed daisies into the ceramic frog at the bottom of the vase.

"He's going again this evening." She snapped a daisy at the throat.

"And when I asked him if it wasn't getting a bit monotonous, he laughed and said, 'Little Dolly Dixon will never become monotonous to me.'"

Nellie stood shoulder to drooped shoulder beside Nadine. Taking the shears from the young woman's hand, she trimmed the stems on the last of the daisies and filled in the gaps left in the arrangement. "This is Friday, and the program changes Monday. Little Miss Vixen will no doubt be on the train out of town by the weekend."

"It's Dixon. Dolly Dixon," Nadine said, and they had another good laugh.

The Monday morning paper featured an announcement that gave Nellie an idea. The revue had been held over; however, a small fire at the theater required repair work that would delay the presentation until later in the evening. Nellie rang up her young relative.

"Why not take advantage of this blaze? Invite Dolly Dixon to spend the afternoon with you and Ned. The surest way of curing an infatuated man is to encourage him. She won't look half as charming off stage. Show Ned you don't care a fig about this silly business."

"How on earth shall I contact Miss Dixon?"

"Go to your husband's office, write a joint invitation on his letterhead, and send it by messenger."

Nadine did as Nellie advised. Then, as arranged, she met Nellie in the shopping district for lunch. One look at Nadine told Nellie that the plan had gone awry.

"Miss Dixon declined the invitation." Nadine shrugged and studied the lunch menu.

"Did she say why?"

"She expressed her regrets and said it was against company rules to meet with theater patrons privately."

"Well then, you have nothing to worry about."

The following Sunday, Nellie joined the couple at their breakfast table. Ned casually mentioned that business would take him to Seattle in the coming week. Nadine tossed her napkin on the table and left the room.

Nellie turned to her cousin. "You are acting foolishly and being inconsiderate. We all know that Dolly Dixon plays in Seattle next week."

Ned reddened and began to sputter. "You think my company conducts business to suit my whims and fancies? I must go when and where I am ordered to go." He stood up and followed his wife out of the room, leaving Nellie alone with the remaining scones.

Nellie got busy with work. She thought she should call on her cousin and his wife to satisfy herself that the situation had been resolved, as she expected it would. She kept putting it off until a chance encounter with Nadine on a city sidewalk alarmed her. The young woman came walking up behind her and tossed off terrible words.

"I am divorcing Ned." She held her chin high. "He has destroyed our home and broken my heart. I have just signed the papers." Nadine kept walking, and Nellie had to increase her pace to fall into step with the visibly irate woman.

"Surely you have no grounds for divorce." Nellie reached for Nadine's arm to detain her. "Listen to reason, or you will have only remorse and regrets."

The words that tumbled from her lips had a hollow ring. Did she regret her own divorce? Of course, the circumstances were quite different. It was not in the heat of passion that she and John had parted but in the cold light of reason.

"Incompatibility of temper. I'm suing him for alimony and division of the property." Nadine stopped in the middle of the busy sidewalk and stood with her arms rigid, her fists clenched. "I will humiliate him and make him suffer." It was Nadine's turn to grasp Nellie's arm. Nellie was tugged into the doorway of a linen shop with a *Closed for Lunch* sign on the door.

"I have shed my last tear." Nadine whistled her words between her clenched teeth. "The papers will be served on him when he steps off the train tomorrow night, and his blonde affinity will receive a copy as well."

Nellie raised her eyebrows and widened her eyes.

Nadine ran her fingers through her freshly bobbed hair. "I have named Dolly Dixon as co-respondent."

Nellie's mouth dropped open. "Nadine, this is all your imagination. Do you have any proof?"

Nadine squared her shoulders and raised herself to her full height, gaining about an inch in her spine. "Well." Her speech was clipped. "If you had been at the Rose Garden Bridge Club and heard the veiled sarcasm and offhand remarks being passed around, you would understand my situation." And with that, the injured party turned heel and marched back down the street.

The next Saturday morning, Nellie's phone rang. It was Ned.

"I am off on a hunting trip. If you are going to be around for a few days, could you go over and stay with Nadine?"

Her questions yielded no answers that made any sense, so Nellie thought she'd better do as he asked. She packed a valise and arrived at the bungalow just as the postman walked up with a registered letter.

A wan and defeated-looking Nadine greeted her listlessly and signed for the letter with little curiosity. "More legal correspondence, I imagine." Nadine grimaced and ushered Nellie into the living room. They sat and chatted for a few moments, and then Nellie nodded her head toward the letter in Nadine's hand. "Legal papers don't normally come in lavender-scented pink envelopes."

Nadine got up, stationery in hand, and went to her desk. She returned with a silver letter opener in one hand, the letter in the other. Slitting the envelope corner to corner, she pulled a single sheet of vellum from its enclosure. She unfolded what Nellie could see was a handwritten letter and read it to herself. Her hand went to her mouth and what little color she had left in her face drained away.

The clock on the wall ticked loudly in the silence that followed. Finally, Nadine spoke in a grim voice. "No wonder Ned left town. I would like to leave town too." Handing the stiff parchment to Nellie, she retreated to her bedroom.

Nellie held the correspondence between her fingers for a moment. Then she moved her eyes slowly across the elegant letters, embellished with loops, curls, and flourishes, that formed the words that sent Nadine into hiding.

Dear Madam:

I have carefully read your divorce complaint, in which you have named me co-respondent. As Dolly Dixon, I deny the accusations, but as Frank Boyd, I am highly flattered.

Kindly be advised that you are slightly mistaken regarding the design of my entity and the nature of the intentions you presume I have toward your husband. In the interests of setting to rest any misunderstanding, I am mailing a duplicate of this letter to your husband.

Sincerely,

Dolly Dixon aka Frank Boyd

"Oh my!" Nellie's hand rose to her flushed cheek. *Poor Nadine.* She moved her fingers to her lips to suppress the giggle that was rising from her windpipe before it played inappropriately on her vocal chords. She would not have a laugh in her cousin's living room at the mortified woman's expense.

Within weeks, the following entry in the *Court Journal* appeared:

Nadine Carter vs. Ned Carter
Dolly Dixon, co-respondent
Dismissed without prejudice

15

A Sandy Footprint

1921

*N*ed and Nadine reconciled. Nellie saw little of them after that. She resolved never again to get herself so involved in someone else's marital affairs. When a quarreling couple patched things up, as so often they did, discomfort with witnesses to their folly was not unusual.

As Opal's star was rising in the community, Nellie found herself less inclined to seek entertainment elsewhere. It was a delight to watch her daughter shine. In just two years, Opal had made such a name for herself that her students danced for private parties and appeared regularly on big theater stages up and down the coast from Marshfield to Gardiner, North Bend, and Portland.

Nellie loved watching Leone perform. Always a featured dancer, she drew gushing reviews. *The Coos Bay Times* reported that during an interval at Marshfield High School's senior ball "the tiny daughter of Mrs. Barry, the Marshfield dancing mistress, executed one of the modern dance interpretations, and elicited unstinted applause for what was a wonderful performance for a child of seven years."

"Seven! Where did they get that I'd like to know?" Leone huffed around the house. "I'm almost eleven."

"Someday you will be glad to have your age misreported like that," Nellie said.

"About your performance, Leone," Opal said, "be careful not lose your technique in the free expression of these new dance forms. Discipline is still required, even in modern dance."

Leone narrowed her eyes at her mother. "The audience loved my performance."

"You know what I'm talking about."

Leone flounced off.

It was true. Her scrapbook was bursting with reviews that never failed to mention the dance mistress's talented daughter. Where she had performed in small auditoriums in Washington, in Oregon she danced on large professional theater stages. Marquees advertised Barry School of Dance programs: "Crowds Turned Away at Recital," and "Dancing by Small Misses Draws Throngs." Newspaper headlines announced sold-out performances.

Leone read every news report to Nellie. Reporters lauded the costumes, scenery, and live orchestration, and never failed to single out Leone for special attention. With her proud mother and grandmother in the wings, Leone commanded the spotlight with fuse-like energy in her feet and radiance on her face. A good outlet for her exuberance, Nellie hoped. A little too hot to handle, Opal feared.

Nellie's hopes extended to Opal as well. She wished her daughter would be content with her success and pay no mind to the men who sniffed around the attractive widow. But one summer night in Portland, after the young misses had been whisked home by their chaperones, Opal had accepted an invitation to go dancing with a man to whom she had recently been introduced. A dapper salesman had impressed work-weary Opal with a box of candy and an ability to tell jokes in both English and French. In a weak moment, Nellie volunteered to take Leone home so her daughter could have a rare night on the town.

What Felix Wolff lacked in stature, he made up for in fast footwork. Fast on the dance floor and fast with the *bon mot*, he put the hustle on Opal and won her heart.

Nellie discouraged her daughter from accepting the little Frenchman's proposal of marriage.

"What do you know about him?" Nellie fumed.

"His family came from Paris and set up business in San Francisco," Opal told her mother. "They are socially prominent."

"What does that mean to us?"

"*Us? We* aren't marrying him, I am marrying him. He's a good dancer, he makes me laugh, and I am going to marry him."

A justice of the peace married Opal and Felix, and they established their home in Portland. The house in Marshfield was sold, but Nellie refused to move in with her daughter and her new husband. Instead, she took a room at a boarding house a few blocks away and began traveling again. Her schedule made her accessible to Opal and Leone between assignments but on her terms. Work eased the ache in her heart over the invasion of the little Parisian into what had, for a short season, been the happiest time of her life.

Late one afternoon, Nellie huddled under the eaves of a hotel veranda in Gold Beach. She watched the Pacific Ocean pound the black-sand beach. If she focused on the forces of nature that put all things in perspective, perhaps the throb in her bunion would not command such undeserved attention. She let her thoughts roll with the tide.

"Why don't you get that taken care of?" Opal asked Nellie the previous week. Nellie had dropped by with a birthday gift for Leone, who was turning twelve.

"I have never been to a doctor in my life, and I see no reason to start now."

Never? A bit of exaggeration maybe, but Nellie had pressed her point. "In my day, women had better things to do than to traipse to the doctor for every little pain."

In my day? Had she really said that? The rumble of the waves below the veranda muted other thoughts. Only this tiny flotsam bubbled up from the deep.

Nellie made it a practice to edit out of her speech any suggestion that the passage of time was slowing her down or affecting her ability to keep up-to-date.

Age is merely a state of mind. The body is a graveyard, but a wise woman exercises mind over matter until her appointed time, she told herself. Best to put her mind to doing what she could to comfort Leone.

Poor Leone. During her visit, Nellie had pulled her granddaughter aside and questioned her about her new stepfather.

"He's okay, I suppose." Leone shrugged and hung her head.

Nellie smoothed the girl's hair, triggering a flood of tears.

"We were doing just fine! Why did she have to marry him and bring him into our house? He smells like cigars. I hate him!"

Why indeed? Nellie shook the rumination from her head. Best to live in the present. Hugging herself against the cold, she moved to the railing. She never tired of hearing the rhythm of the tide. Deep within, she felt the earth inhale oceanic rumblings, hold its breath, and, in a long, slow swish of briny water, exhale some life-giving force back out to sea.

Out to sea. Tears flooded her eyes. Was she losing her moorings? She opened her eyes wide and let the wind dry her tears.

Down the beach, a spectacle of a different sort came into view. A figure trudged up the dune. As an Indian woman drew nearer, her brown face presented a network of wrinkles, her chin striped by three vertical green lines.

The woman was clothed incomprehensibly in a black dress designed for a sylph-like frame. Layers of ruffles strained across her ample hips and fell past her ankles to drag in the sand. The bodice of the gown gapped in front, exposing a broad strip of brown flesh. Three of the largest safety pins ever manufactured bridged the divide. A towering flower-covered hat perched atop her head, and soft, beaded moccasins adorned her feet.

Three baskets rested against her back. As she placed her hand on the gate from the beach to the hotel, she looked up at Nellie and flashed a toothless grin. Ever curious, Nellie swept down the stairs to meet the exotic visitor, who was eager to show her the handcrafted baskets that Nellie knew commanded high prices in gift shops that dotted the coast between Big Sur and Seattle. After some good-natured haggling, Nellie became the proud owner of her first work of art.

The woman continued on her way, and Nellie climbed the stairs back to the veranda, where she encountered the inn's manager, Mr. Norris.

"I see you have been dealing with old Three Stripe," he laughed. "She's quite the business woman."

"Tell me about her." Nellie took a seat on a porch rocker and set the tightly woven basket down on a wicker table festooned with brochures, bowls of fruit and flowers, and a dish of hard candies. She traced her fingers over the intricate ocher parallelograms that twined in the cream-colored weave of ferns and grass and dyed porcupine quills. "What's her story?"

Mr. Norris set aside the small paintbrush he had been using to touch up weathered spots on the door frame. He wiped his hands on his stained buffalo-plaid shirt, sat down on the top stair, and pulled a pipe out of his pocket. He tamped, and he kindled, and he puffed, all the rituals a man performs to gain the undivided attention of a woman before he launches into an anecdote.

"White men stole her from the Nez Perce tribe when she was fourteen. She is a ward of the court. She's had a dozen children by a string of white husbands, all dead now. Kids are all dead too, of whiskey or consumption; they seem to inherit all the white man's diseases but none of their immunities. The county built her a little shack on the hillside and she lives alone now."

"The least they can do for the poor woman." Nellie rocked back in her chair, wishing she could remove her boot and massage her toe.

The innkeeper nodded. "She earns her keep around here. She has a remarkable knowledge of herbs and roots. If she hears of anyone sick, she goes to brewing some of her herb tea and makes it her business to care for them. No one asks her; she just does it." Mr. Norris removed his pipe from between his tobacco-stained teeth and punched the air with the pipe stem. "Believe me when I tell you there is an eighty-mile strip along this coast where there is only one doctor and no hospital." He tapped his pipe on the step to loosen the contents. "And business is slow for that doctor."

Nellie made a mental note to ask Three Stripe if she had a bunion remedy the next time the Indian woman passed by on the beach.

Mr. Norris dropped his pipe ash and dottle into a nearby flowerpot.

Nellie raised an eyebrow. "Good for the soil?"

Norris shrugged and returned his pipe to his pocket. "We had a flu epidemic here several years ago, and the boys at the logging camp got pretty sick. Kept old Three Stripe mighty busy when everyone else was afraid to go and doctor them."

A holler from inside ended the conversation. "That would be the missus. Duty calls."

A few days later Nellie was out for a walk. A motor bus arrived late and an old soldier who looked like he'd seen Civil War service got out. Coughing and hacking, he limped painfully down the road toward the beach.

"A pensioner from the Indian Wars," Mr. Norris explained to Nellie after she passed along the talk she overheard in town.

"People are saying that he has pitched a tent near Three Stripe's shack. That's odd, don't you think?"

"Many of these old codgers drift through town, each telling the same story; unfaithful wife, heartless children, endless government red tape."

"So, he is entirely without funds?"

"He likely has a small pension. He'll pull through. Old Three Stripe will fix him up with some bird soup and herb tea."

Some days later, Nellie strolled alongside the cold and misty beach to clear her head after hours of typing court transcripts. Once again, Three Stripe came trudging across the dunes. This time, she was wrapped in an old army blanket and carried a tin pail. Nellie looked at the milky substance in the pail, and then smiled and cocked her head.

"Goat milk. Neighbor very sick man."

"Ah."

Three Stripe looked down at Nellie's feet. She stared at the place where the shoe leather stretched thin and worn over Nellie's bulging toe and clicked her tongue. The wind carried her words. "Olive oil."

"I don't understand." Nellie looked into the small, warm, dark eyes nestled deep within the folds of skin above the Indian's cheekbones, eyes that spoke where spare words failed, the language of compassion.

"For that bump on your toe." Three Stripe pointed to the protruding bone. "Massage with olive oil, fifteen minutes, once morning, once night. Feel better." And she resumed her walk.

The next week, court adjourned for the year in the small town. Her business done, Nellie returned home.

<hr />

When she returned the following fall, Gold Beach and Nellie were each much the same, except for one happy improvement. Although an ache in her shoulder and stiffness in her hip troubled her from time to time, the pain in Nellie's toe had diminished greatly with the application of oil and regimen of massage. She hoped to encounter the medicine woman responsible for this miracle so she could thank her.

On a trip to the post office to visit her temporary mailbox, Nellie crossed paths, instead, with the old soldier, although not as old-looking as the first time she saw him. He no longer winced when he walked. His clothes were clean, his hair trimmed, his cheeks ruddy with health. He smiled and tipped his hat.

Nellie returned his gestures with a friendly nod. *Three Stripe's ministrations truly are miraculous.* She walked out of the post office with a passel of postcards from far-flung corners of the Northwest, written by people she had met over the years, but it was the letter from Leone that held the most interest. Slipping the cards into her bag, Nellie undid the envelope, pulled out a piece of dime store stationary, and read the letter while she walked.

Dear Grandmother,

I miss you! Mother says I have a saucy mouth and threatens to send me to Saint Mary's for high school. What twaddle! She probably just wants to get rid of me so she and Felix can go out dancing every night. If I am forced to go to Catholic school, I'm sure the nuns will assign me so much penance, no one will ever see or hear from me again. Please come home and defend my case!

Your loving granddaughter,

Leone

Ah, Leone, girl after my heart. Nellie made a mental note to write a letter of encouragement to her granddaughter.

That evening, Nellie chatted with the other boarders seated around the long dining table. Simple meals served family style suited the working class and professionals who wished to end their business day with some semblance of normality. Government workers, union organizers, and others on job assignments that required an extended stay avoided dyspeptic conversation. No debates about the League of Nations occurred at Mrs. Norris's dinner table. Instead, the guests chatted about their travels and the comforts that waited for them at home.

On occasion, Mrs. Norris indulged in town gossip. As they finished their dessert, she announced that the local Ladies Aid Society was privileged to have Mrs. Thrasher, a prominent figure in several women's organizations, speak to their chapter on an issue of considerable concern.

Nellie set aside her fork. "That was a delicious lemon cake, Mrs. Norris. May I inquire as to the nature of the concern?"

Mrs. Norris looked around the table. The accountant checked his watch. The union negotiator yawned and smiled apologetically. The bank examiner placed his napkin on the table, rose to his feet, and thanked his hostess with a slight bow of his head.

"I'm told it's a matter of moral turpitude." Mrs. Norris tried without success to catch the eye of the only other woman at the table. "I don't know the details." She began clearing the table. "At the very least, it will provide an excuse to get some air. Would you like to join me, Mrs. Scott?"

"I believe I will. It's been a long day of sitting for me."

Mrs. Norris looked once more in the direction of the other woman. "Mrs. Wells?"

"Thank you, but I think not." Mrs. Wells left the table, and Mr. Norris was about to do the same when his wife arrested him with a stern look.

"Mr. Norris will take care of the dishes," she said. Then she gestured to Nellie that it was time to go.

The two women walked several blocks to a warehouse in town that served as both a meeting space and an election hall. On the way, Mrs. Norris quizzed Nellie. "Why do you suppose Ida wasn't interested in coming with us? There might be a story here."

"I think Ida is here for a bigger story."

"I suppose our little efforts to preserve high moral standards pale in the face of what the Ku Klux Klan is trying to do."

Nellie's heart began to pound. She slowed her step. "Is that what you think the Klan is trying to do, 'preserve moral standards'? They are lynching people right here in Oregon. There is nothing moral about that."

"Well, let's not get into that. Look, here we are."

Inside the dimly lit warehouse, wooden chairs scraped against the rough timber floor as a line of women jockeyed for the best seats. Others hung back, waiting to see if there might be space on the backless benches that lined the brick walls. Mrs. Norris grabbed Nellie's elbow and guided her forcefully to the front row, where it seemed they might not find a seat. Mrs. Norris stood erect and silent at the end of the row until a pair of women noticed her.

"Oh, Mrs. Norris." One of the women spoke up. "I tried to save a place for you but …"

"I have a guest." Mrs. Norris breathed the words through tight lips.

"Oh, of course." Both women jumped up and fled.

Nellie opened her mouth to protest, but Mrs. Norris jerked her head toward the vacated seats.

"It's the rules."

Wanting no more fuss, Nellie obeyed.

Once they had settled themselves, the society's president welcomed the group and called Mrs. Thrasher to the podium. Although she was well under five feet tall, Mrs. Thrasher was an imposing figure. As she approached, she fixed her eyes on a soapbox that sat in the corner. Then she stood in front of her audience and looked pointedly at the society's president. That lady lost no time retrieving the box and setting it in place. Mrs. Thrasher put a heavy hand on the president's shoulder and ascended her platform. She had no notes that needed assembling. Looking down through her spectacles on the ladies gathered below her, she raised her finger and wagged it in the air.

"Here in your midst, you have a white man and a squaw living openly and notoriously together."

Ladies looked down at their folded hands, shifted position in their seats, or turned to whisper in their neighbor's ear. Mrs. Thrasher launched into a rambling account of the threat such a situation posed to the moral education of the town's children. She then called for the ladies to sign a petition calling for the removal of the debauching menace.

After an uncomfortable silence, a thin-faced woman wearing a clean calico dress ventured a question from the back of the room. "Has anyone ever seen them do anything so very notorious?"

"My goodness, yes." A tall woman in front stood up and turned to face the group. "My husband was over to that shack they're living in and he saw the colonel showing Three Stripe pictures in a fancy magazine and trying to explain things to her."

"What kind of things?" the thin-faced woman asked.

Mrs. Thrasher rolled her prominent eyeballs and pursed her lips. "Use your imagination."

The meeting adjourned, and a line formed in front of the petition table. Nellie had developed too much respect for the role solid evidence played in the administration of justice to be comfortable with the condemnation she had just witnessed. Strangely, a sharp pain in the bunion that the ministrations of Three Stripe had eased flared up.

"The stale air in here is giving me a headache," she told Mrs. Norris. "I will wait for you outside." Then she bolted for the door, but not before the woman in the calico dress made her escape. Nellie would have liked to have talked to her; she admired women who asked questions, but they were rarely the type who banded together. The Calico dress had come late and alone and left at the first opportunity.

By the time Mrs. Norris trailed out of the meeting place, Nellie's bladder was full and her store of patience empty. "Who was that woman to come to town and say such things to those ladies?" she asked as she limped alongside the innkeeper.

"She did get them riled, didn't she?" Mrs. Norris quickly changed the subject to a new recipe for bean soup she planned to try out for dinner the following evening.

The next day, Nellie had to be in court. She made her way through a small crowd and entered the wooden structure that served as a courthouse in tiny Gold Beach. Once a grocery store with a backroom pool hall, the building now stood empty, except for once a year when court was in session.

This Tuesday morning, people poured into town from the surrounding countryside. They had traveled by foot, on horseback or buckboard, motorcar or boat to reach the county seat. A court session allowed them to renew acquaintances and friendships, swap horses, and show off new babies born during the year. It also afforded the opportunity for the young people to do their own kind of courting.

Inside the dusty makeshift courtroom, Nellie found the table that had been set up for her and took a seat. Just before the bailiff said the "All Rise," she spotted Ida Wells in the public gallery. Sitting beside Ida was the thin-faced woman. A slim skirt and a long, loose-cut jacket replaced the calico dress. The two sat apart from a cozy of townsfolk.

Nellie had no time to think what this meant. Court was now in session. She gave all her attention to the judge. The whiskered gentleman with an air of Santa Claus about him winked at her and asked the clerk to read the calendar.

Checking the short calendar as the clerk read, Nellie was surprised to see Mrs. Thrasher's case against the old soldier and the Indian woman on the docket. How had she managed that so quickly? She would put her money on the tall woman with the well-prepared accusation. The two of them must have worked together in secret before the public meeting. What was the use of a petition, then, if the deed was done?

A commotion at the door caught Nellie's attention. She looked up to see several ladies silhouetted against the morning sun that streamed in through the door. Skirts rustled. Boots clicked on the floor. Scents of rose water mingled with the faint odor of dry rot.

The bailiff rushed up and escorted Mrs. Thrasher and several members of the Ladies Aid Society to a long bench behind the district attorney. The district attorney turned and nodded politely to the gallery of women that Nellie supposed were there to give him moral support for the important task ahead. Heat flashed through Nellie's body that she refused to attribute to menopause.

Despite her sneezes, Nellie's pencil raced across page after page in her reporter's notebook forming squiggles and word abbreviations, verbatim transcripts she would later format and file with the county clerk. She set down every word.

The Clerk: Your Honor, we have only a criminal docket.

The Court: Very well, read the cases to be tried and the offenses with which each defendant is charged.

The Clerk: State of Oregon vs. Jim Marks, charged with rape.

The State of Oregon vs. Pete Bean, charged with having in his possession one quart of White Mule.

The State of Oregon vs. David Plummer, charged with maintaining and operating a still.

Four uncontested divorce cases; desertion is charged.

The State of Oregon vs. Colonel Reynolds, charged with living openly and notoriously with Three Stripe, a Yurok.

The Court: I have read somewhere, and I can't seem to recollect where, that the first shall be last and the last first. I think that is a pretty good idea, so we will call the Reynolds case first.

The district attorney tugged a file and a few notes from his overstuffed folio case. Nellie looked over at Three Stripe, who sat on a blanket on the floor. The colonel limped forward to be sworn in and take the witness stand, where he was questioned at length about his living arrangements. Nellie recorded the proceedings:

District Attorney:	Your Honor, I object to the introduction of documentary evidence that has not first been submitted to me.
The Court:	I do not think the court is going to be unduly biased by looking at this paper. I will just take a look here and if I think it is of interest to you, I will ask the clerk to pass it over.

The judge glanced at the paper and handed it to the clerk, who passed it to the district attorney.

District Attorney:	Are you MARRIED to Three Stripe, Colonel Reynolds?
Defendant:	Yes sir. That is what I have been trying to tell you, but you wouldn't let me. Hateya, that's her Indian name, takes good care of me. Your honor, I've been teaching her how to read and write her name and …
The Court:	Case dismissed. The defendant is discharged. Recess until one o'clock.

The judge looked with bemusement at the backs of the women of the Ladies Aid Society, who filed out singly or in pairs. Mrs. Thrasher had slipped away shortly after the district attorney had made the old soldier's circumstances public. A charge of public indecency would hardly stand. The colonel had produced a marriage certificate.

Nellie readied her pencils and notebooks for the afternoon session. Then she caught up with the colonel as he ushered his wife from the room.

"Colonel, I was wondering: what is the meaning of the name Hateya?"

The Indian woman lifted her tattooed chin and spoke up clearly, lisping only on the last word. "It mean, footprint in the sand."

As promised, Mrs. Norris served a delicious bean soup for dinner that evening. Nellie emptied her bowl. As she lifted her napkin to her lips she addressed her hostess. "That was a lovely soup." Then she nodded at Ida Wells." Much tastier than the crow I imagine Mrs. Thrasher is eating tonight."

16

A Growing Family

Portland, 1925

Four years after Opal and Felix married, great joy and great sorrow visited them. Opal gave birth to twin girls, Jane and Jean. Jane lived, but Jean failed to thrive and died a few weeks after her birth.

The progress Felix had made winning over Leone diminished. No more weekend afternoons at the movies or trips to the beach, Felix now had his hands full making funeral arrangements for the tiny infant, fixing bottles for the surviving twin, and comforting Opal. It was Nellie who noticed Leone's barely contained resentment. Leone seemed to have three temperatures. She simmered on sulky, erupted into heated outbursts, and boiled over in defiance.

Nellie didn't wish to intrude, but something had to be done. Felix lacked the will, and Opal lacked the strength to deal with a moody teenager. One Sunday morning, Nellie showed up at their house and shooed the exhausted parents out of doors.

"It's a beautiful day." Nellie held the front door open. "Take the baby for a carriage ride."

Leone shuffled into the front room, her hair in her face, her pajamas limp with too much wear between washings. "I'm not going," she said.

"No," Nellie said, "you're not. You are going to stay here, and you and I are going to have a talk."

Felix mouthed a *thank you* over Leone's head and scooped up the red-faced baby from where she lay on a rug, kicking tiny feet inside the blanket that swaddled her.

"Scoot," Nellie said to Opal. "Go get some air."

The door banged behind them, and Leone rubbed sleep and tears out of her eyes. "Fifteen is a ridiculous age to have a baby sister!"

"You are hardly the first to be inconvenienced by a late arrival."

Leone threw her hands in the air and thrust her face heavenward. "I have been banished to Saint Mary's so Mother can fuss over her new cub."

Nellie clicked her tongue. Leone snickered and fell back on the sofa pillow. "Get it? Wolff. Cub."

"Oh, I get it, Leone." Nellie bent down and patted the girl's knee. "My sister was born when I was seven years old."

"Not the same." Leone thrust out her lower lip and glowered at her grandmother.

"I suppose not. But listen, I have an idea. I have to go to Omaha next month for a meeting of the National Shorthand Reporter's Association. How about you go with me?"

Leone brushed her hair out of her eyes. "What would I do while you are in meetings?"

"You are a big girl. You could wander around downtown and poke in the shops and art galleries. Omaha has the most beautiful playhouse in America. I will get us tickets to see *Abie's Irish Rose* at the Brandeis Theatre."

Teenage Leone was as stagestruck as they come. With such a grand adventure in sight, her mood improved, if only to ensure that the carrot would not be yanked from her grasp. More difficult was convincing Opal, but Nellie had an ally. Felix talked Opal into letting Leone make the trip.

"Travel is an essential part of her education," Felix argued. "She'll be with family. My people made several trips back and forth between Europe and the United States when I was young."

Who were Felix's people? It had never occurred to Nellie to ask. She was vaguely aware that he had family in San Francisco, but this was the first she had heard of connections in Europe. When they married, Nellie had quizzed Opal. What did she know about Felix? His French was more than an affectation; it sounded as if it might be his native language. Opal had been circumspect. Nellie had supposed it was disinterest, but now she wondered. There was no time to probe; all her attention went to what she hoped would be a glorious coming-of-age trip for her beloved granddaughter.

"Count your blessings," Nellie told Leone the day they boarded the train for Omaha. "I was a good deal older than you when I got my first taste of freedom."

"Freedom," Leone growled the word like a wolf ravenous for something long denied. She clutched the handle of a brand new train case festooned with her very first luggage tag.

The trip proved educational for both grandmother and granddaughter. Listening to speeches at the association luncheon, Nellie wished she were young enough to consider becoming more active in the organization. Buoyed by legislation that had given them the right to vote and to be treated equal to men under the law, professional women were stepping into leadership roles. They stumped for safer working conditions and higher pay for themselves. They strove for better education and more opportunities for the generations of women who would follow them.

During the keynote speech, Nellie's spirit soared. What would Amanda have thought of all this? Her mother had realized her highest aspirations when she moved to town and devoted herself to local charity work. What would she think of her daughter working to improve the lives of women across the United States? For the first time, Nellie felt a connection to some higher purpose. A fleeting sense of significance uncurled within her and sought the warmth of approval, but no mother's eyes in heaven smiled down on her, no child's eyes looked up to her, no lover's eyes held her in esteem. Self-approval was cold comfort. What, then, was the source of the glow that flickered inside her, filling her with teasing seconds of contentment and delight? How could she hold onto it? Applause peppered the room and she returned her attention to the podium.

While Nellie attended to business, Leone strolled the prosperous downtown. Back at the hotel as they dressed for dinner and an evening of theater, Leone gushed about straining to get a peek at what looked to be an Old Market speakeasy.

Nellie frowned. "You'd better not tell your mother that. Did you spend some time in the shops and the galleries?"

"Oh sure," Leone said, but further questioning elicited no information on what she saw on store shelves or gallery walls.

Any concerns Nellie might have had about her granddaughter's cultural interests vanished as they settled into their seats at the Brandeis Theatre. Grandmother and granddaughter both enjoyed the new comedy about the Jewish boy and Irish Catholic girl who marry against their parents' wishes. As they were preparing for bed in their hotel room after the play, Leone questioned Nellie. "What religion are we?"

"I suppose we are Protestants. I was raised in the Presbyterian church."

"When did you stop going to church?"

"When I left Kansas."

"Why?"

Nellie thought for a moment. "I felt no need."

Is that true? Something hard and dry prickled. A nameless heartache attacked a bit of damaged tissue and ripped the cover off an unknown hurt.

"Grandmother?"

Nellie pulled herself back. "No, that's not precisely true. I had no desire to let other people tell me how to live. Now go to bed."

It rankled, that silly comedy. A Jewish boy, an Irish Catholic girl, bonded in love and reconciled to their families and a future together. A fairy tale. Nellie lay on her pillow, thinking furiously. A streetlight shot a beam through the part in the curtains. It cast light on the sleeping form in the bed next to hers. Nellie watched the bedcovers rise and fall. She tried to slow her racing heartbeat by tuning it to the rhythm of her granddaughter's soft snoring.

When had she stopped believing the fairy tale? She knew the answer. When Eustace chose Helen. What was the fairy tale? That there was someone who would see her, know her, want her, love her, and set her free from old wounds? Someone who would show her a better way to live?

Had she done so badly on her own? She would not have thought so until this moment. Nellie fought for sleep, calming herself by summoning the gentle clack, clack, clack of train wheels rolling on the smooth track, the flutter of aspen leaves painting the sky in high passes. Her body relaxed and floated on the river of forgetfulness to a dark place.

She lay there, aware of her limbs but unable to move them. She fought to open her eyes, even as a vivid image torn from a familiar dream fixed itself clearly in her vision. Two birds perched side by side inside a wire cage. Lovebirds, she thought. She tittered at them, tapped her fingers on wire bars, but they ignored her. There was something else she could do. Should she? She moved her fingers to the cage door, lifted the latch and pulled open the door, then stepped back. One by one, the birds hopped forward, stretched their wings, and flew away. She stood open-mouthed before the empty cage. Accusations whooshed out of the cage and followed the birds. *You shouldn't have done that! They will die! You'll get in trouble!*

Nellie woke abruptly, her heart pounding. Leone stood over her, shaking her by the shoulder. "Wake up; we're going to miss the train." Morning light streamed through the open curtains.

Nellie threw off the covers and planted her feet on the floor. "Oh no, we won't. We're not going to miss a thing."

17

Payment in Kind

Gold Beach, 1925

Leone started her freshman year at Saint Mary's, and Nellie took her last assignment with the circuit court in Gold Beach. This term, the inn was filled with attorneys, court officials, and a sequestered jury.

Shadows cast by the flames in an open fireplace danced on the ceiling above old Mrs. Erwin and Mr. Ross.

"You are late." Mr. Ross addressed Nellie as she entered the parlor of the Sunset Inn.

"I've been transcribing some instructions for the judge. He is going to charge the jury in the morning. Where is everyone?"

"The attorneys are looking up some fine points of law in preparation for tomorrow. The jurymen are upstairs playing poker, and the witnesses have had to seek other accommodations." Ross leaned back in his chair and propped his feet up on the ottoman.

"The docket is a heavy one this term. Didn't you represent the defendant in every case the court tried last term?" asked Nellie.

"I did, and it cost me money, worry, and a sullied reputation."

"How's that?" Nellie took a seat beside Grandma Erwin, who planted herself nightly on the red velveteen settee. The old lady dropped her knitting in her lap in expectation of a good yarn.

The last of the sun caught the faded lace curtains through the crusted windowpane and dipped below the dunes across the highway. Mr. Norris entered the darkening parlor and bent down to light the fire logs stacked in the cast-iron grate. Ross waited until the innkeeper retreated, the floor-boards creaking under his cautious feet.

Mrs. Erwin fixed her rheumy eyes on the defense attorney. After retrieving a cigarette from a monogrammed case, Ross held the case out to the ladies. The old lady wrinkled her nose and Nellie shook her head politely. The gentleman lit his cigarette, drew smoke into his lungs and held it there. Nellie could almost taste the tang of tobacco, a remembrance of kissing John. As she grew older, the filter on her memory seemed to thin, and recollections passed through unbidden. The fire in the hearth caught and crackled in symphony with the ticking wall clock. Mr. Ross blew smoke rings and began his tale.

"A man in jail asked to see me. Unwashed, unshaven, dressed in a ragged pair of overalls, he was. Accused of bootlegging."

Nellie composed her face in an expression of devout interest.

"He wasn't your regular bootlegger. He'd been peddling his moonshine to get a little money to feed his family, but he hadn't been very successful. At one time, the fella owned a prosperous farm up river, but he mortgaged the property to invest in a machine some engineer invented to separate fine, old gold from the black sand that is up and down the coast here."

"I remember that." Nellie leaned back against a tasseled satin pillow on the settee. "As I recall, that enterprise failed."

Tapping the thin mustache that framed his upper lip, Ross drew a finger alongside the carefully clipped facial hair to the raised corner of his mouth. "Your recollection is accurate, Mrs. Scott."

Nellie met the glow in his amber-colored eyes with a slight play of amusement across her lips. Over the years, she had so disciplined her smile that she had no laugh lines.

"Let the man continue his story." Mrs. Erwin poked an elbow into Nellie's side, jutted her chin at Mr. Ross, and resumed working her knitting needles.

Ross took in smoke from his cigarette in small puffs. The exhaled fumes curled around his words. "I agreed to take his case, figuring the ends of justice would be better served if we turned him loose to care for his family. In payment, he offered me his only possession, a two-year-old black Mexican bull. I declined and told him he could pay me when his ship came in. He told me some cock-and-bull story about a bunch of money he was in line to inherit from an estate being settled in the east. The upshot of it all, I hauled his sickly wife and his five kids into court to gain the jury's sympathy."

Nellie tightened her lips into a line that underscored the sad truth of an all too common situation. Mr. Ross took a final draw on his cigarette and placed it in a small crystal ashtray balanced on his knee.

"The DA pushed hard for a conviction, but I got him off."

The cigarette burned into the filter and went out. The cooling remains produced an acrid stench that set Nellie's nose to twitching. Mr. Ross emptied the contents of the ashtray into his palm. He got to his feet and tossed the ashes into a potted plant near the door. Then he pulled a handkerchief scented with sage and eucalyptus oil from his pants pocket and wiped his hands. Carefully refolding the linen square, he returned it to his pocket and began to pace.

"He insisted I take the bull in payment. He was leaving the county, he said, and he had no more use for the animal. So I hired a guy to drive the bull up to the Kentuck Slough, where I was running some cattle. It took the guy four days to do the job, and it cost me twenty dollars."

"Four days to run your gentleman cow up to the slough?" The old lady cackled. "Your man must have stopped at every watering hole along the way, if you get my meaning."

"Oh, I do Mrs. Erwin. It gets worse." He rubbed his hands together and the pungent odor of spicy herbs filled the room.

Nellie's nose picked up the pleasing scent and her empty stomach began to raise a ruckus. "Do go on with your story, Mr. Ross."

Mr. Ross stretched his arms out wide and arched his back, as if to summon the gods of gab. "Ah," he said when a joint in his shoulder popped. "Well, about six weeks after I got home a young man comes into my office and tells me he's there to collect damages from me. Seems he lives out by Kentuck Slough and has a bed of choice strawberry plants in full bloom, tightly fenced to keep the chickens and rabbits out; a fence that bull of mine tore through to get to the strawberries, and that cost me another twenty-five dollars. You keeping track of what I'm spending here?"

Nellie pulled a steno pad out of her leather satchel bag and began a tally.

"I called a butcher friend of mine and told him to go get the bull and render him into some nice cuts of meat, but he couldn't find the animal. Next thing I know, I got a daddy and his little girl in my office with a sob story about a bull that chased her up a tree and kept her there all day. When her daddy came home to an empty house and no supper, he heard her cries and went to her rescue. That bull charged him, chased him through a flock of clothes hanging out on the line, and the upshot of this was a forty-dollar payoff."

The old lady guffawed and set her knitting needles on either side of her head, pretending to be a charging bull. Nellie added forty dollars to her tally.

"I called another butcher, but his luck was the same. No bull. Then Hans Johnson presents himself and owns up to having shot my bull through the eye. Killed him dead."

The old lady slapped her knee and her knitting tumbled to the floor. The needles, which had long since slipped out of the barely started work, rolled off the thick Persian rug and clinked across the polished wood floor. Ross retrieved one escaped needle and waved it in her direction.

"Turns out, Hans was out courting. It was dark when he started home through the pasture. Wouldn't you know it, that bull came charging out of nowhere. Hans ran, tripped over some tree roots, and, as luck would have it, found a hollowed-out tree stump to hide in."

The clock on the wall chimed six times, and Mr. Norris entered the parlor to pull the chains on fussy table lamps scattered about the room. Ross headed for the decanter of sherry and bottle of scotch Mr. Norris left on the cocktail cart under the clock. He handed the ladies cordial glasses of sweet liquor and returned to the cart to pour himself a heavy-bottomed glass of scotch straight up. On his way back to take his seat, he paused beside Nellie and rested a hand on the back of the settee, just behind her shoulder.

Despite the barrier of the settee back, Nellie could feel the heat radiating from the attorney's body, damp with the exertion of orating in a feverish room. It was not an unpleasant feeling. She twisted in her seat to look up into his face and gave him a half smile that signaled he'd best return to his chair.

Ross whirled around slowly, splashing a bit of Scotch from his glass as he pantomimed the action of his words. "Hans reached for the revolver he always carried. When he caught a flash of the animal's eye, he aimed and he shot."

Nellie wondered if you could actually drop a bull with a revolver and what caliber bullet would be required. She thought better of raising the question.

"I told Hans to go back, skin the animal, and keep the skin as a memento of his bravery."

"That afternoon, Hans returned with a man who owned a large blooded stock farm down the slough and claimed that Hans had dispatched his prize cow instead of the bull. It seems that Hans's sweetie sent him home with a couple of quarts of syrup in an open container.

"Picture this. While Hans is running from the charging beast, syrup slops onto his shirt. He drops the container and shinnies a dead tree trunk so he can drop down into the hollow. Well, the syrup on his shirt gets smeared all over the tree trunk." Ross paused to grin and nod vigorously.

"A sticky situation, if ever I heard one." The old lady bounced up and down in her seat. Nellie took a look at the tally and gave a low whistle. "I hope sweeter times are ahead for you, Mr. Ross."

Ross barreled ahead. "It's dark out. Hans wrestles his revolver out of its holster. The bull stops to lick syrup from the container, but Old Bessie wanders over, attracted by the syrup on the tree trunk, and *bam!* Hans drops her dead. That cost me seven hundred dollars."

"Ho, ho!" Old lady Erwin pounded her tiny hand on the sofa.

Nellie crossed her legs at her ankles and wiggled her foot. "Dare I ask what happened to the bull?"

"I gave a cowboy a ten to hunt down the bull and kill it. But guess what?"

"He never found the scoundrel." Mrs. Erwin hooted.

"I cannot imagine." Nellie sneaked a look at her watch.

"The cowboy found that bull dead in the slough. Apparently, the dumb beast devoured the syrup container along with the syrup, and it didn't go down so well."

"He died of the bellyache?" Mrs. Erwin slapped her knee. "Well, don't that beat all."

Nellie handed a list of the damages to Mr. Ross. "I can see that you are poorer for this misadventure. This will give *you* the bellyache." The sum was seven hundred and eighty dollars. They all had a good laugh before heading into the dining room for dinner. As they went, Mr. Ross leaned over and whispered in Nellie's ear. "I hear we are having steak tonight."

———

A week later, Nellie sat at a small secretary desk in the parlor, catching up on her correspondence. The front door blew open, and Mr. Ross hurried inside, shaking water off his hat. He removed his raincoat and draped it above the puddle of water where the other guests' rainwear hung in a convivial circle around the coat tree.

Across the room, a candle danced breezily on the cocktail table. A bottle of scotch and an old fashioned glass waited for the attorney. Grandma Erwin rocked by the fire, an afghan tucked across her knees against the cold that crept in through the windows, a book in her lap. Mr. Ross poured his drink and came to stand in front of the fire. He lifted the glass in Nellie's direction.

"Would you like to hear the sequel to the bull story?"

Nellie laid her pen down on the letter she had been writing to Opal and turned around in her seat. Her writing hand found its way to the tight place on her shoulder at the base of her neck. Massaging the sore area, she nodded.

"Did you two happen to notice the man I left the hotel with earlier this afternoon? That was Davis."

"The down-at-the-mouth bootlegging farmer who saddled you with a bad-tempered bull?" Nellie asked.

"The very same. He came back to pay me for representing him. I told him about the bull episode, and you know what? In addition to my original fee, he paid all the expenses I accrued."

The old lady's mouth dropped open. "Where did he get the money?"

"His ship came in, just as he said it would. He inherited money from a family estate. Set his family up in Portland, and came here immediately to square things."

"I don't believe that." Nellie stood up and began to gather her papers and pens. "Men with money never pay their debts."

After spending the day transcribing the testimony of others, Nellie was ready to have her own say about what she had observed over the years. "The courts are full of rich men who claim they cannot pay their promissory notes."

In the alcove by the parlor, someone dropped a record onto the Victrola, and strains of "Farewell Blues" snaked long fingers around the polished wood doorframe. Ross threw his head back and drained the last of his libation. Smells of whiskey and candle wax, mixed with the sultry sounds of smoky jazz, served only to ruffle Nellie's ire. "If you told us he put his wife and children to work to pay for his foolish wager, that I would believe."

Ross spoke slowly. "The courts are not 'full of dishonest men,' but of men who disagree, Mrs. Scott. I find that most are honest; my man Davis for example. So state your case."

"That oil magnate you defended, he has dodged his creditors in the courts for the past fifty years. You can't seriously contend he hasn't sufficient money to pay his debts."

"Go on." He folded his arms across his chest.

Nellie walked around the settee that stood between her and the defense attorney. "The automobile manufacturer who has made driving cheaper than walking. He refuses to pay for patents he can well afford." She folded her arms underneath her breasts. That action had the unintended effect of lowering the neckline on the dress she had donned for dinner with the judge, an old friend about to retire from the bench.

Mr. Ross reddened and cleared his throat. He held up a hand to stop her, but she charged ahead.

"Old man Carson who invented the copper ore roaster— the wealthy copper companies used his patent for years and let him nearly starve to death before the court finally awarded him a judgment of millions." Her voice rose. "I tell you, rich men pay only when the court compels them." The forefinger that wagged in the air she brought quickly to rest on her collarbone.

"And yet," Mr. Ross jumped in, "the minute Davis came into possession of his money, he drove one hundred and fifty miles to pay his debt." He tapped his finger on the table to emphasize his point. He looked down at Nellie, six feet of smiling confidence, and delivered his summary. "He is an honest man, and so, I contend, are the majority of men."

Mrs. Erwin nodded her agreement and pointed toward the cocktail cart, indicating her wish for a glass of sherry.

Nellie stood her ground. "If that were so, your caseload would be considerably lighter."

Ross's mouth dropped open. First, a choking sound, and then full-throated laughter filled the room. Mrs. Erwin covered her mouth and giggled. Nellie tried to hold her stern expression, but could not help herself. She laughed with them.

The dinner bell rang, and Mr. Ross escorted Mrs. Erwin to the dining room. Nellie retrieved her papers and climbed the stairs to her room to refresh her makeup before the judge called for her. Having a few minutes to spare, she sat down on the corner of the bed and recorded the conversation in her diary. Perhaps a day would come when she would have the leisure to write about all she had seen and heard in and around the court. Who would believe it?

The wall clock downstairs chimed. By now, Judge Acker must be waiting for her. Nellie checked her face in the mirror, ran her fingers across her cheekbones, and drummed the skin around her eyes lightly with her fingertips. Silly to think she could smooth the years away, but this little ministration refreshed her. What could the retiring judge possibly want to talk to her about?

18

Last Chance Romance

*J*udge Acker's hand at the small of her back guided Nellie into the warm interior of Tuckaway's Seafood Restaurant. They sat at a small table for two where they could look out over the Rogue River while they chatted companionably.

"I had no idea this was here." Nellie slipped a napkin onto her lap and looked over the elegant menu.

"My little secret." The judge winked. "I recommend the Chinook salmon." Two wine glasses and a dusty green bottle appeared. "And a glass of Riesling perhaps?"

Nellie's eyebrows shot up.

"Another little secret. The owners keep a few bottles from my private collection on hand for me."

"You are full of secrets, Judge Acker." The waiter splashed a small amount of sweet wine into her goblet and filled the judge's glass. The judge reached across the table and patted Nellie's hand. "You know, our professional relationship is coming to an end. From now on, please to call me Willem. And I hope I may call you Nellie."

Nellie raised her glass. "To your retirement, then. *Willem.*"

The waiter lit the votive candle at the center of the table, and two plates of hearty grilled salmon steaks with crispy skin arrived. Across the room, a tuxedoed gentleman took a seat at a baby grand piano, and, before long, strains of a Brahms sonata gentled the air.

"Have *you* thought of retiring, Nellie?" Rich juices from the fish pomaded Willem's generous lips. Nellie drew her napkin across her mouth and dabbed away fatty residue that once protected the king salmon in the cold river.

"No. I would have no idea what to do with myself. What are your plans?"

He held up a finger while he finished chewing a buttered roll. "Bread and butter! I read an article in the *Tribune* that says fat is our dietary hard coal, and bread the perfect vehicle for butter." He smacked his lips. "But to your question. My wife and I always planned to travel after I retired, but you know she died a few years ago."

"Yes, I heard that. I'm so sorry for your loss."

A few fish bones and curls of skin were all that remained on their plates. The waiter collected the used dinnerware and reset the table for dessert. "Coffee and cake?" he asked the judge.

"Please." As soon the waiter left them alone, Willem leaned forward. "I'm known for being direct. I'm sure you're aware."

Oh my. Nellie glanced at his wine glass. It was still half full. Whatever he was about to say, it wouldn't be the wine talking. "You are forthcoming; I will say that."

The waiter poured rich black coffee with a flourish and set down two small dishes of pineapple upside-down cake.

"Oh, my favorite." The judge rubbed the palms of his hands together. "Is this the recipe?"

"That won the Hawaiian Pineapple Company award?" the waiter asked? "The very same I'm proud to say."

Willem's eyes grew even bigger and he popped a gooey pineapple chunk into this mouth. Cake crumbs danced on his lips as he returned his attention to Nellie.

"So, I will come right to the point." He jabbed the air with his fork. "I find myself in need of a traveling companion."

His words hung in the air while Nellie tried to digest their meaning. "A traveling companion. What do you mean?" Like a series of short films, several scenarios cycled through her imagination. An assistant to handle details? An attending nurse? He looked well enough. Surely he was not suggesting they travel together as friends, or … *Oh my.*

"I've been alone too long," she heard him say when she pulled her head out of the newsreel. He made his case, laid out logical arguments, and supported them with evidence. They'd known each other for years, were alike in so many ways, could be a comfort to each other in their …"

"Old age." Nellie finished his sentence.

"Of course, for you and me that is a long way off. Admittedly, a longer way off for you than for me." He pushed his chair away from the table, stretched his long legs out in front of him, and leaned back, cradling his head in this hands. "Though I expect we would have many good years together."

Nellie did not know whether to laugh or to reach across the table and slap the old codger. Her face must have shown her confusion because his expression softened. He sat up straight and reached across the table for her hand.

"Forgive me. I can see I have not made myself clear. Nellie, will you do me the honor of becoming my wife?"

Years of experience in Willem's courtroom told her he did not like to have his time wasted, but this was Nellie's first marriage proposal. John had never properly asked her; he had just taken for granted that she would honor her parents' wishes. Surely this time she was due some cross-examination.

"So, we aren't discussing a *business* arrangement."

He chuckled. "No, Nellie, I have too much respect for you, and for myself, to suggest any arrangement short of a proper marriage." As if reading her thoughts, he continued, "Proper in every sense of the word."

"And when was it that you came to feel about me in that way? Until this moment, I have had no indication."

"I've had my eye on you for years."

Nellie tilted her head but held her tongue.

The judge cleared his throat. "Of course I mean the last few years following my wife's death." He made his case. "You are an attractive woman with a good head on your shoulders. I am a wealthy man, not unattractive, women who would love to be in your shoes tell me."

Oh how Nellie wished he had stopped talking before he got to the heart of his intention. Like the young man of privilege who had chosen Helen, the judge wished to bestow himself on a less fortunate soul who would be grateful for the attention. Eustace had done her a favor when he failed to fulfill her dream. Now she would do the same for the judge.

"Willem, you are indeed a most attractive man, and I am honored by your proposal. Regretfully, I cannot accept." She closed her eyes briefly. What possible excuse could she make? Opal's face floated before her. She opened her eyes. "I have family obligations that would prevent me from devoting myself to you in the way you"—she fished for words—"*deserve.*"

Dipping his chin in acknowledgment of her generous act of self-sacrifice, Willem reached for the check the proprietor had set down by his elbow. He took a few moments to inspect the bill for errors and then raised his eyes to hers. "I was not aware you had a personal situation."

Becoming uncharacteristically chatty, Nellie prattled on about a daughter in need of her help and a granddaughter in need of her guidance. When the judge dropped her at the door of the inn, he reached for her hands and held them between his. "Thank you for your delightful company this evening, Mrs. Scott. I am disappointed. Yes. But I want you to know how much I have valued your friendship over the years. I hope we will remain friends."

She assured him they would.

After retiring to her room and preparing herself for bed, Nellie poured her thoughts out in a letter to Jessie.

Dear Jessie,

Tonight I turned down a marriage proposal from a judge, a widower who wished to spend his remaining years in my company. In his retirement, we would have traveled the world together. He is a wealthy gentleman, highly respected in his profession. Even though I vowed never to remarry, I must admit that for a moment, I considered accepting his proposal. Then it hit me. Love was not part of the bargain.

I do not consider myself a romantic. Indeed, I have always prided myself on being a realist. Perhaps love would have grown, but that has not been my experience. I have achieved far more in life than I ever imagined, but I find myself regretting I know so little about love. If it is not a yearning that can be satisfied by proper attention, or a contract two parties enter into for mutual benefit, then what is it?

Looking back, I think I have only seen true love once. Strangely, it was between an old soldier in ill health and an ancient Indian outcast. I saw between them a trust and respect I have never seen before or since. They took joy in meeting each other's needs. They seemed to complete each other. How odd that these two scraggly people should come to mind as the only illustration I have of love.

I used Opal and Leone as my excuse for turning down the judge. As it happens, Leone is becoming quite a handful, and Opal really could use my help. Maybe it's time for me to stop traveling and stay closer to home.

Fondly,

Nellie

19

Poor Clara Ritzwell

Portland, 1928

*A*s Nellie grew older, fewer assignments came her way. Despite what she had always said about making room for younger women to move up through the ranks, it was a bitter pill. If she had not had her family to fall back on—if Opal had chosen to stay in New York— these present times would be even harder.

From time to time she heard from Judge Acker, who traveled in Europe most of the year with his new wife, an Italian socialite he met on a crossing a few months after Nellie turned him down. When he wrote to her, he often inquired about mutual acquaintances. One name came up frequently. Poor Clara Ritzwell.

Nellie told Clara's story whenever she wanted to make a point. Today, Leone was her captive audience, and the point she wanted to make was about poor decisions.

"Stocks are the new gold rush," she lectured Leone, who cared not a whit about the stock market. "And bankers and businessmen celebrate. What many fail to calculate is that as secure as they may feel, one poor decision can impoverish a life."

Leone stood before the mirror in the bedroom she shared with Jane, admiring her new hairdo, a short bob.

"Are you listening? You don't want to be the woman looking backward at a string of bad choices that involve men or money."

"But you said," Leone mocked the words her grandmother often repeated, "'it was the cruel heartlessness of her own sex that caused all the trouble.' Remind me again, Grandmother. Who was Clara?"

Nellie sat on the edge of the twin bed. "An acquaintance. That's of no consequence. What's important is that if she had stopped to think, she might never have left her husband in such haste."

Leone inspected her nails and glanced at her bare wrist. "I need a new watch. Do you know what time it is?"

"Hear me out, Leone. Your friends will just have to wait."

Leone slumped. She plopped heavily on the bed beside her grandmother. Nellie took her hand and launched into the oft-told tale.

"The quarrel was childish. Clara and George disagreed on whose parents' photographs to place first in the family album. Can you imagine?"

Leone shook her head. "That's just silly." She crossed her legs and wiggled her foot.

Nellie slapped Leone's knee lightly. "Be still and listen.

"Clara's mother might have instructed young Clara on what manipulations to employ to bridge the difficulty—"

"'But that lady was in her grave,'" Leone finished Nellie's sentence. "I've heard this story before."

"Not all of it, you haven't. So offended was Clara by George's stubborn insistence that his family tree was all the shelter she required, the silly fool saw nothing for it but to pack her bags and take herself and baby Loraine off to Los Angeles to stay with her grandmother."

"She had a baby?"

"*They* had a baby. And Clara fully expected that George would follow her and beg for forgiveness. She would take him back, and they would live in a state of marital bliss built on a foundation of mutual respect."

"She should have put those cards on the table in the first place." Leone snickered and smoothed her short skirt over her knees.

"Perhaps. Anyway, Clara's grandmother was a querulous soul; stiff joints, small mind, living on a widow's pittance. She welcomed Clara into her home."

"I'll bet she did. She needed a nurse." Leone stood and began to pick up her clothes piled on the floor. "How old was this tootsie, anyway?"

"Three or four years older than you. Girls married early in those days. Anyway, weeks turned into months, and Clara wearied of caring for a cranky old lady on top of tending to a baby, but she was too proud to write to George. A year went by, and George divorced her on the grounds of desertion. And that was that."

"You mean she never saw George again? The baby never saw her father again? Clara had to live permanently with her *grandmother*?"

"Awful thought, isn't it." Nellie laughed. "That's right. And she was isolated from the life a young woman should have. Her only moments of peace were her walks in the park with Loraine while her grandmother descended into a narcotic abyss."

"What kind of narcotics?"

"It's well you ask. Laudanum. Doctors prescribe all sorts of medicines that seem to do more harm than good. But that wasn't the worst. The old lady didn't know that her income barely sufficed to pay for her medicine and put food on the table, or that her mortgage payments were in arrears. Clara blamed her grandmother's spartan life on her parsimonious spirit. Neither of them anticipated the financial disaster that was about to fall."

Leone frowned. "How do you know this woman?"

"In my position with the court, I became acquainted with many people's circumstances. I have been known to drop an occasional hint to cause someone to reconsider the wisdom of doing nothing."

Leone opened her mouth to retort. Nellie held up a hand. "But a person of Clara's intrepid character often requires more than a hint." She leveled her eyes at Leone. "A bold nature wants a bolt of lightning to turn them from the path of destruction. I was nearing the end of my career. I simply could not summon that energy, and so I said nothing. I regret that."

"What happened to her and her baby?"

"I did keep tabs on Clara and Loraine as they struggled to overcome Clara's ill-advised decision to let her marriage die of neglect. You would think that would have been enough of a lesson. She should have learned to think through her actions in light of the possible consequences." Nellie tapped her temple.

The clock in the living room sounded the quarter hour. Leone walked to the tiny bedroom closet, dropped a stack of folded clothes on the floor and reached for her coat. Nellie kept talking.

"It was in the park where she often walked to clear her head that Clara encountered Mr. Frank Brown, a wealthy tobacco dealer on vacation."

Leone pulled her coat from its hanger and draped it over her arm. She moved to the doorway and turned to face her grandmother.

Nellie matched her granddaughter's impatience by continuing her story with exaggerated slowness. "Innocent flirtations led to equally innocent assignations. They both had older relatives to whom they were beholden, she for her very survival, he for the honor of a promise he had made to his widowed mother: he would not marry as long as she lived."

"Clara didn't see that as a sign of trouble ahead?" Leone leaned into the doorjamb and placed a hand on the thrust of her hip.

"Sadly, no. A year passed in which Clara and Loraine were happy for the diversion that Mr. Brown offered when business brought him to town; an outdoor puppet show to amuse the child, a discreet dinner in the city on the rare occasion that Clara could slip away. Then Clara's grandmother died."

Leone pushed herself away from the doorjamb and stood up straight. "And she was free from her obligation, and ..."

"And I was there when she learned the unhappy truth of her situation. No provision had been made for her and her child."

Leone's eyes widened. "You mean they were out on the street?"

"I was in court the day poor Clara Ritzwell discovered her grandmother's house had been seized to pay her debts. In the proceedings, it came to light that her husband had left her and Loraine penniless in the divorce. Not the decent thing to do, but it was his right. When court recessed, Clara was waiting for me in the hall. She asked for my advice."

"You told her to get a job, didn't you?"

"I did, but she complained that she had no trade or profession. Well, she was complaining to the wrong person, wasn't she? Everyone has some useful skill they can employ. It just wants imagination.

"Self-pity will not serve you well," I told her. "Take nurses' training and go to work in a hospital. That's my advice."

"And did she?"

"Pshaw! Who takes my advice? She wanted to know how she would pay for training. Women in my day were resourceful. I asked her if she had a friend who might help. I knew she did. I came to regret that piece of advice."

"Let me guess. Clara turned to Mr. Brown, and he helped her, but at some terrible cost."

"Smart girl. The gentleman proposed a plan of his own. Instead of investing in a solution that would lead her to employment and independence, he talked her into letting him move her to his hometown. They could see each other more often. He would provide all her necessities and many luxuries she had missed during the years they had wasted."

Leone's hand flew to her mouth. "She became what your generation called a *kept woman*."

Nellie clicked her tongue. "What does your generation call it?"

"Gold digger."

The clock announced the half hour. Nellie waved her hand in the air. "Either way, when people do not observe proprieties no good comes of it. In fact, Clara was not a wanton. She was merely a woman wanting a bigger dose of common sense than the good Lord gave her."

Nellie stood up and walked through the bedroom door into the living room, and Leone followed. They sat side by side on the sofa, waiting for Leone's friends.

"How did they fare in their new home?" Leone craned her neck around to look out the front window. The street was empty.

"As you might imagine," Nellie said. "From the very first day that Clara settled in, the virus of gossip worked against her welfare and the happiness of her child. I received a tear-stained letter telling me that when Clara gave a birthday party for Loraine, not a single classmate attended."

"Oh, that's terrible. Children should not be mistreated for the sins of their parents." Leone folded her arms and rocked back and forth. Her movement disturbed the black and white cat snoozing among the sofa pillows. The cat stood, arched his back, and rubbed himself up against Leone's arm. Sparks flew.

"Ouch, Mouser!" The cat leaped from the sofa, nicking Leone's arm with a claw as he scooted. She raised her arm to her mouth and sucked at the small puncture wound that began to spurt blood. Mouser disappeared around the corner.

"Keep pressure on that. The blood will stop in a minute." Nellie returned to her story. "I advised Clara to enroll the girl at the Sacred Heart Academy, where few questions are asked."

Leone put a finger over the place on her arm where a spot of bright red blood continued to pool. "Poor tyke. Did Clara find something to do with herself?"

"She made a courageous effort I'll give her that. She tried to affiliate with a local church, but was turned away because of her reputation as a woman with no visible means of support; she offered to help private charities with their projects; she applied to the Eastern Star for membership in hopes that her father's tenure as a Mason would help. All her efforts to build a social life met with chilly rebuff. She was entirely without companionship, save for the nightly visits of Mr. Brown."

Leone's face twitched at the suggestion of impropriety. "Well, maybe that' s all the companionship she needed. And she had her daughter."

Nellie shook her head. "She finally decided to take my advice. Although a life emptying bedpans held no appeal, she thought she might like working at a counter in a little shop, chatting with customers who would not care a fig about her living situation. With Mr. Brown's help, she took a business course and opened a small consignment shop. She stocked it with cast-off finery that attracted quite a business from the Front Street ladies."

"Front Street, as in waterfront, as in …?"

"Yes. At first, those ladies were generous in their patronage, but they proved to be a fickle lot. When their numbers dropped off, her business venture failed."

The clock chimed the hour. Leone looked up, alarmed. "Grandmother, I have to go. I should walk to the corner and meet my chums."

"My story is near the end. Loraine graduated high school, but could not find a job in the town where her mother was stigmatized. She went east, took her grandfather's name, obtained employment in a brokerage, and married respectably. Clara next tried to open the home Mr. Brown provided her to the orphaned children of a distant cousin who lost her life in a motor accident. The arrangement suited the children's alcoholic father quite well, but not the courts. The children were taken from her and sent to a proper foster home. Then the inevitable happened."

"She died?"

"That would have been a blessing. No; the one thing Clara never doubted was that Mr. Brown would marry her when his obligation to his mother ended. But the old lady was still living when the gentleman suffered a stroke and was placed in a private sanitarium, where *he* died. That ended Clara's monthly allowance and her tenancy in the house he had provided her. Mother inherited the house from son, and the first thing she did was evict Clara."

"No! So, she really did end up in the street. Grandmother, you should write this story down. It would make a terrific exposé of economic inequality in *McClure's Magazine*. All these people that tried to keep poor Clara in her place—"

Knuckles drummed on the front door, putting an end to the storytelling. The door strained at the hinges and popped open. School girls dressed in party clothes filled the room with their chatter.

"Leone, we got tired of waiting for you."

"Oh, hello, Mrs. Scott."

"Let's go, Leone. Don't forget your *stuff*." A crafty wink led Nellie to believe that Leone's friend wasn't talking about a sweater and a handbag.

"Off you go then. Enjoy your evening." Nellie's hip popped when she rose from the sofa to pick up the coat Leone had left there in a heap, but the young women were out the door like trick-or-treaters on the hunt for sugar. Nellie stood in the center of the empty room, staring at the closed door. She pictured Leone on the other side of the door—hands pushing, feet flying, careening into life—careless of the doors that might one day be closed to her if she followed her heart before using her head.

It is the way of the world. Nellie closed her eyes and recalled the last time she chanced to see Clara; the proud back, the thin shoulder blades, the unkempt lock of hair that escaped from under her hat and stuck to the back of her neck as she walked down a lonely street and faded into memory.

PART 2

Leone

20

Depression

Portland, 1929

*I*f Nellie and John had stayed married, today would have been their fiftieth anniversary. Nellie sat at the kitchen table in the small foursquare house Opal and Felix had managed to buy. To pay the mortgage, Felix was on the road much of the time. Gregarious by nature, he enjoyed the glad-handing that secured him the top salesman position in most business quarters. In his absence, Nellie sat happily at her daughter's house, pecking away on her Royal portable typewriter, enjoying the peace.

How like the box house John had built her in Kansas—this little place. Memory rattled the back screen door and blew in on a breeze. Back then, her fingers had ached from the hours of sewing and scrubbing, slicing and chopping. Now Father Time jabbed his fingers of shooting pain into her knuckles and joints. It took more than a good night's sleep to erase the discomfort, but, in her practiced way, she bent to her task and ignored the insistent complaining of age-stiffened muscles and thinning bones.

Nellie was deep in her story when the screen door banged again, and Leone appeared in a duster of windblown hair, ill-fitting clothes, and painted red lips. Dumping her schoolbooks on the table, the girl went to the icebox and returned with an orange drink.

Nellie stopped her furious typing and raised her head. "And hello to you, too. You'd better remove that lipstick before your mother gets home."

"Sorry. Hello. How was your day?" Leone smiled sweetly. Turning again to the icebox, she pulled out a bottle of near-beer and dangled it. "Want one?"

"I wouldn't mind."

Leone popped the tops off the bottles and plopped in a chair across the table from her grandmother. "Another story?"

"Hmm." Nellie leaned over her work and reread the half page she had just typed.

"Why do you write here instead of where *you* live?" Leone leaned back in her chair and gulped down half of her bottle of soda.

Nellie kept her eyes on her work. She threw the carriage across the typewriter and resumed her rhythmic tapping.

"Too many people coming and going where I live. The light is better here."

"Is that your assignment for class tonight?"

"Hmm; Leone, let me finish this."

"I wish I were taking a creative writing class instead of final exams." Leone cracked a textbook and began to take notes in a binder. Nellie's fingers danced across the typewriter keys, stopping only to advance the paper in the roller or sip the poor excuse for a drink.

When Leone finished her refreshment, she reached over and grabbed her grandmother's near-empty bottle, pulled it up to her lips, and threw her head back quickly. A few drops of amber liquid trickled onto her tongue. Slamming the bottle back down on the table, she wiped her mouth with the back of her hand and adopted a merchant seaman's voice, "That'll wake up your taste buds, matey!"

Nellie made a sour face. *Tap, tappity, tap, ding!* She looked up at Leone, elbows planted on the table, chin cupped in the heels of her hands.

"Grandmother, did you know that Amelia Earhart is preparing to fly an airplane around the world? A woman; think of it!"

Nellie snorted. "Flight. When I was your age, that's all I thought about."

Leone stared at her. "You wanted to fly a plane?"

"I wanted to escape the hold other people had on me. Just like Amelia wants to escape gravity. She yearns to cut the tethers others would use to keep her in her place."

"So you know who Amelia Earhart is." Leone leaned back in her chair and doodled her pencil on her notepaper.

"Of course I do. Do you think my brain has shut down because I'm not working at the moment?" Nellie knitted her fierce eyebrows together and pursed her mouth. *Tap, tap, tap*, she finished up and snapped the page from the roller. Holding it up in front of her face, she scanned the copy while addressing her granddaughter from behind the legal-sized paper. "I'll have you know, I have just accepted an offer of employment from an insurance office." She lowered the paper and leveled a penetrating look at Leone.

"You are going back to work? Why?"

"Because I have rent to pay. I will not be beholden to your mother to keep body and soul together. A woman should use her professional skills for as long as possible."

"Who is going to watch Jane in the afternoons while mother works?"

"Your mother will figure out something." Nellie gathered her papers into a portfolio and placed her writing tools in a pencil box. Another gust rattled the screen door. She shivered.

"It is always cold in this house. Leone, why don't you go shut the back door and light the stove?"

"It gets stuffy with all the doors closed. And when I start the stove before dinner, Mother complains that I'm wasting fuel. She tells me to get up and move about to get warm."

"You do that. Move to that door and close it." How did the girl manage to say so much with just the stubborn set of her shoulders and a loose, sassy walk? Nellie pressed her prim lips together and shook her head in amusement. She looked up at the antique German wall clock somberly ticking away. Nellie had passed this inheritance from Amanda onto her youngest. It looked substantial, hanging here in Opal's kitchen against a wallpaper pattern of airy white blossoms and feathery Paris-green ferns. Nellie stretched her arms and reached for her loosely constructed, fancy knit sweater.

Leone flounced back to the table, plopped in her chair, and flipped opened her modern poetry textbook. "I've discovered a new poet: Ezra Pound. May I read you one of his poems?"

"If you must."

Leone pulled herself up tall. Hands in constant motion now, words spilled from her mouth. "Pound is a composer of words." She let that sit. "He plays by ear, not by musical training."

She punctuated her statement with a nod of her head and then took off soaring. "Without the constraint of rhyme, reason and affection marry! Every word contributes to an intellectual and emotional coupling—"

Nellie stood up, retrieved her satchel, and slapped it down so hard the table rocked on the uneven floor. "Poppycock, Leone!"

She opened the heavy leather bag and jammed her portfolio and pencil box inside. "Alice Meynell, now there's a poet. 'A Letter from a Girl to Her Own Old Age': rhyme *and* reason."

Leone's eyes caught fire. She opened her mouth to begin her rebuttal, but Nellie raised her finger. "How words sound. How they make you feel. That's not nearly as important as what words teach you. Rhyme has a purpose, Leone. Its purpose is to help you remember life's hard lessons."

Leone shook her head so hard that her bobbed hair swung into her moist eyes. "You can't discount the mystical power of sound, free from constraint, to inform the heart ..."

"Mystical power? Informed hearts? Leone, I tell you, if some of the women I saw in my twenty years in the courts, the women I'm writing about, had paid more attention to the life around them instead of feelings inside them, they would not have found themselves in the predicaments they did!"

The back porch door squeaked and slammed. Opal bumped into the kitchen, shouldering a heavy tote, trying not to trip over the whippet that trotted behind her and the cat that circled her feet. She set an armload of groceries on the counter and bent down to pull off her street shoes, digging into her dance bag to find the ballet slippers she always wore in the house. She winced as she slipped into them. Then she stood up and tucked a wilted white blouse back into slim black pants, shiny with wear.

"I could have used your help at the studio this afternoon, Leone." Opal moved the empty bottles from the table to the sink. The dog danced in circles, his nails clicking on the worn linoleum floor.

Nellie began packing up her typewriter. The cat leaped onto to the counter and picked her way through the oatmeal-crusted breakfast dishes.

Opal opened two cans of pet food, wrinkling her nose at the smells of liver, fish, and sour milk. "Did either of you remember to put the chicken in the oven?"

Nellie looked at the clock.

Leone's hand flew to her mouth. "Cripes! I forgot."

"Better get to it then, missy." Nellie stood up and stashed her typewriter in a kitchen cabinet.

Leone executed a military-style about-face and marched to the stove to light the oven. She grabbed the chicken from the icebox, threw it into the roasting pan, salted it, and shoved it into the oven.

Nellie sat back down at the table and pulled a bus schedule out of her satchel. She was consulting the timetable when Leone change-stepped past, chin in the air, swinging her arms stiffly.

"I have to do everything." Leone sighed dramatically.

Nellie reached her foot out and tripped her. Leone fell into the table. They looked at each other and burst into laughter.

"You two." Opal looked at them with a mixture of exasperation and love.

"Guess we'll be eating late tonight." Leone collected her textbooks and escaped to the front room."

"Never mind about me, Opal." Nellie headed for the door. "I'm catching the bus back to the boarding house. They are expecting me for dinner tonight."

Leone arranged herself on the Davenport. Her books lay unopened on her lap, her eyelids drooped, and the day's petty annoyances receded. She was snoring when her mother's voice woke her.

"Where is your sister?"

How should I know? Leone tried to keep the growl out of her voice: "In her room, I guess," she offered. "Or out on the front lawn playing, maybe? That's Grandmother's job to watch Jane in the afternoons, not mine."

Opal appeared in the kitchen doorway, crossed the room, and disappeared down the hallway. When she returned, she leaned against the doorframe and swiped a hand across her forehead. "She's fallen asleep on her bed. Now I'm going to have a hard time getting her down after dinner."

Leone turned a page in her book. In the silence that followed, the clock ticked loudly and the evening newspaper hit the driveway. She got up to retrieve the paper, but Opal stopped her.

"Leone. If I can't count on the two of you to watch Jane while I teach class, things are going to fall apart around here."

"Sooner than you think, I'm afraid. Grandmother told me this afternoon that she is going back to work."

"Well, I guess that's no surprise." Opal looked at the clock, then headed back to the kitchen. "Wake your sister at six for dinner."

Leone called for the whippet, and they took to the front porch steps together. She sat down on the last step and watched Roxie do her business on the lawn. When the dog came to sit with her, Leone threw her arms around the pup's neck and whispered in her ear. "It won't be long before they have one less mouth to feed around here, Rox. After I graduate from St. Mary's in June, I'm going to LA. I've had enough of my mother's new family."

The mostly absent husband, the whiny sister, and the grandmother were never much help. Leone confided all her grievances to the one person in the family who wouldn't talk back. She pulled gently on the whippet's ears.

"Mother and I do all the work around here."

Leone let Roxie back in the house and stretched out on the sofa with her schoolbooks. Glancing toward the kitchen, she inched her foot underneath the Copen-Blue and rose-colored knitted afghan heaped atop a thin spot in the upholstery. When her toe knocked against a hard object, she pulled herself upright.

"Dinner! Leone, wake your sister."

No time to investigate the small box she had pilfered from a closet a few days ago, and stashed in the folds of the afghan a few minutes ago. Like everything else in her life, it seemed, she would have to wait until prying eyes were distracted.

Jane crabbed through dinner. The chicken was too dry, the green beans tough and stringy, the chunks of carrot and celery in the gelled orange salad hard to chew. Leone left half her food on her plate and escaped again to the front room.

Sounds of water filling the sink and the smell of soap assured her that the day's dishes would occupy her mother for awhile. Had Jane finally settled down, or would she be running back and forth? Leone craned her neck until she caught sight of Jane's shadow at play on the kitchen wall, a small hand choosing a color, a tiny finger pressing crayon to page in her coloring book. Likely that was "Children of Many Lands," a gift from Felix, purchased on his last sales run. Jane always colored inside the lines, so that would keep her busy.

From the rumpled folds of the afghan, Leone retrieved the box she had found one day while poking around in the coat closet. Grandmother stashed boxes of her belongings all over their house. Leone grimaced at the thought of her own possessions piled so deep in her tiny closet that she had to throw her weight against the door to get it to latch.

She let that thought go and turned her attention to the wooden box inlaid with a shell design nested in the blanket on top of her knees. *There's probably nothing in the box Grandmother hasn't told me about, but I've never actually seen her letters.* She ran a hand over the English walnut parquet lid and traced the shiny white cottage roses with her finger. Turning the tasseled key that had been left in the lock, she held her breath and lifted the lid.

A stack of envelopes, brittle with age, lay on top. The letters Leone had expected to find, but the tooled leather journal that rested underneath was a bonus. She stifled a small gasp and looked around quickly.

"So long until tomorrow," Lowell Thomas signed off the scratchy radio news broadcast her mother listened to every night. A pan scraped across a stove burner, and kitchen utensils clattered in the sink.

"Leone, come in here please and dry these dishes. I have to put the garbage out."

Leone pulled the slim journal out of the box and hid it between the pages of her history book. "Can't you let the dishes air dry? I'm doing my homework," she yelled. Then she shut the letterbox and shoved it out of sight.

A chill entered the room from the poorly sealed front windows. Careful not to uncover the box, Leone pulled the afghan up across her legs and opened the textbook that sheltered the journal.

She read quickly through her grandmother's account of the familiar story of Eustace and Helen, her wedding to John, the trip west. She slowed down when she came to an entry that puzzled her.

Dear Diary,

Although it pains me to admit defeat, I cannot remain in this marriage. I can no more abide being a carpenter's wife in Los Angeles than I could stand being a farmer's wife in Kansas. The fault is mine. I did not marry for love. I lacked the will to disobey my parents and the imagination that there might be any other path for me.

As long as John has his brothers, his boy, and his fishing boat, he is content. Meanwhile, I wither. Like one of my mother's rosebuds that never blossomed, I droop and rot. Not a pretty example to set for my daughters.

I can wait no longer. I have decided to take the girls and go up north where they say job opportunities abound for people with my skills, even for women!

Mabel is ready to try her wings; Opal, I worry about. She is more of a homebody and dotes on her older brother. But I want to try my hand at making my way in the world before it's too late. Is that selfish? No more selfish than John was, marrying a girl fourteen years younger than himself to secure his job and give him children, and then refusing the opportunities to better himself and his family.

I admit, the prospects of starting over in California dazzled me. I never stopped to consider that John has only his hands with which to make a living, and it made not a whit of difference to him whether he carouses with farmhands or day laborers. I'm the one with wit to see that if I took office employment, we might improve our station in life. We could live nearer the city center. He won't hear of it.

He wants to keep me captive on this patch of dirt outside of town.

I won't seek a divorce just now. I will just say I am taking the girls to visit Jessie in Spokane for the summer. It will be hard to leave my spirited boy, but he'll want his father, that's obvious. The girls are easier to manage. And I still have a chance to set their feet on higher ground.

Some days I quake in fear over what I am about to do. Most days I am elated!

Leone sat stone still and let the truth wash over her, seep into the loam of her being, and feed her discontent. Her grandmother had not been forced to go to work because her husband had divorced her, she had divorced her husband because she wanted more out of life. Grandmother, so concerned with the proper way to behave, had up and run away. Hardly the brave doyenne holding together a fractured family by sacrifice and hard work; no, she was a reckless adventuress having her way with the world.

The radio switched off. Crayons spilled back into the cigar box. Leone returned the journal to the letterbox and arranged herself so it rested in the curve of her knees under the afghan.

Her mother walked into the front room, drawing her thumb-sucking, shuffling child by the hand. Sharp-eyed Jane threw Leone a mean look.

"What are you hiding?" Jane stiffened her knees and planted her feet on the floorboards.

"Very sharp teeth, Little Red Riding Hood." Leone narrowed her eyes and bared her teeth at her sister. Jane burst into tears.

"Leone, that's enough. Now I'll never get her to sleep." Opal scooped up the four-year-old and whisked her off to bed.

Leone lay back on a fussy satin pillow covered with lace crochet and pondered her new knowledge. Her grandmother had run away from home! *Little wonder she offers no argument when I threaten to leave home. And my mother? She lit out for Broadway before she even finished school. They have no right to stop me.*

That her mother had regrets, she was aware. Leone supposed it was her birth that had ruined her mother's stage career. The young Opal Nellie Scott who posed in photographs, wearing dance costumes trimmed with ribbons, looked at the world through eyes brimming with hope. The older O.N. Wolff who juggled a teenager, a toddler, and an entourage of students took them in with tired eyes filled with concern. Except when she stood before them with her rubber-tipped teaching stick. The years fell away when she corrected a young dancer's form or demonstrated an *arabesque.*

The only other thing that lit up her mother's eyes was Leone's report cards. Why did her mother harp so on education? Education opens doors, her mother said. Doors to what? Not to anything Leone cared about. She rolled her eyes up to the ceiling and focused on tiny specks that appeared to move slowly toward the light. They might be specks in her eyes, but nearby a spider's web rippled in the soft rhythm of an unseen bellow puffing cold air through a gap above the door. The spider tucked herself up in the corner and watched her progeny roll away.

Leone folded her fingers around the lovely writing pen she had discovered under her grandmother's letters. Of course, she planned to return the pen at some later date. After all, the sheaf of stories she uncovered at the bottom of the box wanted closer examination.

A voice droned through the thin walls that separated the front room from the bedrooms, her mother reading bedtime stories to Jane, saying prayers with her. Before Leone began attending Saint Mary's, she had never heard a prayer. When had her mother started to pray? In Leone's growing up years, when it was just the two of them, had she prayed for God to send her a second husband, the tedious Felix? Was a traveling salesman the answer to her mother's prayers?

Leone reached into her pocket and pulled out the crumpled story her grandmother had left on the table. She pulled herself back up and sat forward, smoothing the paper. Another piece of the puzzle. *Why not use this new information in my family history assignment? Ha! That should get a rise out of Sister Isabel.*

Sister Isabel, 3rd Period English
Family History Assignment
By Leone Barry

My Grandmother's New Life

At the turn of the century, my grandmother, Nellie Belle Scott, traveled to Spokane and recast herself as "a woman who had lost her husband and had children to support." No one in her new life needed to know she "lost" him in a divorce she initiated herself.

She abandoned her only son to the rakish ways of his father and took her daughters to live with my Aunt Jessie while she got on her feet, as they say. My Aunt Mabel (whom I never knew) graduated from high school, got a job, and moved into a boarding house. But then tragedy struck. Aunt Mabel drank creek water and died.

My grief-stricken grandmother moved herself and my mother into the new Hotel Ridpath, a modern building that housed many people who were moving into the city. She found a job as a stenographer in a law office at the nearby Rookery Building. My mother went to school and gave dancing lessons to the children who lived at the hotel. She was only ten years old, but hard-working parents were happy to pay her to occupy their children while they toiled in offices and kept shops. She used her wages to pay for her dance lessons, and when she was sixteen, she set off for the vaudeville stages in New York, Toronto, and Chicago.

My grandmother was devastated. She had lost both of her daughters! She could not bear to slave away any longer in the stenographers' pool. By the grace of God, she was given the opportunity to travel with circuit court judges and report the lives and crimes of people who required their day in court.

A young girl who once rode her horse across the plains of Kansas in search of a lost book, spurned the marriage proposal of its wealthy owner, and lived in an orange grove with a tinker and their three children, now wrote her own ticket in a world of law and disorder in the Wild West.

My grandmother is writing a book about her adventures as an itinerant court reporter. As soon as I finish school, I plan to follow my own star and move to Hollywood.

The End

A week later, Leone received her assignment back from Sister Isabel, a familiar judgment printed in fat, red, block letters on the last page: *This is not a life that our Lord would bless. Your story does not have the ring of truth.* The sister had pulled her aside and delivered a verbal reprimand as well. "Family history is fact, Leone. When you let your imagination get the better of you, the result is drivel—lies, and fiction."

Leone stared at the letter grade in the corner of the page until the U blurred, divided in two, and made her dizzy. Unsatisfactory. *Well, what is grace, then, if not to lift a person out of despair? How dare Sister Isabel condemn my grandmother to a life of perpetual sorrow!*

21

Discontent

*H*er last week of high school, Leone had babysitting duties every afternoon. Today she sat on the front step minding her sister while her mother taught a class. The boredom of having to babysit and the sting of a bad grade from Sister Isabel stirred discontent.

What is the truth, anyway? Leone reached into her school bag and pulled out the assignment that had earned her a U. Brandishing the papers in the air, she raised her voice. "Who are the nuns to tell me that my story about *my* grandmother, if not entirely accurate, isn't mostly true?"

Roxie rolled her big brown eyes in anguish. Rump down, the pup cocked her head and thumped her tail on the paved walkway that led to the house, a dwelling indistinguishable from its neighbors but for peeling paint.

"You don't care, do you; you just want this." Leone stood up and pulled a treat from her pocket. Roxie's tail thumped faster. Leone balanced the biscuit on the dog's nose. Roxie went rigid.

"Wait." She held up her hand. The dog trembled.

"Wait." Roxie fixed her eyes on the end of her nose.

"Now." Roxie flipped the biscuit into the air and snapped it between her jaws. Two crunches and she bounded off.

Wait. That's all I seem to do. Wait to graduate. Wait to grow up. Wait to get out of here. Leone scowled at the offending letter grade. Sister Isabel had scribed the U so heavily into the top margin that Leone could feel the mark with her fingers from the backside of the paper.

"Some parts of my story are facts." She shouted at the white tip of the black tail that disappeared around the side of the house.

Throwing her head back, she spread her arms wide and addressed the gray clouds passing overhead.

"The parts I don't know, I made up." The clouds ignored her. "So what? That's what makes a good story."

Something in the bushes snorted. Leone straightened up and glared at the rustling branches. Jane dragged herself out from under a scraggly rhododendron and came to stand in front of Leone.

"You are just like Roxie, always wanting attention." Leone looked down at her sister. Sunlight bounced off the top of the little girl's short straight bob, hair so white it made her head look like a waxing gibbous moon. The child looked up at her with sullen blue eyes and began to retreat.

"Oh come on, Jane, I didn't mean it. Sit here by me and let me tell you a thing or two." Leone sat back down on the cracked concrete porch step. Cold moisture seeped through the skirt of her school uniform and dampened her white cotton underpants. Jane took a few steps to stand in front of her, but she refused to sit.

"Old Sister Isabel called me a liar." Leone held up the offending pages.

Jane stared at the red mark and mouthed a *U*. "That's a *U*."

Leone steamed. "We aren't doing your letters, Jane. The old hag thinks I'm unsatisfactory because my truth doesn't fit her virginal view of a world where women have two choices: serve God or serve men."

Jane's smile took on a knowing air. "What does *virgin-al* mean?" She cocked her head. Wisps of her white hair fanned out in the gathering breeze and were illuminated against a peek of sunlight just before the sun disappeared behind a dark cloud.

Leone glared at her. "That's hardly the point. Listen to what I'm telling you. The truth is, the women in our family arrange evidence to support whatever story they choose to tell. And no one knows better than Grandmother that the evidence does not always support the truth of a matter."

"You sound like some of the attorneys I used to work for."

Leone froze. The voice came from inside the house, just behind the screen door. Grandmother must have left work early and snuck in the back door. Leone jumped to her feet, and Jane scooted away.

"I'm looking for my letter box, Leone, have you seen it?"

"No, Grandmother, but I'll help you look." Leone reached around to unstick her skirt from the backs of her legs. She tugged at the rotted elastic that barely held her underpants together. *Might as well not wear any.*

Once inside the house, Leone made a show of going room-to-room, opening drawers, and poking into corners. She managed to slip into her bedroom to retrieve the box.

"Grandmother, I found your letter box in that old trunk you keep in the closet. You must have missed it." Leone placed the box in Nellie's outstretched hands.

A knowing smile crept slowly across Nellie's well-maintained face. "That's my girl. I think I'll just take this back to my room at the boarding house. Less temptation." She looked directly into Leone's eyes.

Leone reddened and lowered her gaze to the stitching on her stylish high-heeled shoes.

Nellie followed her gaze. "New?"

Leone swept her foot along the floor in a circular movement and brought it to rest lightly where her grandmother could get a good look. "For my graduation."

"Pretty." Nellie leaned back on her heels. "Now I must go. I have class tonight."

After dinner, after Jane fell into a sound sleep in the twin bed next to hers, Leone tugged the chain on the small dresser lamp and leaned into the mirror to examine her face. She had her mother's smile, her grandmother's sharp cheekbones and no-nonsense nose, and the same deep-set brown eyes as both, eyes that sparkled with intelligence in her grandmother but reflected some deep sadness in her mother.

I am your girl, Nellie. And I am not sticking around this joint to lead a boring life of work, child rearing, and husband pleasing.

Leone pulled a nightdress over her head and crawled into bed. She lay on her back and fit the thin coverlet up under her chin. Through the naked front bedroom window, the moon threw light on the ceiling. In the wind, a budding lilac tree scraped the stucco wall outside the room, its branches casting shadows above her head. *Whoosh:* they trembled and swayed. Stillness: they came to rest, unbent, unbroken. Leone, who said prayers by rote in school throughout the day, consulted no one but herself at night. *I'm going to be a dancer and an actress. Or maybe I'll be a writer.*

She turned over on her side, tucked her arm under her head, and tried to remember all the places her grandmother had described in the stories she found in the letterbox. *Good thing I read them before Grandmother caught me prying.*

Has an artistic (so-called) ending of grim realism, someone had scribbled in red pen at the bottom of a story titled "The Miner's Wife." Leone kicked at her covers, flipped over on her back, and lay stiff. That detestable red pen! She forced herself to relax and smiled up at the ceiling. *I rather liked the grim realism.*

Good possibilities; however, we doubt the ability of this drab, sad-eyed woman to succeed as you describe, the red pen pronounced. Leone's jaw tightened. Her head throbbed. Do teachers not read newspapers? The news was full of stories about people who rise above their circumstances.

Make her success more plausible. The red pen ran into the margin and stopped. *Fiddlesticks!* Leone's heartbeat drummed in her ears. *The less plausible, the more interesting.* She sat up in bed and hugged her knees.

A few feet away, Jane snored in the soft, looping way of children. Muffled voices vibrated the thin wall that separated the bedroom from the front room. Felix must have returned from his monthly round of sales calls.

How could this drafty house feel so airless? *Implausibility.* Her new watchword. She would not rest until she had made headlines.

"Isn't that the girl you gave a *U*?" the nuns would say to Sister Isabel.

"Leone Barry has written a novel of great promise," critics would hail. "One day, she will be known to all the literary world."

One day, to be known. Her body warmed, and sleep soothed her brow with a soft hand. She fell back into her pillow.

Behind closed eyes, her mind would not release her body to slumber. Grandmother wrote with the detachment of a tourist traveling through strange events of life, or a reporter, which, of course, she was. As far as Leone knew, only she and the red pen wielder had read the stories. *Why should it be different for me?*

I'm starting out younger, and free as a bird. But hadn't her mother started out with both those advantages? What if her mother had not succumbed to the attentions of a fellow dancer and returned to Spokane with her infant self? *Well, I wouldn't be here, would I?* What if her father had not mysteriously died en route to join his family when his contract was up? *At least that is what Mother told me. Very suspicious.*

Enough *what ifs*. A ghost-like Indian woman walked a beach; a young wife lay dead in her honeymoon cabin--the strange-but-true stories that raised doubt in the minds of stodgy academics raised hairs on the back of Leone's neck. Yielding to sleep, she entered the stories. The grave markers for the miner's wife and the hunter's bride morphed into books on a shelf. They bore eulogies that floated off the page, hung in the air, and dissipated like skywriting. *Stories are a library of life the locusts cannot destroy.*

Leone fought to open her tightly shuttered eyes. The last image she saw before Morpheus administered the final dose was the gravestone of the forgotten child on a lonely hillside.

To be forgotten. The god of sleep and dreams murmured. *Isn't that the harshest reality of all?*

It will be different for me. I will not be forgotten.

22

Graduation

Leone sashayed into the living room where her grandmother sat fingering the grosgrain ribbon on a black straw hat. "*Très chic.*" She pointed to the hat and executed a pirouette. "How do *I* look, Grandmother?"

The skirt on Leone's simple white dress skimmed her shapely knees. Nellie looked her up and down. From the top of her head of curly bobbed hair to the toe of her white-kid one-strap pumps, she looked angelic, but for one detail.

"I think you can get away with the mascara, but the red lipstick? Your lips enter the room before you do. The monsignor will have a heart attack."

Leone laughed and used a tissue to blot her lips. "Better?"

"Come here."

Leone approached her grandmother and bent over to present her face. Nellie held out her hand for the tissue. Leone stuck out her tongue for Nellie to wet the tissue and rub off more color.

"There."

Leone and Nellie sat together in companionable silence, waiting for the tardier members of the family to finish dressing for Leone's graduation ceremony from Saint Mary's.

"Grandmother, remember that story you told me about the woman who got tossed out onto the street because her lover died and his mother took revenge? What happened to her?"

Nellie pulled a compact out of her pocketbook and checked her face powder. She smoothed an eyebrow and patted a wave of hair into place.

"Grandmother? Did she write to Loraine and tell her what happened?"

Nellie clicked the pocket mirror shut and picked up her story exactly where she had left it.

"Clara did not wish to be a burden on her daughter."

"But surely Clara let Loraine know of her desperate situation."

"What a memory you have. Clara was a stubborn, proud woman, but yes, she wrote to Loraine."

"And she went to live with her?"

"Her letter was returned, stamped *No Longer at This Address*."

"You mean to tell me she never saw her daughter again?"

"That's right. Clara lived out the rest of her days at the Salvation Army Home that I helped her get into. When she died, she was buried in a potter's field."

"What's that?"

The measured click of mid-heeled shoes down the hallway alerted the two women that their conversation had likely been overheard. Opal walked into the room, pulling a hairpin from between her lips. She laced it through a few strands of hair that had fallen loose from a carefully sculpted curl.

"Potter's field is the final resting place for people with no means of support, Leone. What your grandmother is trying to tell you is that family ties are fragile and easily broken. Of all the connections you make in this life, it is your family you should be able to count on when times are hard." Opal glanced over at Nellie. "It takes work to keep those connections."

Jane skipped awkwardly through the doorway wearing shoes a size too big for her. She twirled the flounces of her skirt in the flirty way of young girls and trained her large blue eyes on her sister. Receiving no response, she turned her charms toward Nellie, touching the shiny blue ribbon laced through her short bob and tied in a fetching bow just above her ear.

Nellie stood up and put on her hat. "That's not at all what I'm saying. I'm saying, don't ever count on a man to take care of you. Take care of yourself."

Leone stood up and walked over to link arms with her grandmother. "That's what I intend to do, take care of myself, but

I have to graduate first." She ushered her grandmother toward the door. Then she turned to hurry the others.

Jane's lower lip quivered. Opal held out her hand to her small daughter. White patent leather sandals scraped across the floor until she found shelter in the folds of her mother's dress.

"Jane, don't drag your feet like that." Nellie looked at Opal. "Where is Felix?"

"Waiting for us by the curb; he's warming up the car."

———❧———

The women paraded through the door. Leone, aroused by hope for her future, enjoyed the sensuous swish of her skirt against her silk-stockinged legs. Nellie, bolstered by memories of the past, balanced her steps in practical shoes she had broken in for the occasion. Opal, lithe and flexible, managed the present moment and all its implications with quiet grace. And Jane dragged her small feet in nameless fear.

———❧———

Fifty-two young ladies graduated from St. Mary's Academy. After the solemn ceremony, presided over by the archbishop of Portland, the young women joined their families. Faces shiny with a sense of achievement and endless possibilities, they sparkled at restaurant tables and home gatherings. Private parties would follow.

Leone's circle of friends was small but intimate. After a dinner Felix had arranged in Portland's Chinatown, she would sneak away to a party in a stately home, a bottle of fine bourbon whiskey stowed in her handbag. It was a gift from Felix, slipped to her after the ladies left the table to take Jane to the restroom. On the occasions that the dapper little Frenchman treated Leone like an adult instead of a schoolgirl, she almost liked him. Because her mother and grandmother would disapprove, the subterfuge was even more delicious.

During a dessert of green tea ice cream and fortune cookies, Nellie presented Leone with a new Elgin watch, its square face attached to a black-ribbon band. Opal handed her a fancy card with a check in it, and Felix slipped a legal-sized envelope by the side of her napkin. Another gift? Leone reached for it, but Felix placed his hand on top of the envelope and shot her a warning look.

"Save that for later." He flashed a jovial grin to his wife and his mother-in-law and then returned his attention to Leone. "Read us your fortune, why don't you?"

Leone was used to Felix's teasing ways. She picked up the crisp twist of sweet-smelling cookie and cracked it in two. Carefully unfolding the paper inside, she frowned. "I'm not sure I understand what the cosmos is trying to tell me." She handed her fortune to Nellie.

Always observe propriety, but not at the cost of your higher nature. Nellie recited the words to the family. "That's true. If there is one thing I learned in my career, that is it."

"But what does it mean?" Leone asked.

"It means behave yourself, but don't be a sellout," Felix said.

"I think it means you best mind your manners and follow the rules, but do not allow others to rob you of the passion God has placed in your heart," Opal said.

What a thought, the idea that God might be the author of the feelings that swirled inside of her. Leone screwed her mouth sideways. Nellie leaned over and patted her hand. "Be kind to others. Be true to yourself. Give the Almighty His due. That's all your mother is trying to say."

"You all make it sound so easy, but Einstein says that the cosmic religious experience is a challenge to make clear. You have to believe in the rationality of the world structure to experience faith." All eyes were on Leone now. She sat up straight and floated her words above the din in the restaurant. "Einstein says it is the function of art and science to keep hope alive."

Felix swiveled his head from the table on their left to the table on their right. He lowered his head and squinted his eyes. "Is that what they taught you in Catholic school?"

"Hardly, but as the convent is not my vocation, I took it upon myself to read other points of view."

Jane dropped her ice cream spoon, and Opal bent down to pick it up. "Are you going on vacation?" the child piped up.

Leone dabbed her lips with her napkin. Setting the cloth stained red with her lipstick aside, she looked around the table. She lifted her chin and prefaced the speech she had been preparing for weeks with a few words to Jane.

"It's *vocation*, not *vacation*. A vocation is a calling to a profession you feel suited for. I agree with Dr. Einstein that the hope of the world lies in the pursuit of art and science. I believe that my calling is to be an artist."

"You mean dancer?" Opal wiped the spoon she had rescued with her napkin and handed it back to Jane.

"What about a writer?" Nellie spoke up. "The field of journalism is a door worth knocking on."

"Neither of those occupations pays very well." Felix signaled the waiter and reached into his back pocket for his billfold.

Leone gave her stepfather a withering look. "There are worlds without money, Felix. I will get by."

Felix sputtered a mouthful of coffee out through his nose.

"You got coffee all over my new dress!" Jane set up a howl. A waiter rushed to the table and began to clear the dishes away. It seemed the appropriate time for the small party to gather their coats and for Felix to pay the bill. The rest of Leone's speech would have to wait.

After Nellie had been dropped off at her boarding house, after Felix chauffeured his wife and daughters back to their cottage, Leone popped into the house to drop her gifts in the bedroom before heading out for a round of parties. The envelope in her handbag remained unopened.

Felix sat on the davenport, his short legs splayed out. He waved a hand at Leone as she passed through the front room into the hallway and then summoned his wife, patting the cushioned spot beside him. Opal dropped down with a sigh and pulled off her shoes. Leone paused in the hallway where she could observe her parents without being noticed.

"What did you give Leone for her graduation?" Opal pulled her feet up onto the sofa cushion and massaged her aching arches.

Felix took a cigar out of his shirt pocket and rolled it between his fingers. "I gave her a train ticket."

23

Discovery

Hollywood, 1929

*T*he summer after she graduated, Leone spurned the lead roles her mother continued to offer her in the popular Barry School of Dancing recitals.

"The thought of one more polka or tambourine dance at the Odd Fellows Hall depresses me beyond measure, Mother. I need a bigger stage." Leone reached up to the top of her small closet and pulled down a valise she had recently purchased using her graduation money.

"You know I've rented the Orpheum Theatre this year." Opal's perpetual hopefulness annoyed Leone. Laying out the valise on top of a tangle of sheets on her bed, Leone turned to face her mother. Opal's small frame presented an obstacle that prevented her from retrieving her clothes from the dresser drawers, so Leone reached for a piece of paper she had concealed in a novel on her nightstand and held it out for her mother to see.

"An appointment slip. See?" Despite her best intentions not to lose her temper, she raised her voice. "Look here." She held the small ticket up by the corner tips in front of her mother's face. "This is a memorandum for artists." She slipped the coveted record of her first employment outside her mother's dance studio into her handbag. "I'm an artist, Mother, not a fancy dancer. I have an engagement next week at the Palace Hotel in San Francisco. In the Gold Room." Now was as good a time as any to let that cat out of the bag.

Opal's face froze. Leone followed her mother's eyes, glazed with moisture, as they searched the room for something to focus on and found a framed photograph on Leone's nightstand. In the photo, Opal sat posed in a chair. Felix stood on the right behind his wife, chest puffed out, one hand resting on her shoulder, grinning into the camera. Jane sat front and center on her mother's lap, looking solemn. Leone stood off to the left, hands hanging down—a stranger, Leone thought. She recognized the expression on her face. It was the smile she practiced in the mirror, a sweet smile, the one she switched on when the occasion required.

Opal rubbed her temples, pressed her lips together for a moment, and then said, "You will dance in the chorus, I imagine. What kind of dancing?"

"A Spanish dance."

"Fancy." Opal swiveled and left the bedroom. Leone followed, her fingers balled into fists. In the front room, Opal gathered her music books and dance bag. Leone peppered her mother's back with a volley of words.

"You don't understand. It's a start."

"Oh, but I do understand." Opal turned again to face her daughter. "I was younger than you are now when I went to New York. It's a hard life, Leone. If you start in the chorus, you will end in the chorus. And chorus dancing is a short career. At least get your education first, and start preparing for a career that can sustain you when you can't dance anymore."

Leone's face turned red. "You have to take the fun out of everything, don't you! I'm meeting people. Important people who can help me get roles in Hollywood. I'm not just a dancer. I'm going to be an actress too."

"Oh for pity's sake, Leone. Is that what you want?" Opal released the overstuffed dance bag from her shoulder back down to the floor. "We are in a depression. I might lose the studio. We might have to move to San Francisco to help take care of Felix's parents. You think you are going to just trip off to Hollywood?" Opal folded her arms and waited for an answer.

"Well." Leone lowered her voice and spoke her words slowly. "I can tell you this. If you are planning to move to San Francisco, then I am moving to LA sooner rather than later."

"Let her go, Opal." A chair scraped along the kitchen floor, and Nellie appeared in the doorway. "At least she's not going clear across the country like you did. We won't be so far away if she needs us." Nellie walked over and stood beside Leone, who reached for her grandmother's hand and squeezed it.

No one had noticed Jane's presence. During the argument, the little girl had snuck into the room and buried herself under the afghan on the davenport. She sat up now, pulled the covering off her head, and narrowed her eyes at them. She turned green, clutched her stomach, and with a wail, threw up her breakfast.

"That child." Nellie shook her head.

Leone glared at Jane.

Opal rushed to the kitchen for wet towels.

Nellie paid for Leone's room at the Hollywood Studio Club out of the meager savings she had squirreled away. Young women poured in from every region of the United States, seeking employment in the entertainment industry. The newly renovated residence hall sheltered wide-eyed ingénues from rural America, a comfort to their parents.

Leone's new life was a whirlwind of dance classes and auditions. Evenings she would compare notes around the communal dinner table with young women from small towns and big cities across the country. In the beginning, she did more listening than she did talking. A Catholic education and one trip to Omaha had not prepared her for the sophistication of the New England girls, who had years of summer stock experience under the slim belts that circled their small waists. Nor for the soft speech of their southern sisters, a smokescreen for steely resolve. Queen of the hive at Saint Mary's, more often now, Leone found herself buzzing about on her own.

She was by herself the day she ran to catch a trolley to the dance studio. Out of breath, she set her foot on the step and lost her balance when the streetcar started rolling. She slipped. She tumbled into the street and landed hard on her left arm. Pain shot from her wrist to her elbow, and she blacked out.

As soon as the driver realized that a girl lay in the street beside the trolley, he braked. When Leone came to, the hand of a kind stranger reached out from among the bystanders gathered around her. Slowly she regained her senses as she felt herself being tugged to her feet and handed up into the car.

Leone ignored the murmurs of sympathy and sat very still on a bench seat, taking stock of herself. Her arm hurt like the dickens, but everything seemed to be in working order. Several blocks later, though, as she stepped back down onto the street, she experienced an odd sensation. She could not feel the pavement with her left foot. By the time she reached the dance studio, she was limping badly.

Madame Smolina, the ballet mistress, stood in the center of the classroom. "And one, and two, and three, and four." She counted in heavily accented Russian. She didn't have to look up to detect the halt in her favorite student's step.

"Leone, what has happened? The class continued their battements, *en avant, à la seconde,* and *en arrière.* Madame glided to Leone's side.

"A slight accident, Madame; I'm feeling quite weak on my left side."

"Tell me."

Leone described her mishap. Trying to make light of it, she joked. "I was seeing stars, Madame, and not the kind that show up in class between auditions and performances."

Madame frowned and clucked her tongue. "Tell me exactly what you felt."

Leone tried to recall what had happened. "When I fell, a sharp pain gripped my hip. I think it weakened my leg. The pain shot up my arm and exploded in my head."

"Stand up straight and let me have a look." Madame reached her slim hand out and touched Leone's hip with two graceful fingers. It was as if she had pulled a rug out from under Leone's feet. One minute, the injured girl was telling her story, and the next minute she lay crumpled on the floor, her eyes darting wildly, her body unable to move. She could feel her lips attempt to form a response to Madame Smolina's anxious questions.

"What are you saying? I can't understand you." Leone could hear her own words, but they did not seem to reach the teacher's ears. Madame's lips were moving, but she sounded as if she were speaking from the depths of the Pacific Ocean.

Leone's eyeballs continued to dart around in their sockets, desperate to hold onto the light, but now the teacher's face loomed like a featureless moon above her. Then the light dimmed and went out, and Leone was sucked into a darkness from which she would not emerge until a voice she did not recognize called her forth.

For a week, Leone lay in a Los Angeles hospital bed, trapped inside her body, unable to move, see, hear, or talk: utterly senseless. Hospital physicians could not explain how a minor injury led to such devastating consequences. Despite their reluctance, after exhausting all their resources, they called in a psychiatrist.

Years later, Leone would wonder why the long wait to consult their esteemed colleague? Then she would remember. He was not esteemed by the hospital staff. Dr. Cecil Reynolds was a celebrated student of hypnotism. As such, he was highly suspected of selling snake oil.

It was not the nature of Leone's accident, its dire consequences, or her miraculous recovery that conspired to give her the headlines she had so desired. It was the celebrity of the man the medical establishment finally summoned. A leading proponent of the physiological theory of hypnotism, Dr. Reynolds also happened to be personal physician to Charlie Chaplin. Thus the stage was set for a dramatic recovery.

What was it like, to be called out of darkness? An odor like fingernail polish remover laced with alcoholic sweetness seeped into Leone's consciousness. She became aware of her body, but she could not move. Neither could she see, speak, or hear.

Get up now, and walk.

Her limbs like dead logs began floating downstream. By what volition she maneuvered her body from the grave of her bed to the bank of pillows that now supported her in an upright position, she did not know.

Get up now, and walk.

She reached for the arms of an unseen partner. Her legs swung over the side of the bed, and her bare feet slipped onto the floor. Weightless, she emerged from a dense fog and stumbled into the arms of a nurse, who supported her weight and murmured into her ear, "That's very good; rest now."

Over a period of a week, this exercise repeated itself. With each halting journey from Leone's bedside to Dr. Reynolds' arms, her body grew stronger. Still, she remained in darkness. How she yearned for light. Toward week's end, the step of her feet lightened, but a gray blur continued to cloud her vision.

Will I see again?

Each day, Leone stepped briefly into a hazy clearing until one day, she stayed. When the haze cleared, the first thing she saw was the doctor's handsome face.

"Welcome back, Leone." Under his imposing, heavy, dark eyebrows, the doctor's warm, brown puppy eyes pooled with compassion. The nursing staff clasped their hands to their hearts. The attending physicians whispered among themselves. Voices! She could hear voices, but not her own.

Will I sing again?

A few days later, doctors surrounded the bed where she lay. An anesthesiologist administered a mild sedative that lulled her into a waltz-like state of well-being. By now she trusted Cecil so completely that she had no fear of regressing. She studied the faces that crowded around her bed, the raised eyebrows, the pursed lips, the jutting chins and tilted heads. Only Cecil smiled and leaned in to search her eyes with his. Speaking magic words, he turned the lock on her vocal chords a notch. Her throat let go, and a few raspy sounds escaped her lips.

The nursing staff that stood behind the doctors pushed closer. Cecil touched her hand, nodded his head, and the lock on her speech clicked over another notch. Sodden words strung together in a senseless phrase that fell from her mouth. The doctors rubbed their chins, blinked, and shook their heads. The nurses nodded encouragement.

Cecil caught up her hand in his. "Speak, Leone. Tell me how you are feeling."

The latch on her voice sprung open. "I feel very well, Doctor." *Oh my stars, what a lovely sound! That's my voice. That's me. Speaking!*

24

Disappointment

*L*eone left the hospital and walked into a new life. Newspapers across the country hailed her as the pretty little dancer, hurled by accident into a hysterical paralytic condition, healed by the power of suggestion while under hypnosis. Some nameless fear had caused her to imagine a physical problem where none existed. That, and her youth provided the ideal set of circumstances for healing through hypnosis, Dr. Reynolds explained in interviews and lectures. Some would say it was a miracle. He maintained it only proved the veracity of French physician Hippolyte Bernheim's theory of suggestibility, which led Dr. Sigmund Freud to believe there could be powerful mental processes that remain hidden from the consciousness of man.

Powerful mental processes indeed; when Dr. Reynolds pulled back the curtain on this unfamiliar mental and emotional terrain, Leone stood blinking in the public spotlight. She dared not consider what forces had stripped her of all sense. It seemed more prudent to just accept her fame as a gift.

"A year ago, I was battling the nuns at Saint Mary's over illicit cigarettes and illegal booze." Leone laughed as she handed a copy of the *Cumberland Evening Times* to Madame Smolina. "Look here! A full page, with pictures."

Some of the dancers continued to prepare for class, lacing up their toe shoes. Others drifted over to glance at the headline, "The Very Strange Case of Pretty Leona Berry."

"I see they spelled your name wrong." A tall dancer with sharp elbows smirked.

"I've been in the papers lots of times, but I've never had a whole page devoted just to me." A short dancer with plump knees bent over to examine the article.

"Oh, I know." Leone bestowed a sympathetic smile on her admirer. "My name has been in the society pages before, but only as a featured dancer in my mother's dance recitals. Now I'm photographed with Hollywood stars. I get callbacks from most of my auditions, and soon I'll have my Actors' Equity card."

Madame Smolina turned away. She clapped her hands, and the dancers took their places at the barre.

Bragging is an unattractive quality in a woman. Nellie's voice reverberated in a deep recess of Leone's mind. She moved to join the dancers at the barre, but they arranged themselves in such a way that she had to look to Madame to chastise them.

"Leone, you may use the back of the folding chair I keep in the closet for those times when it seems the room is not big enough to accommodate one of us."

Back home, the responses to Leone's renown were equally chilly. Opal expressed her skepticism in a letter. *I'm wondering how you could hear that charlatan if, as you say, you were deaf,* she wrote. *I've read that this Dr. Reynolds is star struck. Do not allow him to use you for his own purposes.*

Nellie added a postscript: *Pay no mind to naysayers. Whatever the doctor's motives in thrusting you into the limelight, use this time to your advantage. Whatever you set your heart on, with hard work you will achieve it.*

Leone did not waste time considering her mother's skepticism or her grandmother's advice. Cecil had given her a new life. Oh yes, he returned her to health, but more than that he introduced her to powerful, talented people who drew her into their circles. A dangerous temptation or a golden opportunity? She cared not a fig. Finally, she had a chance to kick up her heels and have a little fun.

Leone dropped her weekly letter from home into the wastepaper basket beside the stool where she perched, one long net-stockinged leg stretched to the floor, the other balanced on the stool rung. In the dressing room, dancers pressed shoulder to shoulder, adjusting costumes, buckling dance shoes on their feet, fastening feathers in their hair. Leone leaned into the brightly lit mirror and lined her eyes with a Kohl pencil.

The sting of her mother's criticism still hurt. *Mother danced vaudeville in New York and Chicago before she had me and came back to the West Coast, minus the husband and father I never laid eyes on.* She outlined her lips in red pencil and filled them in with a brush. *Who is she to say dancing vaudeville is no life for me?* Sitting back, she admired the results.

Just because it didn't work out for her doesn't mean it won't work out for me. Look at me! A Catholic schoolgirl just two years ago, and now I'm a featured dancer in the Los Angeles Theater District! Whistling an infectious new tune from *Chasing Rainbows*, she snapped her makeup kit shut.

"Happy days are here again," a lovely voice sang out from the doorway. The commotion drew all eyes to the exquisite person of Letty Randall Webb, and then back to Leone.

"Leone, darling, I just popped in to let you know that Charles, Cecil, and I are in the audience tonight, wishing our little dancer the very best." Letty leaned on the doorpost and fiddled with the white fox fur collar of her evening jacket. All chatter subsided, and the dancers gathered in front of the actress.

"Miss Webb, I saw you at the Belasco last week. You were magnificent."

"Miss Webb, what is it like to work with Maurice Moscovitch? The *Los Angeles Record* raved about him. They said his characterization was perfect."

Still seated on the stool next to Leone, an unimpressed dancer muttered under her breath, "But his acting is archaic." Leone slipped off her stool and bumped the rude dancer's arm as she passed, causing the girl to poke herself in the eye with her mascara wand.

Lights flickered, the signal to queue up for the next number. Letty flashed her high-wattage smile at the group. "No more talk about my performance. Tonight is about your performance."

The dulcet tones of Letty's voice sent a thrill through Leone. The actress drew close, slipped a finger under Leone's chin, and lifted her face. "And yours, my pet." Long eyelashes fluttered. Warm lips touched both sides of Leone's hot cheeks. "Cecil says to tell you to dance your heart out tonight. Show the world that you are cured." One more peck on the cheek and she turned for the door, a whirling dervish of frothy taffeta and fox fur.

"Gosh," one of the dancers said. "Every time I see Letty, my heart just stops. She's as pretty as a cupcake topped with an inch of shiny pink fondant frosting."

Leone flushed. Of late, it wasn't stage lights that put the stars in her eyes. It was Letty Randall Webb.

———

In Hollywood's Biltmore Hotel, Leone and Letty rolled on the bed, howling.

ARE YOU AFRAID TO LOVE?

Perish the Horrid Thought!

IF YOU ARE SATISFIED WITH YOUR SEX LIFE, READ NO FURTHER!

"Oh, oh, oh, my tummy hurts." Letty sat up and clutched her stomach.

"The Gittelson Brothers have truly outdone themselves." Leone waved a theater program in the air and dropped it into her lap. She ran her finger over the advertisement that was giving them such a giggle. "Would you listen to this!

"Just tell the lady you ordered your tickets from Gittelson Brothers— and remember—if she says No, she means Yes—if she says Maybe, she means No—and if she says Yes, she ain't no lady."

"Are you?" Leone turned up the corners of her mouth in a coy smile.

"A lady?" Letty smoothed her hand over her blondish curls.

"Satisfied with your sex life?"

"Maybe." Letty rose from the bed in the hotel suite where she and Charles were staying while he directed a new film. Sinking her exquisite bare feet into the lush white carpet, she floated over to the desk that sat below the plate glass window and drew back the sheer to gaze down at Pershing Square.

"Leone, have you ever seen Dolores Del Rio? She's just stunning. She's starring in this movie Charles is directing." Letty continued to stand at the window, her back to Leone, her arm resting gracefully against the window frame.

Leone stared at the curve of Letty's spine beneath her sheer silk dressing gown. Sensations she had allowed herself in the cocoon of Catholic school—intimacies explored under the sheets during sleepovers; secrets shared with like-minded girlfriends looking for safe places to find out what all the fuss was about; titillations they assumed would one day transfer to the opposite sex—these feelings now rose up and squared off over a woman who wore sexuality as casually as she draped her marabou boa off one shoulder. Desire came out from a corner of Leone's mind. Danger danced out of another corner.

When Letty bent over to open the desk drawer and fish around for something, Leone dropped her gaze to the actress's pert bottom but lifted her eyes quickly when she felt her face flush. *Whoa. Slow down.*

"Does Charles find her stunning?" Leone asked.

Letty straightened up and turned around. She was holding an eight-by-ten photograph. "Of course he does. That's why he cast her. She is perfect for the role of the duchess. She's positively regal." Letty narrowed her eyes. "What are you suggesting, Leone?"

Leone straightened her shoulders and sat up tall. "Is that what you like? Regal women?"

"I thought we were talking about what Charles likes."

"Charles." Leone wrinkled her nose. She stood up from the bed and threw a tasseled shawl over her shoulders. "Military hero, business tycoon, London producer, Hollywood director."

"And my husband."

Was there a hint of smugness in her smile? Leone's eyes moistened.

"I have something for you, darling." Letty extended her arm and waved the photo she held in her hand in *come-hither* fashion. "I thought of you while the photographer was snapping away."

Letty, fresh-eyed Kansas farm girl, slipped her musical voice into a smoky register that sent shivers into nascent parts of Leone's body, a response she was just now coming to understand. Leone brightened and took hold of the photograph.

In the sepia-toned picture, the actress stood sideways, head thrown backward, gray eyes seeking an audience. Her soft curls hung down her naked back. She wore a black mermaid gown of textured lace and held a tapestry in a round frame. Across the nondescript artwork, Letty had written: *To lovely Leone, held very high in my thoughts. L.*

Leone kept her head bent over the photograph. Her face burned. *Not exactly where I want to be held, but her message is clear: Back off.*

"All right girls, snap to it." The dance captain ended his tête-à-tête with the stage manager and snapped his fingers in the air. From the second row of the chorus that backed up the principal dancers, Leone executed yet another bored bump and grind. Principal dancers were allowed to try their hands at a little acting, a small speaking part to support the slinky star. Their role was to sidle up to some Johnny and spew the sarcasm audiences mistook for wit.

"Okay, take five, girls." The stage manager dismissed the chorus. "You, third from the left in the second row."

Leone slowed her exit and tapped her chest with her finger. *Moi?* She mouthed.

"Yeah, you. Could ya try *lookin'* like you're having a good time?"

Leone crossed her eyes and flashed the bony man dressed in black an exaggerated smile of impure glee.

"That's more like it, honey. Hold that thought."

Leone walked off the rehearsal stage tugging at an elastic panty-leg band that was designed to cup her buttocks and stay in place. Was it costumes or budgets that were getting skimpier? Both, she imagined.

A snatch of conversation from a huddle of dancers in the wings reached her ear. "She can dance circles around any of us, and her voice isn't bad, but that one? No acting chops."

Leone raised her chin and moved past them. She supposed they were talking about her, but it didn't matter. It was true. She had no talent for the nuances of acting, but what difference did that make? The worse things got in the American economy and European politics the faster Hollywood churned out sharp-edged, bawdy entertainment. Hard-pressed to put food on the table, men fantasized about the tough-talking anti-heroes who knew how to put a nagging dame in her place. To appeal to their wives and lovers, producers kept a stable of dames who knew how to stand up to a man; women like Garbo, Harlow, and Hepburn.

As hard as she tried, Leone could not ignore the facts. If Hollywood could cast a triple-threat dancer in the chorus, one that could step into a stronger role if need be, why not? Younger, prettier girls who had "lead in the high-school play" on their resumes showed up every day at the Hollywood Studio Club.

Leone changed out of her rehearsal clothes and pulled on a tailored shirt and the straight-hanging, mannish-cut trousers she preferred. She sat on the stage-door steps and smoked a cigarette.

Someone pushed through the heavy door and dropped down behind her. Fingers wove themselves among the close-cropped curls at the back of her head.

"Want to come out with us tonight?"

The stiffness in Leone's shoulders relaxed. She put her hand on top of the hand that Rosemary rested on her shoulder. She hadn't felt close to anyone since Letty blew into her life, and out of it just as fast. Letty. Her postcards had stopped coming months ago. Leone's phone calls went unanswered.

Others pushed through the door, hurried down the steps, and grouped around Leone. Leone threw her head back and grinned her signature saucy smile.

"C'mon sister, let's go drinking." Rosemary offered her a hand up. Leone rose quickly to her feet and fell in with her new companions.

25

Derelict

*A*lcohol-fueled parties could not assuage Leone's fear. The darker the cloud grew in Europe, the brighter Hollywood glittered, but mere blocks away bread lines grew longer. Her savings exhausted and callbacks dropping off, Leone found herself one rent check away from joining that line. The thought of being dependent on a handout filled her with fury.

"Can't you ask your family for help?" Rosemary linked her arm with Leone's as they climbed the back stairs to a suite in the Chateau Marmont.

"I would die first."

"Oh, I doubt it will come to that." The two stood on the landing patting their hair into place and adding layers of lipstick. "We creative types always find a way."

Down the hall, a door opened. A large man stuck his head out of the doorway and peered right and left. Spotting Leone and Rosemary, he beckoned to them. "Girls, come right this way." Rosemary swept ahead, and Leone followed.

That worlds without money existed Leone could attest to, but there was always a price to pay. Hollywood was growing bawdier. Although Leone could count on free food and liquor at parties, where she was always welcome, the price of admission was acquiescence. Wasn't that what she had left home to avoid?

Anything Goes was not just the name of a Broadway show set to open at the end of the year; it was the battle cry of the bohemians.

Free booze, free drugs, free sex, and free artistic expression—and the purveyor of the last two services? Herself and her friends. Let them expect whatever they wanted. She would dress the part and accept the free food and drinks. Soon enough they would figure out that her spirit was not as free as Isadora Duncan, a modern dancer who, given enough scarf, broke her neck when one end of her signature wardrobe piece flew into the wheel of the convertible she was riding in and garroted her.

Does free spirit mean "Damn the consequences, full speed ahead?" From her perch on a settee where she sipped absinthe and sized up the other partygoers, Leone let her mind wander.

Or does it mean freedom to follow your inner wisdom? Her grandmother's voice. Try as she might to silence that voice, what Grandmother would think always lurked in a closet of her mind.

And who informs inner wisdom? Leone asked, pleased with herself. She was holding up her end of this internal conversation quite well. Despite the muddle she was in over her future, she had not lost all reason.

God: some would say. Like a tiny bird suddenly alert to possible danger, Leone held very still, all ears. That was not her grandmother's voice. What was that?

"A penny for your thoughts." The party host leaned over the settee. He held a sugar cube nestled in a slotted spoon in one hand, and a pitcher of chilled water in the other. Leone lifted her Pontarlier glass and allowed him to pour chilled water over the spoon into her drink.

"They do this in Paris." His voice was as smooth and cultured as the drink.

"*Mmm.*" Leone swirled the milky green liquid around in the glass, raised it to her nose, and breathed in the anise sweetness and tangy herbal undertones. Only in sophisticated cities like Hollywood could one appreciate a culturally iconic drink such as absinthe prepared in just the right fashion and served in just the right glass.

Her host put his lips to her ear. "If you want to light up your brain, see my man over in the corner. He'll take you into the back room and fix you up."

Leone looked up and spotted a young man standing apart from the crowd. He wore a suit much like the one she wore, loose pants and a two-button jacket with wide lapels. What set them apart was her makeup. She wore her party face; eyebrows extensively tweezed and defined with a thin pencil line, lips painted to look like they had been tattooed on her face.

"Mmm." She slid her eyes up toward the man with the silver spoon and blinked once, slowly. This affectation of boredom lent her an air of mystery and excused her from conversations she did not care to have. Her host patted her shoulder and glided off.

A couple balancing glasses of champagne sat down across from Leone on a sculpted, cream-colored sofa with angora mohair seat cushions she had been admiring. The man extended his hand across the small cocktail table that separated the couch and the settee.

"Hi, I'm Dunham Thorp."

His companion took the cue. "And I'm Marion."

She was lovely. A little vacant, but that could have been due to something she had ingested.

"Actress." Dunham jerked his head in his wife's direction.

Leone dipped her chin toward Marion and took Dunham's hand firmly in her own. "Dancer. Unemployed."

"Writer. Same."

Marion came alive. "And I paint and look after our daughter, Ella." She slipped her forefinger along the sleek marble-top cocktail table until it stopped at the base of Leone's glass. "And that looks delicious but dangerous."

"Mmm. What do you write, Dunham?"

"Press releases. Scripts. I'm working on a novel, but I have a deal in the works that is going to get us out of here." He put his hand in his pocket and came up with a lighter for the cigarette Leone had pulled from a pack sitting on the table.

"Why would anyone want to leave all"—Leone drew smoke into her lung and then gestured around the room with her hand—"this?"

Three sets of eyes surveyed the room. Ears inclined toward moving mouths; arms slipped around female waists; hands thumped male shoulders; hips caught sharp table edges; lips caressed cheeks;

drinks spilled. Snatches of conversation could not be traced to their source. It was like a watching a movie with an out-of-sync soundtrack.

Dunham leaned in and rested his forearms on his knees. "I'll tell you why. There's no space for artists like us in Hollywood anymore."

Leone sat up straight and leaned toward Dunham. "What do you mean? This room is crowded with artists."

"Ah yes, but creating *meaningful* work requires solitude and a supportive community."

Leone took a drag on her cigarette and leaned back. "Isn't that an oxymoron?"

"You would think so, but we've found a community of people who support each other and give each other space at the same time. 'Individuality within Community,' that's their motto."

Marion laid her hand on Dunham's knee and fixed her huge brown eyes on Leone. "It's on the coast. A doctor lives there who can help our little girl. She had polio."

"I'm so sorry." Leone crushed out her cigarette in a cut-crystal ashtray. She turned toward Dunham. "So, what's the deal?"

"I have a friend who is starting a magazine, a conversation in print, if you will, about issues of the day. He wants me to be managing editor."

"A news magazine?"

"Definitely not. A monthly journal of ideas. We'll recruit people with new and stimulating points of view. We'll encourage friction among thinkers of all persuasions: political, religious, sexual—"

Marion broke in, "And artistic. Gavin wants a poetry section."

"I write poetry." The words slipped out before Leone could discipline her tongue. *Who is Gavin? I should have asked.*

Dunham leaned back and crossed his leg over his knee. "Do you type?"

———✦———

Back in her dormitory, the rich food, strong drink, and stimulating conversation fueled vivid dreams that robbed Leone of badly needed rest. Because she could no longer afford lessons at Madame Smolina's studio, she began sleeping late. When she woke, her body ached—whether from hard living or lack of exercise she wasn't sure. She started a routine of stretching and strengthening exercises on her own, something she had seen her mother do when the ballet studio closed for holidays. Her resolve lasted a week. Her mother possessed a disciplined spirit that must come from something other than regimen. Despite her troubles, her mother had a wholesomeness about her that perplexed Leone, angered her even. What did she lack?

Leone began to dream of long walks on the beach. She longed for overcast skies to envelop and protect her while she figured out how much of her life was an act, and how many of her deepest desires she could satisfy without losing her soul. She pulled away from the party set and began attending rallies, lectures, and poetry readings, sometimes with Rosemary, sometimes alone. She met people like the Thorps who introduced her to intimate salons where the literati gathered.

In tasteful living rooms in Pacific Palisades, she met European artists who had fallen out of favor under Hitler's looming shadow. Hollywood was an Ellis Island for emigrating writers, composers, painters, and filmmakers pouring in from Europe on every ship that crossed the Atlantic.

"Stay and be killed, or start over." A bespectacled young man in his early thirties spoke in a thick German accent to a small group of graduate students who surrounded him. "My products are here"— he tapped his head—"in my mind. So, I will just set up shop in a bar." He scanned the rapt faces who hung on his words. "Do you know of one?"

"Who is that?" Leone asked Dunham, who showed up often at the salons with Marion by his side.

"Bertolt Brecht. He's a poet, playwright, and director. The Nazis just kicked him out of Germany."

Marion stood next to her husband and stared off into space. The dark-haired, elegant woman often appeared to be in a trance. There were days, like this one, when a misbuttoned blouse or uncombed hair marred her physical perfection. "Everyone is looking for a haven." She addressed the air.

"It's true," Leone said. "The entertainment industry may not provide the refuge a true artist requires. It is a business, after all."

Dunham cupped his chin with his hand. "You know, Leone. Moy Mell may be just the place for you."

"Is that the community you told me about?"

"Yes. Why live hand-to-mouth in Hollywood? Talent needs a big starry sky, and that we have out in the Dunes. We take our food from the ocean and the produce fields that stretch for miles. We do the work that pleases us, and we look out after each other. I could use your help getting our first issue of *Dune Forum* out.

An appealing idea. Better to fend for herself and find a way to contribute the fruit of her imagination to the betterment of mankind, than wait on Roosevelt to ladle soup into her bowl or employ her in the Professional Products Division of the Works Progress Administration.

"One of the Dunites knows about a hut on the cliffs above the ocean we could probably get for you. The old guy used to live there, but he prefers camping in the Dunes."

"The Dunites? Who are they?"

"Free-thinking people who want to live a simple life." Marion stared into her cocktail.

"All kinds of people, really." Dunham took up Marion's hand and patted it. "Hermits who wish to be alone with their demons dig in for years. Hobos wander through the community. They eat our clams and warm themselves by our fires. And Gavin's friends. Gavin collects artists the way his grandfather collected books."

"You have mentioned him before. Who is he?"

"Gavin Arthur is Chester Alan Arthur III, the grandson of our twenty-first president. You won't be in a room with him for five minutes before he lets that fact drop." Dunham laughed. "But he's a great guy. There is a chair at his table for everyone, whether it's John Steinbeck come by to read to us, or Upton Sinclair wanting help to eliminate poverty in California, or Leone Barry who writes poetry."

Dreamy-eyed Marion stirred from her reverie. "Come with us and see for yourself."

26

Dunes

Oceano

$\mathcal{N}$othing in her life had prepared Leone for the wild freedom of the Dunes. Where theater life had been a tight schedule of classes, auditions, rehearsals, performances, and parties, life in the Dunes required only that she learn how to feed herself. That her hut on the cliff removed her from daily life down in the sand hills that formed the Dunes presented a challenge, but not an insurmountable one.

Barter and glean, that was the economy that sustained the community. Hermits built their cabins of willow branches and scraps of wood that washed up on shore. They dug for coveted Pismo clams and sold or traded them. Leone mended their clothing for a bucket of clams.

The sparse, largely male population of misfits found a solace in this otherworldly place where they could nurse their alcoholism, delusions, or desire to be left alone. Some were hiding from past misdeeds or soured family relationships. Others, worn down by poverty, found renewed health in the rigors of daily life in the Dunes.

Living alongside the hermits, a collection of artists and intellectuals gathered around Gavin Arthur at Moy Mell and enjoyed an abundance of food and drink provided by their host. Her first week in the Dunes, Leone was a frequent guest at his table. The burgeoning utopian community nestled beside a grove of eucalyptus trees attracted visitors from across the United States. From Gavin's spacious cabin, heated by a wood stove, guests could walk through a tunnel of blackberry bushes to reach the Community House. Visitors were always an occasion for feasting, music, dance, and discussions that lasted until exhaustion numbed them into incoherence.

At times when she wasn't helping out at the Community House, Leone retreated to her hut where she ate simple meals of fried clams and local vegetables. She cooked outside over an open fire and slept on a clean pallet she fashioned from packing crates, cardboard, and thin quilts distributed by charities. Quiet days stretched out before her, unmarked by any routine other than waking at dawn, fixing her coffee, and tidying up. Some days she settled into an upholstered chair with ripped seat cushions the previous tenant had pulled outside and placed on the precipice overlooking the Dunes below. Here, she read an advance copy of Vita Sackville-West's eagerly anticipated *Collected Poems* Gavin had lent her. In the distance, the vast ocean moved in froth-tipped, icy-colored aquamarine waves, kneading the shore in long, powerful strokes. Entranced by words and waves, Leone drifted in and out of sleep.

Other days she stayed inside and wrote at a table pushed up against the wall under the hut's only window. Tape held one windowpane together where the glass had shattered. Blowing sand had etched and clouded the other three panes. She wrote from early light until the sun passed over. After a few weeks, though, she became restless. She walked into Halcyon, got a ride out to the Dunes, and reported for work.

"It's about time you showed your face." Dunham looked up from the table where he was sorting through stacks of handwritten manuscripts. "I'm ready for you now. Did you bring your typewriter?" He ran his fingers through the thick, curly, dark hair that fell across his brow.

Leone threw her hands up in the air. "You were serious about that? I imagined that my writing and editing skills might be more useful to you."

"Gavin is the publisher; I am the editor; Gavin's friends are the writers; and *you* are the typist. Your job is to make sure the copy we submit to the printer in San Francisco is perfect. It's an important job. Let's go get your typewriter."

Sounds like third row in the chorus line to me. How had her grandmother managed her way out of the steno pool? *Not by lollygagging around at home, missy.*

The next morning, Leone arrived early at Moy Mell. Most residents and guests were still asleep, so she walked over the dunes toward the ocean. Walking on the sand deposits delivered from the mountains by creeks and rivers was hard work, but her calves were conditioned for it through years of dance. She would be able to catch up with Dunham who would be out clamming with his small daughter.

She thought she spotted the girl in the distance, whirling around on the wet sand. Dunham popped up from behind a dune not far away and hailed Leone.

"What is she doing out there?" Leone asked.

"*Shhh.*" Dunham put his finger to his lips and squatted down so he could not be seen from the shore. "The fish and game warden is about."

Leone dropped down next to him. "What is Ella doing out there?

"She's clam dancing." He looked delighted. "She learned it from one of the hermits. You whirl around in the sand on one leg, and your foot burrows down in the wet sand until you feel a clam with your toes. You should try it."

"What happens if the warden catches her?

"Oh, he will. He'll inspect her bucket to make sure the clams are legal size and then wish her a good day. Children don't need a license to clam."

"Ah." Leone peeked over the dune. Sure enough, the warden was having a lively conversation with the girl. A few minutes later, he drove off down the beach, and Dunham stood up and waved Ella over. She moved slowly over the dune, her muscles still weak from her bout with polio. Dunham reached for her bucket and then for her hand. The three headed back to the Community House, where Dunham would cook a big breakfast while Marion slept.

"Gavin approved your poem for our first issue." Dunham looked straight ahead.

"He did?" Leone could hardly breathe. "Would you thank him for me?"

"Thank him yourself. He's giving a party tonight. Ansel Adams will be here this afternoon to photograph the Dunes for a future issue of the magazine. You can meet him."

Leone spent the day at the Community House helping prepare Thomas A. Watson's essay, "An Engineer's Idea of God," for the printer in San Francisco. By the time the fog rolled in, the weekend guests had arrived from the Bay Area, and a fire in the fireplace brightened the room. Gavin left his seafood stew to simmer in the Dutch oven on the stove and sequestered himself with Ansel.

Marion wandered into the room. Blue paint speckled her bare arms.

"How did your painting go this afternoon? Leone asked.

Marion looked down and touched a dried fleck of paint on her elbow. "When I get more paint on myself than the canvas, it's a good day." She drifted over to the Victrola. Picking up a record, she began to sway back and forth. "We'll having dancing tonight, I suppose."

"We will indeed," Gavin came through the door, followed by Dunham, Ella, and a pretty young woman with long dark hair. "I have new records, the Ray Noble Orchestra and the Billy Cotton Band."

Ella let go of the young woman's hand and rushed into her mother's arms. "Marion," she squealed. "Guess what? I helped core apples for the cider Dunham is going to make." Marion sat down and pulled her daughter onto her lap.

Cars arrived and people crowded into the room. The party was in full swing when Ansel returned from his walk and announced he intended to return during the next full moon. The young photographer was gone before Leone had a chance to approach him.

"He's quite famous, you know." Marion looked at Leone with her soulful brown eyes. "He's just opened a gallery in San Francisco." Ella, sleeping heavily in her mother's arms, shifted position. "And he's just had his first child, a son."

The malaise Leone had managed to keep at bay the last several months returned. How to describe it? Like a flashback. It wasn't like traveling back in time, but more like a flash and the room whooshing back from her. She saw them all through a dark mirror, her face a ghostly imprint on the glass, a faint image through which she strained to keep sight of them all. The salty smell of Ella, circled in the warm safety of her mother's arms, made Leone's eyes water. *Who is going to take care of that little girl when her daddy takes off with the barefoot brunette? Marion lives in a daze.* A sneezing fit banished the scrim that had darkened her view.

Gavin came by with a bottle of expensive whiskey.

"I must be catching a cold." Leone raised her glass.

"I've got just the medicine to fix you up." Gavin splashed the burnt amber liquid into her glass.

Someone dropped "Jog Along," a fox trot, onto the turntable, cranked the Victrola, and set the tone arm down carefully. The women got up and took practiced steps around the room. As the noise level rose, the men left off their conversations and joined the dance.

Leone stood alone in a corner. Weak and shaky, she opened her eyes wide and focused on a light beaming softly through the window across the room. Headlamps focused on the distant road? Someone finding their way with a flashlight? She went to the bar, refilled her glass, and slipped outside.

In the moonlight, the dunes took on a pink glow. Ella's dog Dribble rose from his resting spot on the porch and padded alongside Leone. Together they made their way out on the dunes.

"You get left outside too?" Leone stretched out her hand and patted the top of the dog's head. *Outside.* How often had she felt left outside? Outside the norm when she was a little girl without a father; outside her body when she was in the hospital in LA; and although no one knew it, outside any group of people, no matter how hard she tried to fit in.

Far off, the glow of a campfire beckoned. When Leone and the dog arrived at an old hermit's cabin, her glass was empty. The hermit sat cross-legged in front of the burning woodpile, feeding sticks into the blaze. Crackling flames from the fire lit his craggy face. He nodded toward Leone's glass.

"Ya look dry." He patted the sand next to where he sat, and Leone dropped down to sit beside him, but not too close. She pulled her knees to one side, and the dog settled near her feet.

The hermit passed her a cracked clay jug full of some unnamed home brew. "Come to join my party, have you?"

Leone filled her glass and raised it in tribute. A swig and a wince drew a laugh from the hermit. "I see you're used to the good stuff. Why are you out here?"

"Why are you?" Her second small sip of the liquor seemed less raw.

He looked up at the three-quarter moon. "I been out here a long time, asking myself that question. I think I finally come to an answer. It don't much matter *where* I am; it's *who* I am that matters."

Leone scooched herself a little closer to the fire. "And who is that?"

The hermit rolled up on one knee and reached for a Mexican blanket that lay in the sand. Careful to avoid the open fire, he tossed it in her direction. She pulled it around her shoulders, arranging it across her knees while she waited for his answer.

Across the dunes, light from the big house filtered through the eucalyptus and cast eerie shadows on the sand. "Well it ain't one of them, that's for sure." He nodded toward the house.

"Hmm." Burrs stuck in the blanket scratched her skin. Her ragged fingernails caught on the twisted cotton threads as she picked the stickers out and poked them down in the sand.

"Nope." The hermit jabbed the wood in the fire pit with a stick. Sparks spit into the air. "They're the highbrows. We're the blessed poor."

A burning ember floated down onto the blanket and smoldered. Leone beat her fingers on the smoke-blackened wound that ate into the loosely woven fabric. "That's your answer? That's who you are? A poor man?"

"Course that's who I am. Honey, you can't live a simple life unless you make peace with your lack." He poked a stick in the fire till it caught, then pulled it out and watched it glow. "Your fancy friends come out here, looking for what? They bring their wealth and talent and ambition with them. What's different?"

She stared at the curly gray hairs that smattered across his chest. That he could sit out here, bare from the waist up, astonished her.

"Don't get me wrong girlie. Them folks been mighty generous to us, but they fool themselves to think there's magic in this"—he threw his hands out toward the dunes—*"place."* He tapped his sternum. *"This* is the *place."*

The old man reached out, took Leone's arm in a tight grip, and shook it. "Honey, you have to know what you lack before you can find room in your heart for"— he lowered his voice to a whisper— *"magic."* He let her arm drop.

Even though it didn't hurt, Leone rubbed her arm. Dribble raised his head and then tucked his nose under his tail.

"They want to change things." Leone's voice wavered. "They're smart people who want to make life better for all of us."

He snorted. "Listen to me. Some things you just can't figure your way to. You get so far, and then you got to just let the magic happen. It don't happen if you're all filled up with yourself. Know what? In a few years, they will move on. Us? We'll die off. The sand that blows on these dunes will cover all trace of us. What will be left? A few pottery shards resting alongside shell mounds the Chumash left behind."

Again he fixed his fierce gaze on Leone. His eyes were like fingers of bright light probing deep and dark and painful places. "You can't change anything if you don't change yourself first. And you can't change yourself if you don't know what you lack."

In the distance, car doors slammed. The old man got to his feet and began to scatter the dying embers. "Tide's coming in. If you're leaving tonight with any of them, you best get going."

Leone looked at him through eyes blurry with drink or tears or both. "Thanks." She got up on unsteady feet and faltered a little when Dribble stood and shook himself. They made their way back, and Leone shooed the dog up the porch steps. She walked around the side of the house and approached one of the cars idling in the parking area while the driver consulted a map. She tapped on the window.

"I can show you how to drive out of here if you will give me a ride into Halcyon."

27

Packing and Moving

Portland, 1934

The Great Depression may have ended Nellie's career in the courts, but ample opportunity had presented itself elsewhere. Insurance firms like the American Fire and Casualty Company had taken a longer investment view, selecting stocks with more stable earnings. In her seventh decade, stability was more appealing than before. Her job in an insurance office, while not challenging, paid the bills and that was all right.

Most Saturdays, Nellie took the bus to Opal's, and they shopped together, but today she sat at her daughter's kitchen table while Opal wrapped dishware in newspaper and stacked them in boxes. Felix had succeeded in his campaign to move his little family to San Francisco. He wanted to be near his aging parents, who struggled to keep their Union Street art and frame shop open.

Something niggled at Nellie. "I thought you told me that Felix was French."

"Well, they emigrated from Paris."

"But Union Street, that's the Fillmore district. Isn't that the Jewish part of town?"

Opal pulled another coffee mug from the cupboard. She held it in her hand as if weighing the bulky piece of brown Buckeye Pottery, one of many mismatched pieces Felix had brought back from his travels.

"I don't know; it might be." She wrapped the mug and shoved it into the box. "We don't talk about things like that. In this country, the Wolffs are just shopkeepers. Business people."

"Well, you better start talking about it. The anti-Jewish sentiment in Europe could come to our shores."

Opal froze. She turned to face Nellie. "Is that why you won' t come with us? Because Felix is Jewish?"

Nellie drew herself up. Her left hand shook where it lay on the table, and her dark eyes glittered. "You know better than that. How could you say such a thing? I didn't know until this moment that his family is Jewish."

"Then why?"

Nellie slumped. She placed her right hand on top of her left to calm the bothersome tremor. Her voice shook. "Because I don't want to be the old lady living off her daughter." She fidgeted with a ring on her finger, a turquoise set in silver. "Someday it may come to that, but I'm not ready."

Opal sat down at the table and reached for her mother's hands. "I know, Mother, but please remember, you will always have a home with Felix and me if you need it."

"Hmm." Nellie pressed her lips into the barest of smiles and pulled her hand away. She pushed herself up from the table. "Can I help?" She carried her coffee cup to the sink, rinsed and dried it, wrapped it in newspaper, and set it in the packing box.

The two women worked together in silence for a moment, then spoke at the same time.

"Where did Felix take Jane?" Nellie asked.

"Have you gotten a postcard from Leone yet?" Opal wanted to know.

"Not a one."

"Felix took Jane to the beach." Opal glanced up at the clock and then washed her hands under the tap and began to make sandwiches.

Breathing hard, Nellie walked back to the table and lowered herself into a chair. "Do you have any idea where Leone is?"

The screen door rattled. Opal went to let the pawing tabby out and the eager spaniel in. The luscious scent of lilacs competed with the daily drama that played around Opal's ankles—a hiss and a slap, followed by a yip and the clatter of toenails trying for traction on the floor. She continued to stand in the open doorway.

"I'm going to miss Oregon. We have been a family here. It will never be the same." Opal drew in a deep breath, shut the door, and reached for a towel. Bending down to wipe the dog's paws she said "But to answer your question, a postcard came last week. It didn't say much. The postmark was Oceano. That's about two hundred miles north of Los Angeles, I think."

"Do you think she's left Hollywood for good?"

Opal shrugged. "May have. She didn't give me an address. I have no way of letting her know we're moving. Maybe we'll never see her again."

"Not likely." Nellie snorted. "What *did* she say?"

Opal pulled the card out of her apron pocket and handed it to Nellie. It was a black and white reproduction of a photo, a house set among sand dunes. Nellie looked at the image briefly and flipped it over. Her eyebrows inched up as she read aloud the one sentence scrawled across the back of the card. *My oasis in beautiful mountains of sand. L.* Nellie stared at the message for a long minute. Then she set it down on the table.

"That's all she said? Her handwriting has gotten sloppy."

"That's all you have to say?"

"Looks like she spilled a drink on it. See here?" Nellie pointed to a dried splotch that had caused the signature to bleed into something unrecognizable. "I don't think that's tears. Whiskey is more like it."

Opal hugged herself. "We know so little of her life. I don't know what to think. She seemed so happy her first year, even after the accident. When she stopped writing, I figured it was because she'd gotten so busy."

"You kept writing to her, didn't you?"

"Of course, but six months ago my letter was returned. Someone had written *No longer at this address* on the envelope."

"You didn't tell me."

"I didn't want to worry you. I figured we would hear from her eventually."

"And now you have. Opal, she is a young woman finding her way. She's no different than you or me at that age."

"You can't say that. I wrote to you every week."

"Until you got pregnant."

"You don't think she's pregnant ..." Opal's hand went to her mouth.

"No. Not likely." Nellie reached up and pulled Opal's arm down. "Don't cover your mouth like that. I can hardly hear what you're saying."

A car door slammed in the driveway. Sounds of sobbing filled the air, growing louder as footfalls approached the door. Felix burst through the door carrying Jane, who had a trickle of blood running down her leg.

"What happened?" Opal grabbed a cloth towel, wet it and hurried over to blot the blood on the child's knee.

"Oh, she fell on a rock and got a little cut on her knee, that's all." Felix handed the girl over. "She'll be fine."

Jane cried harder, gulping air and gripping her mother's neck tightly. Opal set her down on the kitchen counter. She extracted herself from Jane's chokehold and gently examined the wound.

"It's just a little scrape. Calm down now." Opal patted Jane's shoulder, and the red-faced, teary-eyed girl's heaves settled into snuffles.

"I'm going now." Nellie stood up and pulled on her sweater.

Opal wiped the child's tears away with her hand and reached for a tin of Band-Aids she kept ever at the ready. As Nellie passed by mother and child, she reached around Opal and patted Jane's uninjured knee.

"Buck up there, little lady. You have to learn how to take the bumps in life. There will be a lot of them."

Jane wiped her eyes with the backs of her hands and sniffed hard. She glared at her grandmother and jerked her knee away.

Nellie touched Opal's shoulder lightly. "And you stop worrying. Leone is a smart, talented girl; she's one tough cookie. She'll write to us soon enough. And when she does, she'll have stories to tell."

28

Disillusion

Oceano

*L*eone made fewer trips to the Dunes. She kept to herself in the hut, making no attempt at home improvements. The first copy of *Dune Forum* sat on the table next to typewriter. When she blanked while writing, she would turn to the poetry section in the magazine and stare at the page.

Symphony of Water
by Leone Barry

It lies there ...
As a brown hurting giant,
With the features of it
Thrust and sharp and static.
It is the thing between
An asking and an answer.
It is the shore....

The eye of a star is flashing us.
We are wailing, washing, wishing.
We are water.
O, waves that reach and waves that twist,
O, strange far promise of a fire....
It could be the last deceit.
It can last as long as night.

O, silver burning, silver eye....

Sing, you forms of foam.
We have toiled in blue deepness
And you are more than our dreams,
Careless and white,
Fading on the tide.
We are beauty.
We have mated with the sun
And our children lie
As young golden lights
Along our power.
A strangeness is with us.
It trembles to us.
It asks, it tells.
Shall we hate it with our storm,
Shall we love it with our peace?
Shall we....
O, straining, certain, sinking sea,
O, things that have been and will be....

Mother, mother,
Nestle us.
We fear the things we are.
We fear the things we do.
We do not understand.
Our laughter lives and dies.
Our sorrow lives on
And in and on.
Things fall to us.
And we to them.
And we wonder, wonder.
We would be soft and sweet
And satin on your breast.
Mother, nestle us.
Father, we have broken our brother....
It has become the terrible shine,
The shining terror

Of our motion.
Father....
A greatness has entered us.
It is almost a sound.
And yet....
Be still.
It is the voice of us,
So sighing, sobbing, singing,
That we have not known it as our own.
"We are going, we must go.
We are going. We must go."
Knowledge breaks.
We gather the things that we are.
And we are tears, and we are dew,
And we are rain, and we are sweat.
We are every running river,
We are every soaring sea.
We belong, we belong....
O, blood of every sorrow
Beating, beating.
O, blood of every joy
Racing, racing.
We are wailing, washing, wishing.
We are water.

It lies there....
It knew our going,
It knows our coming.
And it waits,
With open, splendid arms.
We move .. .
Our life beats us on
In blue and green
And great final gray.
We kill
As we rise and rush.
We die

As we flash and fall.
We live
As we go on and on and on....
O, star beyond our reach,
O, pain beyond our soul.
It lies there ...
We break and writhe
And fade upon it.
It is the thing between
An asking and an answer.
It is the shore....

Would she ever be able to write something so beautiful again? She turned back a few pages and reread her credit.

LEONE BARRY lives not far from the Dunes in a little hut perched on a cliff where she is writing a novel of great promise. She is twenty-three, and the DUNE FORUM banks on the fact that one day she will be known to all the reading world.

Gavin made that up. He knew nothing of what she was writing. Still, it was good of him to publish her poem. The first issue had attracted much attention and submissions from well-known poets piled up on his desk. She glared at the empty paper in her typewriter.

The old hermit's words had stayed with her. She had always thought of lack as the absence of something you needed or wanted, but he seemed to be addressing some universal character deficiency. She stood up from the table, water glass in hand. In the few steps it took her to get from the table to the washstand basin, the glass slipped from her grasp and shattered on the rough wood floor. Earlier in the day, she'd dropped and broken her coffee mug. Not only did she lack imagination for the morning's work, she also seemed to lack the ability to hold onto cups and glasses.

Leone swept up the broken glass and tossed it into the garbage alongside the brown pottery shards. Perhaps a walk down the winding dirt path and a visit to the thrift shop would lift her spirits.

Halfway to town, she spotted something shiny nestled in coastal buckwheat and deep-pink verbena. Stepping off the path, she bent down to investigate and pulled a dented tin cup from the bristle of foliage. Tossed aside by a hobo; it would do. By the time she returned to the hut, she was breathing hard from the uphill exertion. She dropped into her chair at the table and set the cup in front of her. Round with a broad handle, it looked like the cups soldiers used in movies she'd seen. She stared at it. Stained and dirty. Empty. What had the hermit said? Something about magic A prayer formed on her lips. *Fill my cup with magic.*

Voices outside jolted her from her reverie. No one ever came to the hut. She looked out the window and then threw open the door. Two young women leaned on each other, panting.

"How did you find me?"

"Good God, Leone, whatever possessed you to live up here?" Rosemary pushed through the doorway.

"We're on a little holiday. We thought we'd look you up." Rosemary's companion followed.

"How did you find me?" Leone stepped aside. The room soon filled with chatter that had become unfamiliar to her.

"We bandied your name about town. We should have asked how far up the trail you were. We had to park the car and leave it."

"Do you have any water?" Rosemary's friend gasped and held her side. "Oh boy, I must be out of shape."

Leone washed out the tin cup and filled it from a stone jug with a train painted on the front. While her friend downed the cup of water, Rosemary swigged directly from the jug and set it back down. "Before I forget, I have a message for you. Your mother called the Studio Club asking for you. She didn't seem to know you'd left LA."

"What did you tell her?"

"That I would give you the message."

"What did she want?"

"She wanted you to know that they have moved to San Francisco."

Rosemary's companion refreshed the tin cup, dipped her fingers into the water, and patted her forehead and cheeks. "Whew."

"Who's your friend?" Leone narrowed her eyes at Rosemary.

"Sorry, thought you'd remember. Evelyn moved into the club just before you left. But listen, your grandmother is still in Portland, and I guess she's not doing well."

"Hey," Evelyn barged in. "What say we all walk back down to the car and drive out to the Dunes. I'm dying to see Moy Mell. I hear the parties out there last for days." She looked around the room. "Where's the bathroom?"

Leone opened the front door and pointed toward a small grove of eucalyptus trees.

"You're kidding."

"Watch out for the poison oak."

While the two women were gone, Leone packed up her typewriter and a valise of clothing. Before she zipped the bag, she shoved the tin cup inside. Shutting the door behind her, she fell in step with her friends as they walked past the hut. Rosemary eyed the valise and typewriter case. "Going somewhere?"

"I'll show you around the Dunes. After that, I'm going to try to talk you into driving me up to Portland."

29

Visit

Not long after the Wolffs left Oregon, ill health forced Nellie to surrender and allow Opal and Felix to make room for her in their small California bungalow. When it was time to pack up and leave Portland, Nellie looked through her letter box for the collection of short stories she had titled *Leaves from a Reporter's Notebook*. She didn't find them. Her creative writing teacher had seen promise in her last assignment, the one about Clara. Although it was not Nellie's favorite, the instructor had encouraged her to develop Clara's tale of woe for publication, going so far as to suggest a title:"The Woman with no Visible Means of Support."

Is that what she looked like now? After years of supporting herself and setting aside money for her old age, her small savings were proving inadequate. Today she was being ferried back to California in Felix's DeSoto, her few worldly goods stuffed in the trunk. Felix lit an El Producto and launched into a monologue.

"George Burns' favorite. Opal won't let me smoke them when Jane is in the car. Bothers her asthma, she says." He raised the cigar in the air and looked over his shoulder at Nellie. "Might do her good to smoke one, I say. What do you think, Mother Scott?"

"I think it's a good thing for all of us that Opal found a neighbor to watch Jane."

What am I going to do with myself at their house? Nellie considered her options. Her favorite fashion magazine, McCall's, had recently started to publish fiction. Perhaps she could sell her stories. She'd have to find them first.

While Felix drove, window down, puffing on his infernal cigar, Opal sat in the backseat beside Nellie, her hands folded in her lap.

"Mother, there is more in life you may rely on besides money."

Nellie stiffened. Was Opal a mind reader? Sitting straight, allowing no contact between her spine and the back of the seat, she inspected the stiff fabric of her shiny black dress, dusting away the occasional white speck of cigar ash that fell on her skirt.

"How does Felix afford such a fancy car?" Nellie asked. "What make did you say this is?"

"A DeSoto Airflow." Felix volunteered an answer in his loud, cheery voice—compensation for his small stature, Nellie always told herself. "How's the ride back there, Mother?" The top of Felix's derby hat bobbed up and down to a tune the tires played running over ruts in the road.

"The ride is quite comfortable, Felix." Opal smiled at her mother. "Felix can afford this car because, in good times or bad times, people always want candy, and Felix is an excellent salesman."

"My customers love me, Mother. Don't you worry."

Nellie pulled her shawl tightly around her shoulders. "I make it my practice not to give myself anything to worry about, Felix, but a little worry might do *you* good. A steady diet of cigars and candy cannot be good for your health."

Felix laughed and pulled open the ashtray to rest his cigar. "Got to have my smokes and my sugar, or life's not worth living. Say, what do *you* do for fun?"

"Fun is not something that has ever concerned me. Fun is for children." Nellie leaned forward and peered over the top of the front seat. "Felix, put both hands on the wheel! Your car may be new and modern, but it won't drive itself."

Opal placed her hand gently on her mother's forearm. "Don't worry, Felix is a good driver."

"I'm not worried." Nellie clenched her teeth and pulled her arm away, adjusting her seating to be closer to the window. Felix began to whistle "Love Is Just Around the Corner." He flipped on the car radio and started adjusting the knob. "A little Bing Crosby, ladies?"

Has it come to this? Relegated to the backseat and forced to listen to a litany of love songs? Nellie steeled herself by staring out the window. She focused on the cliffs and dunes that towered above US 101 and fell into a reverie.

Leone had lived in a hut perched on a dune somewhere in California. Her granddaughter had come to see her a few months ago; just showed up one day in an old jalopy with another young woman. If there was anything to worry about beyond how she was likely to fare as a ward of the Wolff family, it was what was to become of Leone.

Nellie leaned her head against the car window, closed her eyes, and summoned Leone to her thoughts. The soft lips that used to turn up in her granddaughter's teasing smile now pulled down into a tight jaw. No amount of makeup could conceal the puffiness around her eyes. Girlhood was gone, but it was more than that.

Looking back, she had to admit that the last time she had seen her granddaughter, she should have chosen her words more carefully.

◦◦◦

"You look tired. Are you getting enough sleep?" An innocent remark, but Leone had looked like she'd been slapped. During Leone's visit, the girl seemed to take everything Nellie said as a criticism. *No wonder she didn't make it in Hollywood.* Not a charitable thought.

Leone had pulled her fingers through her closely cropped hair and forced a smile. "I don't sleep very well these days. I lay awake at night worrying. How will I ever find a place in this world? It was easy for you, Grandmother. You always knew what you wanted to do. The world opened its arms to you."

So that was it. Petulance had not been one of Nellie's character traits until age had got the better of her self-discipline. The response that had formed in her head, she did not voice. *How old are you? Twenty-four? I was close to forty before I saw an opportunity, and I had to walk over a perfectly good husband to take it.*

But the time for lectures was over. By the end of her visit, Leone had relaxed enough to give her grandmother a glimpse of her new life. To Nellie's way of thinking, her granddaughter appeared to be living in a ragtag community of poets, politicians, and polygamists, or whatever they called sexual adventurers. Passing hoboes, migrant farm workers, wandering mystics, and artists seeking each other's company drifted to a colony some rich man had formed.

"Famous people come to see us all the time." A bit of the sparkle returned to Leone's eyes.

"Like who?"

"Like Upton Sinclair, John Steinbeck, and Meher Baba."

"Humph. Sinclair and Steinbeck I know. Who is Baba? A baseball player?"

Leone did not choose to enlighten her grandmother. Instead, she repeated the history of the Dune community. "Gavin says that Moy Mell is a place where money means not much and ideas mean a great deal," she told her grandmother.

"Gavin Arthur, the grandson of former President Chester Alan Arthur? That's easy for him to say. He's got both."

"You've heard of him? Why do you say it that way, 'he's got both'"? Leone imitated Nellie's cynical tone.

"Money and ideas; he can afford to bandy words around. It's not an easy way to live when wild ideas are your *only* currency."

Now it was Leone's turn to seethe. Nellie regretted her remarks, but it was increasingly hard for her to bite her tongue. Who replaced Leone, the happy hoofer that went to Hollywood, with this changeling? What caused this strident young woman to spew angry words about a dizzying array of social and political issues? Where were her manners?"

Nellie expected that her granddaughter would stay several days, but Leone cut her visit short with an excuse that her friend Rosemary had set up job interviews for the two of them in San Francisco.

"I'm disappointed you can't stay longer. What sort of job?"

"Oh, something in a publishing house." Leone slipped into her coat.

"Well, you'll be near your mother. That's good."

"Hah, I hadn't thought of that."

When Nellie reached up to give Leone a hug goodbye, she felt the girl stiffen. It was true: Nellie rarely embraced members of her family. It wasn't how she was raised. Tears came to her more easily these days, and she let them fall.

"I love you," she whispered. The words felt foreign on her tongue, but they had an effect.

Leone's body relaxed into hers. One arm hugged now-stocky shoulders; one cheek rested briefly on the thinning hair atop Nellie's head. Smells of cigarettes and peppermint chewing gum and the lemony scent of Jean Naté invaded Nellie's nostrils. Her granddaughter's husky voice vibrated low in her ear. "Go live with Mother. I worry about you."

30

Ditched

San Francisco, 1935

Late one misty morning, Leone pushed through the swinging doors into the Black Cat Cafe at the edge of San Francisco's North Beach. Ten-year-old Jane followed.

"We can get some lunch in here." Leone bumped past the checkered, oil-cloth covered tables and headed for the bar. Jane coughed and reached into her coat pocket for a tissue to wipe her eyes.

"It stinks in here." Jane planted her feet on the barroom floor. "It smells like cigarettes. Mommy wouldn't like it if she knew you brought me here."

"She doesn't have to know, does she?" Tugging on the sleeve of the girl's wool coat, Leone coaxed her toward the bar. She slapped her hand on a barstool. "Up you go."

Jane placed her slim hands on the watermarked black counter, stepped her foot onto the stool rung, and hoisted herself up. Her hands rested flat on the bar for a moment. They stuck out of her navy blue coat sleeves like salamanders peeking out of a dark cave. She turned them over and inspected her palms.

"This counter is sticky." Jane unfolded a stray cocktail napkin sitting on the bar and began to wipe her hands. "Why did you bring me here?"

Always those accusing eyes. Leone shivered and dug around in the pocket of her loose trousers for a packet of Lucky Strikes. "You know Mother has asked me to keep an eye on you. She needs to find a place that will take your father."

"Is he going to die?" Jane lowered her eyes but turned her head slightly to hear the answer.

"What? Speak up. I can't hear you when you mumble like that."

Jane raised her head and repeated her question. Her solemn blue eyes shimmered, but she held her lips tight.

Leone set the cigarette package aside. She sat down on the barstool next to Jane and was quiet for a moment. Then she reached for her sister's hands.

Jane's small, cold hands lay limp and weightless between Leone's palms. Leone squeezed Jane's icy fingers between her own warm hands.

"I'm going to give you a straight answer. It isn't likely that your father will ever recover from his stroke. Mother can't continue to play nursemaid to your father and work swing shift in the cannery to make ends meet. A nursing home is the only answer."

Jane made no move to wipe away the tears that escaped her eyes and ran down her cheeks.

Leone raised two fingers and signaled the bartender. "Scotch, up please." She put a finger under Jane's trembling chin and lifted her face. "Think of it this way. At least you got some time with your father. I never even met my father."

The bartender put a rocks glass down in front of Leone and slipped a coaster underneath. He pointed at Jane.

Leone nodded. "Give her a Shirley Temple, Lou. Thanks."

Lou got busy behind the bar, pouring sticky red juice into a glass, pulling the soda, loading maraschino cherries onto a toothpick. "I'm glad that's not for me." Leone nodded toward Lou's ministrations. She turned to Jane. "I have no taste for sweet stuff."

Lou made a show of arranging Jane's drink on a napkin for her. "Who's the little lady?" Jane straightened her spine and shot the bartender a stony look.

"My sister. She's older than she looks." Leone turned to Jane. "You like tuna fish?"

Jane nodded.

Leone ordered a sandwich. "Take your coat off. You're going to be here awhile."

"No. I'm cold." Keeping a wary eye on Leone, Jane poked at the bubbles in her glass with a plastic mermaid swizzle stick.

Leone took a long pull on her drink and lit up a Lucky. "Felix was okay. I just hate to see what he's putting Mother through. I mean, she's got Grandmother to take care of now, and you. The two of you can't help her. She's stuck in that little house on the peninsula. They should have stayed in the city where there are hospitals and nursing homes close by." Leone finished off her scotch.

"Why don't you help her?"

The question hung in the air. Leone looked toward the door. "Because I have my own life. I help her by staying away."

Lou set a sandwich in front of Jane and swooped up Leone's empty glass. "Another?" He held up the glass. Leone looked at the door and nodded.

"You got it. Say, Leone, you found a job yet?"

"Aren't you having a sandwich?" Jane set the second half of her sandwich down and pushed the plate away.

Everybody's got questions. Leone downed her glass of courage and picked up the portfolio she had brought with her. "Not yet, Lou. I'm working on it." She turned to Jane. "I have to see a man about a job. He's an editor, and he's looking for an assistant. You can tell Mother about that. The job opportunity, I mean. Don't tell her I had to leave for a few minutes to meet … to go to an interview."

Two heads poked through the swinging doors. Rosemary hailed her to join them out on the sidewalk. Leone threw a few bills down on the bar. "Lou, I won't be long. Would you keep an eye on Jane for me? Give her a magazine to read."

Lou looked over at Jane. She shrugged. It wasn't the first time Leone had made bad on a promise. "Okay, but go sit at a table, kid. I can't have you sitting at the bar when people start coming in. "And you"—he jabbed a finger at Leone—"you behave yourself and don't make us have to come looking for you, you hear? Aw, go have fun. The kid can sit over there and do some people watching." He pointed to a small corner table with one chair that backed up to the wall. "Nobody will bother her. Okay with you, girlie?"

Jane pointed to her empty glass. "I'll have another." Without looking at Leone, she slid off the barstool and took her uneaten sandwich to the corner table.

Jane had not been able to help herself. One day it just slipped out, the story of how Leone left her at the Black Cat bar until the after-work crowd was well into its second martinis. After that, Leone did not see much of her half-sister.

Opal found a place that promised around-the-clock care for Felix in a home for the aged in San Francisco. The tiny but affordable vacation cottage they had purchased on the peninsula became home to Opal, Nellie, and Jane. It meant they couldn't visit Felix very often, but the bedroom community provided a safe environment for Jane and employment opportunities for Opal and Nellie. Nearby San Jose boasted the largest canning and dried-fruit packing center in the world. Nellie insisted there was no reason why she couldn't sit and cut cots along with the other women while Opal packed prunes. They got along.

31

Dogs

San Pedro, 1936

*W*hen jobs failed to materialize for Leone and Rosemary, they moved to Rosemary's hometown, the working class port of San Pedro in Los Angeles. One morning, the two women spread the weekend newspaper out on the kitchen table in their rented apartment. Rosemary clipped grocery coupons while Leone poured over the want ads.

"What kind of a job are you looking for?" Rosemary asked.

"I don't know." Leone dropped another sugar cube in the battered tin cup she drank her coffee from every morning.

Rosemary wrinkled her nose. "Are you sure you won't let me buy you a proper coffee mug?"

Leone shook her head.

"If it's the money, I could bring one home from the restaurant. They let us take dishware after it gets too scratched up to use with customers." Rosemary reached playfully for the cup. Leone batted her hand away.

"I've told you, no. It's my talisman." Leone put her hands around the cup as if it were a priceless treasure instead of a hobo's castoff."

"You're a funny one, Leone. I've never known anyone quite like you. So, what's the story with the cup?"

"No story. It just reminds me of something a hermit once told me. Whenever I'm tempted to think too much about myself, I look at this old cup. Empty as I feel, dented as look, I can still hold out hope."

"Now you're getting philosophical, but you still haven't answered my question. What kind of a job are you looking for?"

"At this point, anything. Are there any jobs at the diner? I could tend bar."

"I don't think that would be a very good idea, do you?"

"I suppose not." Leone thought about the shot of whiskey she had slipped into her morning brew and wished for another. "What about the pet store your parents own. Do they need any help?"

"As a matter of fact, they do." Rosemary brightened. "They just lost their dog groomer. Do you happen to know how to groom dogs?"

"Do I ever! There is not much about dogs I don't know. I grew up with dogs. Dogs love me."

"I'll go make a phone call."

It was as if someone handed her a hat and a rabbit jumped out of it. A week later, Leone stood behind the counter at Critter Cove Pet Shop, selling canned pet food and dog biscuits. "I can't believe this," she told Rosemary. "I get paid to play with dogs."

Pet food was in short supply. Wealthy people from Los Angeles found their way to one of the few pet shops that had managed to keep the doors open. A month after she started, Leone's work schedule was filled with grooming appointments. She was not above working her connections. Hollywood starlets sent their Silkies, Shih Tzus, and Yorkies out to Critter Cove where they could be sure no small paw would suffer the nick of a nail clipper.

A dog groomer. Leone never expected this would be her life's work, but it fit her. In some senses, she had stepped into her dream. When she wasn't working, she roamed the Palos Verdes beaches with her own Yorkies. Although the muse had largely left her—her novel lay uncompleted in a bottom drawer—she contributed opinion pieces to the local newspaper. Sometimes the ones she wrote when she wasn't drunk got published. Once, she submitted a poem to *Dog World*, and they published it.

Rosemary was her biggest fan. "You know, Leone, stay off the booze, and I bet you could get paid for what you write. You express yourself well."

"We all have our demons."

A similar conversation repeated itself often, and one day Rosemary took Leone on.

"We may all have our demons, but you don't have to be so cozy with yours, do you?" From lawn chairs where they sat in the backyard, they watched the dogs play in the grass. Leone had just poured her third scotch, in violation of her agreement with Rosemary.

"Ha," Leone answered, setting the glass aside for a moment. "It seems I lack the will to banish them, so I befriend them instead."

"You're being flip."

"I suppose."

The slurring wouldn't start until later in the evening after she'd finished the bottle. Then she would make phone calls she would regret and vows to stop, and she would, for awhile. She never told anyone about the demons' promises to fill the empty place with warmth and light. She knew it was a lie. There was no courage in the bottles she hid from Rosemary.

On her best days, Leone knew that magic was not an elixir. Magic was the joy she felt from the nuzzle of a dog, the peace of shared moments of domesticity—the first tomato from the garden, a taste of Rosemary's *bolo de bolacha*, coffee-soaked wafers layered with buttercream and tangy fruit compote. For these fleeting moments, she was grateful.

As the years passed, Rosemary would ask Leone why they spent all their holidays with her family. Why did they never visit Leone's family? "We will," she would answer, but they never did.

32

The Last Ride

Los Altos, 1939

When did Nellie's heart begin to fail? While Felix languished in a rest home, Nellie lay in her small twin bed in the back bedroom of the house, never quite sure whether her eyes were open or shut, or whose face loomed above her, whose voice murmured in her ear.

Eustace leaned in to kiss her. She was blind. No, no, those were John's thin, dry lips pressed to hers, his mustache a not unpleasant tickle under her nose. Tucked up under his arm, wearing a light cotton dress, her body warmed to his on the porch of the new house he had built for her in Kansas.

In the yard, Johnny stirred up dirt practicing his rope tricks. The girls played dolls on the wooden steps. Wood steps? No, that was the soddie. Never mind. Focus. There was Mabel, giving instructions to her cornhusk doll, and baby Opal gathering fistfuls of dirt, letting them fall from her hand and blow away in the wind.

Stone still, Nellie lay in her bed and let memories tumbleweed past. Steam whistled in the distance. When did her affection for home and hearth boil away? A copper kettle dragged across an iron burner; wheels clattered on rails; burnt coffee grounds prickled in her dry mouth. She thrust her tongue past her parted lips to receive the ministrations of soothing icy coolness amid snatches of conversation.

Look here; see the lines on the bullets and the casings. What was the question? What was the answer?

The scent of roses and the whisper of words; *we wanted you as a witness to our marriage.* Who stood under a bower of roses?

A hand on her back; a handsome lawman. *Did she?* Nellie's outstretched hand was taken up, fingers pressed rose petals into her palm and gently moved her hand toward her nose.

"Smell these, Mother. These are from the rose bush you and I planted last spring. It's a Harison's Yellow rose."

Nellie's eyes flickered. So seldom had she used her voice in the past few days she hardly recognized it as hers. "Tell me."

Opal sat on a chair by her mother's bed. "It's a vigorous, hardy rose, known for resilience and resistance to disease."

"Good stock"—Nellie squeezed Opal's hand— "like us."

"Yes, like us. It's also called the Oregon Trail Rose because the pioneers carried it west."

Her speech came easier now. "Did we have roses in Kansas?" Nellie blinked away tears that protested the bright sunlight shining through the window.

"I seem to recall that we did." Opal took a tissue from her pocket and dabbed at the corner of her mother's eyes. She stood up and walked to the window to lower the shade.

"I should have brought some root cuttings with me when we left Kansas." Nellie's arm fell to her side and the petals Opal had placed in her hand scattered onto the cream chenille bedspread. Real tears fell in earnest now. "Do you blame me for leaving your father?"

Opal took her mother's hand and placed it gently under the covers. "I missed Johnny very much."

"Your brother."

"Yes."

"But not your father?"

"Well, yes, but I didn't know him very well."

"I don't think I did either."

Nellie closed her eyes. Some minutes later, a ragged noise in her throat choked her. She struggled for breath, her eyes opened, and she tried to sit up. Opal pulled a pillow from the foot of the bed and helped her mother lean forward so she could fit it behind her. She held a glass of water to her mother's lips, but Nellie refused it.

"What will you do, Opal? With Leone on her own now, and Felix. He can't last much longer." Nellie coughed and wheezed with the effort of speech.

Opal put her finger to her lips. "Don't try to talk." She took a long, deep breath and raised her eyes to the partially shaded window. Outside, the morning glory vine stretched along the window ledge, its flowers tightly closed against the heat of the summer day. "Felix is in God's hands. I've made my peace with that. God has been good to me. I have Jane. We take care of each other. I have my students. I have my little house. My life is full of blessings."

A shadow passed across Nellie's face. In a spurt of energy, she wrestled her hands free from her covers and grabbed Opal's arm. "It isn't dying I'm afraid of, Opal. It's leaving you to fend for yourself."

Opal sat very still. She pulled her arm out of Nellie's grasp and placed her hand on her mother's forehead, smoothing a few thin strands of hair. "Mother, if there is one thing you taught me, it was how to fend for myself. Don't worry about me. Jane and I will be okay."

Nellie relaxed into her pillow. "And Leone?"

Opal slumped a little and then pulled herself up. "All I can do is pray that God is watching out for her."

Nellie closed her eyes and Opal slipped out of the room to get a vase for the roses. The room darkened. Stillness laid a hand on Nellie's chest and pushed her back into her pillows. She fought to hang onto her thoughts … Leone and Jane … Jane had been a twin. What had happened to that baby? Her name had been Jean. No. Helen, that was her name. Helen couldn't see either.

A honeyed smell filled the room; sweet like grass; sour like hay; musky like her Indian paint pony. Racing across the Kansas plain, her long dark hair whipped across her cheeks. Her legs wrapped around his belly, she urged her pony toward the horizon and drew her last breath.

PART 3

Christine

33

Discord

Los Altos, 1956

I t wasn't easy for Leone to talk Jane into letting her take ten-year-old Christine for the weekend. Jane sat stiffly beside her husband on a beige sofa in a beige living room and brought it all up again, the irresponsibility, the drunken midnight phone calls, the loan requests.

"I don't remember asking you for money."

"You did. You took money from our mother too." Jane's face was a stone.

"I'm sure I did not do that." Leone was getting nowhere. She would have to change her tactics. She looked over at Christine, who stood near the front door rising up and down on her toes in her effort to contain the energy that buzzed in her body. Leone could feel the child's excitement. She tried one more time.

"She's an antsy one, isn't she. I bet that gets on your nerves after awhile. You could use a break, couldn't you?"

In the hallway, Christine nodded her head vigorously. Jane glared at the girl and shook her head.

Leone attached another lure to her line. "And by the way, I'm not strapped for money. My business does quite well. I'll take her shopping for school clothes. You can give me a list."

It was not lost on Leone that her half-sister's husband had set her up nicely in one of the new tract homes the government helped veterans get into, but they appeared to have the basics, nothing more. She was willing to bet that Jane kept a tight rein on the purse strings.

"Mom, I want to visit with Aunt Leone." Christine slipped out of her shoes and stepped onto the carpet. Small feet in thin white socks tiptoed across the room to stand next to Leone, which did not please her mother.

"Why do you want to do this, Leone? You've never shown any interest in me or my family." Jane raised her chin and tightened her lips, erasing the natural prettiness of her face.

Be careful. You will freeze that way. It is the very same expression I saw on Grandmother's face the last time I saw her. The two of them are so like each other, stubborn and complicated.

"I like your daughter. She's got spunk. Tell you what. Let's scotch the idea of my taking her back on the train to San Pedro." *Poor choice of words.* "I'll spend a couple of more days at Mother's. It will be a *supervised* visit."

Christine knew better than to turn her pleading eyes toward her mother. Instead, she locked eyes with her father.

"Let her do it, Jane." He placed a hand on his wife's knee. "I can drive them over to your mother's, and if Christine decides she wants to come home later she can telephone us, and I'll go get her." He stood up and took a couple of steps toward a stain on the rug. Bending down, he rubbed his fingers into the fibers, pulled his fingers up to his nose and sniffed. "I think we need to shampoo this carpet, Mother. I'll take care of that when I get back."

He calls her "mother." How odd. I never really thought of Jane as motherly.

"Can I go pack a suitcase?" Christine asked in a small voice.

"Take one out of the closet." Her father sat down on the couch again. He took Jane's hand in his and rubbed it gently. "I'm going to go back the car out of the garage and check the oil. I might stop at the gas station after I drop them off." Another knee pat, a nod to Leone, and he escaped to the garage.

"Can I use your telephone to call my friend, so she knows she doesn't have to pick me up here at your house?" Leone was halfway to the desk phone when she turned around and faced Jane. "You have a nice home here. A nice husband. Nice children. Don't you think you could find it in your heart to forgive me for all the mistakes I made?"

Jane stood up. "Make your phone call, Leone. I have to make lunch for Carolyn. She'll be waking up from her nap soon."

"You're a lot like her, you know?"

"Carolyn?"

"Our grandmother. Nellie."

Jane turned red in the face. "I'm *nothing* like her. She was a mean, bitter woman."

"No, she wasn't. You didn't understand her. She had a sense of decorum, that's all."

"Yes, well, she liked you. She didn't like me. She thought I should never have been born. She tried to get my mother to do something about it."

"What are you saying?"

A commotion in the hallway cut off further conversation. Christine dragged her suitcase into view, her little sister tagging along behind her.

"That's the other one?" Leone pointed to red-nosed Carolyn, who was sick with a cold.

"You make it sound like I had a litter of puppies."

The two women glared at each other; then Leone burst out laughing. Jane's eyes brightened. Despite her best intentions, the corners of her mouth turned up. Leone shook her head slowly. "You are *just* like her. Wicked sense of humor. Neither one of you lets a person get by with anything."

Christine set her suitcase upright and sat on it. Carolyn hung back, eyeing Leone with suspicion.

"Go to the kitchen, Carolyn. I'll fix you some soup. How's your throat?"

Carolyn rolled big blue eyes from her mother to her aunt. "You don't look like sisters."

"We're half-sisters. Never mind that. It's time for your cough medicine."

Carolyn fell into a paroxysm of coughing. "I want the orange flavor cough syrup, not the cherry flavor."

Leone shooed them into the kitchen and made her phone call. Then she leaned on the kitchen doorframe, waiting until Jane looked up from the stove.

"Thank you for letting me come. And for letting me take Christine for the weekend."

Jane spooned a little of the chicken soup she was stirring to her lips and turned off the stove. "When are you going back to San Pedro?"

"Monday." A car engine revved in the driveway, choked, started up and settled into a rough idle.

Leone continued to stand in the doorway while Jane ladled soup into a bowl, then set it before Carolyn. They looked at each other: one blue-eyed, fair-skinned, and tense as a mouse; the other brown-eyed, weathered, and wary as a possum. It was Jane who broke the silence.

"I'm glad you came, Leone. I have a favor to ask you."

Leone pushed herself up from the doorframe. "What's that?"

"Would you please call or write to Mother more often? She worries about you."

"I will try to do that."

Two short blasts of a car horn moved Leone to the front door where Christine sat on her suitcase, jiggling her foot. When she saw Leone, she jumped up and shouted over her shoulder, "Bye, Mom." Leone picked up her suitcase and led the way out the door.

34

Disconnect

*O*pal lived alone in the cottage now. Earlier in the week, Leone had asked her how she was getting by.

"Social Security. Plus a small income from a few private dance students helps put food on the table."

"You're still teaching?"

"That surprises you?"

"I don't know. I figured that Jane would take care of you."

"Is that where you think the money I send you comes from? Jane?"

What to say? She could not recall a moment when she thought about it at all. She remembered nothing of the blackness that rolled over her, invited by too much booze and too many regrets. In her lucid periods, she attended only to those sensations that carried her from one moment to the next, the smell of a freshly shampooed pup, the featherweight feel of a shell picked off the beach, what else? So little satisfied. *It was a mistake to come here.*

Opal was still talking. "And a part-time job as a companion puts gas in the car; I don't need anything else."

"A companion?" Leone had never considered that her mother might have anyone in her life besides family and a few neighbors. "Who?"

"I make lunch for an old gentleman whose family needs someone to keep an eye on him. After lunch, we play cards and watch the early news on the television." Opal threw Leone a knowing look. "Then I go home."

"Sounds pretty chummy."

"Yes, well, he did ask me to marry him, but I suspect what he really wants is an unpaid nurse not a wife. Besides, I will never marry again."

"I should hope not. What are his kids worried about, anyway?"

"Sometimes he gets it in his head to pick up his shotgun, go outside, and shoot it down the gopher holes on the front lawn." Opal laughed. "If he should miss and shoot himself in the foot, my job is to notify the family."

They had a good laugh, and then Leone asked, "What does Jane think of this arrangement?"

"Oh she likes him. She has us both over on Christmas morning. He brings presents for the girls."

A familiar pain had flashed in Leone's chest. "How cozy." The words escaped before she could strangle her naked resentment. *I've never had an invitation to Jane's house. I had to invite myself.*

Today would be different. Today Leone walked into the cottage with Christine as a shield. Once inside, her husky baritone voice filled the room. "Mother? I've got Christine with me for the weekend." She shooed Christine. "Get busy with something for awhile. We'll go shopping a little later." Then she dropped the girl's suitcase in the living room.

Opal appeared in the kitchen doorway. "I bought you a couple of comic books and a Mars bar," she told Christine. Opal pointed to the kitchen table, where the groceries still sat in bags. Christine retrieved her goodies and started to pull out a chair, but Opal put a gentle hand on the girl's shoulder and guided her through the back door. Why don't you go out back for a little while? I'll call you when we are ready to go." Then she turned to Leone.

"Why did you bring her here?"

Leone pressed her lips together in puzzled bemusement and shook her head. "I thought you and Jane would like it if I showed an interest."

"Oh, Leone. Do you feel an interest?" Opal began to unpack her groceries and put them away.

"I feel like a drink. Do you have any beer?"

"No."

The back door squeaked open and nails clicked on the worn linoleum floor. "Scochie wants to come in." Christine's voice came through the door.

The door slammed shut, and a Chihuahua scuttled into view. Spotting a stranger in the kitchen, Scochie squatted on her haunches and peed. Leone dropped down to sit on her ankles and held out the back of her hand. The little dog trembled, sniffed the air, and inched forward on dancing feet. Leone crooned, and the dog swooned, rolling onto her back. Leone massaged the dog's tummy with gentle fingertips, causing the dog's eyes to roll back in her head and her leg to tic like the second hand on a clock when it gets stuck.

Opal handed Leone a paper towel to wipe up the mess the dog had made.

"Dogs like me." Leone blotted the puddle with the towel. Scochie jumped to her feet and shook her hindquarters in appreciation. "I don't know anything about kids. It was probably stupid of me to agree to take her."

"Jane asked you to take her?" Opal unwrapped the cold cuts and began to spread mayonnaise on slices of bread.

"The other kid is sick. This one is better off here, don't you think?"

"I love having her here."

Leone stood and watched Christine from the window. The girl sat on a swing seat, knees pressed together, head bent over a Betty and Veronica comic, pulling her fingers through her ponytail. "That's good," Leone said. "We'll have a nice visit. You can watch her tonight, okay?"

"Where are you going?"

"To the city. Can I borrow your car?"

"I'd really rather you didn't. Opal set a plate of sandwiches on the table and poured milk into three glasses. "Why didn't you drive your car up from the coast?"

Leone pulled in her chin and silently mouthed, *milk* Then she scowled. "My car is on the fritz. What is this, the third degree? Never mind. I can call a friend."

The screen door squealed again. "Is lunch ready yet? I'm hungry." Christine stayed out of sight.

"Come on in," Opal said. "Lunch is on the table."

So motherly. Without alcohol to dull annoyance, Leone fought the demon of discontent. The girl came in and sat down, pulling one leg up underneath her. She set about pulling her sandwich apart to inspect the cheese. Leone left her sandwich untouched. She stared at Christine, her mind clicking like a slide projector. An old slide dropped into view, her teenage self seated at the table with her grandmother, mother, and Jane. She searched the image for motherliness.

Sit up straight. Don't play with your food. Nellie's voice.

You never play with me. Jane's voice.

Where was her mother's voice? She struggled to hear it. Leone examined the faces that floated before her; a matriarch's displeasure, a mite's dissatisfaction, and between them, a mother's patient forbearance.

A soft feather of sound brushed past her ear. It took her back to her beach-combing childhood when she sought protection from buffeting winds by leaning against her mother's body. Not a soft body to pillow into, it was more like a strong gate you could swing on, a gate that never unhinged under your weight, never locked you out. But when her sister was born, she saw that the love that drew her in and spoke words of comfort was indiscriminate. Not special, not just for her, it was offered to all. She shut down her mental projector, picked up her plate and her milk glass, and took them to the sink.

"I'm sorry; I can't eat this." The plate clattered in the sink. Milk poured down the drain.

Opal looked up from where she sat next to Christine. "Can I fix you something else?"

"No, no. I'm just not hungry. I'm going outside for a smoke." Leone forced a smile. "When I come back in, let's play a game of canasta, shall we?" She patted Christine's head, and as she passed by, Opal reached for Leone's hand.

It had been years since she had allowed a touch from her mother. Inwardly, she recoiled, but she let Opal squeeze her hand. The warm flesh of her mother's palm was soft as butter, but the strength in the fingers that closed around hers was surprisingly powerful.

The grasp was firm, but not bruising; quick, but not abrupt. Opal dropped Leone's hand before she could pull away.

⸙

They played canasta at the kitchen table in this house that held no history for Leone. Being an uneven number of people, they drew and discarded and melded their cards individually. Christine had an irritating way of snickering when she was ahead. Anything but pokerfaced, she would knit her eyebrows together and purse her lips for long minutes before she laid down her cards and slapped the table with glee. As Opal gathered the cards to deal another round, Christine turned to Leone.

"Nana told me you used to be a dancer and a writer. Did you ever write a book?"

"That was a long time ago." Leone scraped her chair back from the table, stood up, and left the kitchen. In the bathroom, she leaned her head against the thin wall and listened to the muffled conversation taking place at the stove on the other side of the wall but inches from the toilet. A spoon clattered against an aluminum pan. Her mother was making hot chocolate. Christine must be standing at her elbow. A nonstop talker, that one. All those questions followed by a litany of noncommittal answers. "I don't know. I really can't say. You need to ask Leone about that."

When Leone returned to the kitchen, three cups of steamy hot chocolate sat on the table. While Opal sorted the cards for a new game, Christine pulled a stack of hard chocolate chip cookies out of a blue cellophane package and piled them on a plate like poker chips. Leone put a magazine she had tucked under her arm down in front of Christine, opened it, and tapped her finger on the masthead.

"This is the first issue of a magazine I helped bring out, *Dune Forum*."

Opal dealt the cards.

"Look here." Leone flipped over to the credits and pointed to her biographical note.

As Christine read, her eyes widened, then narrowed. "This was a long time ago. Did you really write a book?"

"I really did, but it was never published."

"What was it about?"

"Shall we start this round?" Opal scooted the card deck into view.

"Nothing a girl your age would understand."

Christine scrolled her finger down the table of contents and found Leone's name. Then she leafed through the magazine and found her aunt's poem, *Symphony of Water*. She read it out loud.

Opal gathered up the cards, put them away, and went to feed the dog.

"I don't understand this poem, Aunt Leone."

Leone shrugged.

Christine re-read a few lines out loud.

> *Knowledge breaks.*
> *We gather the things that we are.*
> *And we are tears, and we are dew,*
> *And we are rain, and we are sweat.*
> *We are every running river,*
> *We are every soaring sea.*
> *We belong, we belong ...*

"I get it! It's about not understanding. Like trying to understand who we are and where we come from, and why stuff happens to us."

Did I write those words? Leone stared out the window. Her eyes rested on a rose bush in full bloom. Something she couldn't see was making a commotion under the bush, causing the branches to shake and the blowsy yellow roses to drop their petals.

Christine babbled on. "In the poem, you ask the mother for comfort. You don't ask the father for anything. Why not?"

"What? Are they teaching psychoanalysis in grammar school?"

"What's that?"

"Never mind."

"We study poetry." Christine lost her smile. "I am good at it." Her eyes hardened briefly, in the way that a friendly dog who receives an unexpected slap turns feral and then catches itself before it snaps.

In retort, Leone recited another few lines from her poem.

"'It is the thing between. An asking and an answer. It is the shore …'" Some of us prefer to sit on the shore, Christine. We don't ask, and we have no answers.

"You never ask God for answers?" Christine seemed at the ready to supply the answers, but Leone stopped her.

"I have never asked God for anything, and He has kindly obliged me."

"Are you sure about that?" Opal spoke with quiet, heartfelt finality.

Leone's throat tightened. She supposed her words were sacrilege. She felt like a cattle rustler in a Western film, standing on the scaffold with a rope around her neck. Did she have any last words on the subject?

"I am fairly certain I have never asked God for help unless you count the times I swore at Jesus and asked Him to get Sister Isabel off my back. But you are right. I can't accuse Him of not trying to get my attention. He has tried. Several times. I guess I just don't have it in me to respond."

Something moved in the periphery of her vision. Foe or friend? Was it creeping toward her or darting away? Time to leave, now, before the floor fell away under her feet.

Leone reached over and pulled the magazine out from underneath the girl's scrutiny, but not roughly. She shoved it down into the overstuffed green canvas bag that stood on the floor. "I have to go change now." She looked at her watch, then held out her arm. "Look at the time, would you. My friend is picking me up in just a few minutes."

"So I guess we aren't going shopping." Christine's voice was steady, her words less a question than a statement of fact.

Opal dropped a hand down on the girl's shoulder. "It's getting late. We'll go tomorrow. You have time to go outside before dinner if you like."

"Yes, tomorrow." Leone shooed Christine away from the table. The girl walked to the back door and pulled open the screen. Her feet tripped slowly down the stairs. Before long, the rusty chain on the swing set began its complaint.

Leone hauled her canvas bag to the bedroom and reappeared moments later wearing high-waisted dungarees cuffed at the ankle and a green buffalo-plaid shirt, worn thin. She stood by the living room window, looking out to the street. "Hey." Her raised voice echoed. "How come you don't have any furniture in here?"

Opal came out of the kitchen and stood in the center of the room, her feet falling naturally into third position. Unaware of the habit, Leone was sure, her mother checked her posture in the mirror and straightened her shoulders.

Leone looked around the room as if seeing it for the first time; the mirrored wall, the bare floor, the ballet barre. Her eyes froze. She pressed her lips together, biting them between her teeth until the inside of her lower lip felt raw.

"I'm still working, Leone. We talked about this. This room is my dance studio. I have students during the week."

"That's right. You did say that. Still teaching the neighbor kids proper posture and social grace?"

"Dance steps go in and out of fashion, but people always have the need to present themselves well to others. After what we have all been through, this world could use a little grace, don't you think?"

"I suppose it could, but what do I know about grace? Once I danced in Hollywood and read my poetry in North Beach bars. Now I'm a dog groomer. I didn't tell that to Christine, but Jane knows. I'm sure she'll tell Christine first chance she gets."

Opal reached a hand out to touch Leone, but this time, Leone flinched and pulled back. Opal let her hand fall in a way as natural to her as closing a dance movement. Leone gave her mother a hard look, but somewhere, in the recesses of her mind, the beauty of the music that sustained her mother registered. The agony of knowing that beauty was so close and so unattainable to her made Leone desperate for a drink.

Opal spoke quietly. "It's an honorable profession, caring for animals. We've always loved dogs. Jane can't handle them now, but both you girls loved dogs."

"Jane can barely handle her girls."

Opal's dark eyes shimmered. "I do what I can to help her. Christine spends a lot of time here with me. It's good for both of us."

Leone turned her face away.

"I know you had dreams that didn't come true." Opal ignored the sound of a car engine that slowed to an idle by the mailbox. "But working with something you love, the way you do? That is no small accomplishment."

The car turned and pulled up in the driveway.

"Don't wait up. I'll be late."

"The door will be unlocked."

35

Passing Torches

*C*hristine propped herself against a pillow on her twin bed in the back bedroom. She finished a chapter in her library book and let it fall shut. Turning her head toward the other bed, she studied Leone's slouchy canvas bag that spilled out reading material, notebooks, and odd-looking clothes.

Why did Leone look so different? What did Nana mean when she said that Leone had lived a hard life? Dancing in Hollywood, living and writing at the beach, it all sounded fun, but Leone's eyes guarded secrets. Her eyes were dark, like Nana's, but the sadness was different.

Nana's eyes were like cups of warm cocoa. You knew sadness lay in lumps at the bottom, but as you drank, the lumps dissolved and added flavor. Was sadness like that? She thought about the sweet whipped cream Nana always spooned over her cocoa. The cream floated on top and melted slowly into the warm drink. It took the bitterness away.

Christine had heard about her grandmother's sorrow: two dead husbands, a dead baby, but there was some other kind of sadness. Even though Nana never complained, she must be sad that both her daughters were so ... angry.

A sudden thump jolted her from her thoughts. Sadie, the solidly built, black and white bobtail cat came out from underneath the bed and jumped up to settle at Christine's feet. Opal peeked her head in.

"Time to tuck you in and say your prayers?"

Christine yawned and set her library book aside on the night table.

"Is that for school?" Nana was always interested in her studies.

"No. I'm reading *Oliver Twist* for myself, but I can't keep my eyes open."

Opal sat down on the bed next to her granddaughter. Sadie opened one green eye, stretched out her front legs and showed her claws, and then tucked her paws under her chest. She rested her chin on Christine's outstretched legs and went back to sleep.

"Do you want me to review your Sunday school lesson with you?"

"Sure." Christine reached for the paper tucked inside the Bible that lay in the stack of books on the nightstand by her bed. Her library books traveled back and forth between her house and Nana's house, but her Bible and her comic books were treasures she kept here.

Opal glanced at the paper. "You haven't done much with this."

"I read it. I just haven't filled it out yet." Christine lay back on her pillow while Opal read through the lesson.

"Do you know what the root of evil is?" Opal asked her.

"I know that one. It's money."

"Is that the answer? I'm not sure that's true." Opal reached out and lifted up the tiny gold cross Christine wore around her neck. She worked it back and forth on its chain, then gently laid the cross back down on the child's chest, just above her heart.

"I think the root of evil is bitterness. If you have any of that in your heart, confess it when you say the Our Father. Are you ready to say your prayers?"

Christine nodded, but she wasn't quite ready. "What is bitterness?"

Opal thought a moment. "It is the sin of Cain."

"He's the one who killed his brother. So, wouldn't murder be the sin of Cain?"

"Murder was the result. Cain's sin was disappointing God and refusing to make amends. Instead, he let anger grow in his heart. That is bitterness."

"Oh." Christine closed her eyes and started to say the prayer her grandmother had helped her memorize. Before she made it to "Thy will be done," she was asleep.

In the early morning hours, the springs on the twin bed next to Christine's squeaked and groaned. Or it might have been a low, cursing moan that woke Christine, or the thud as the green canvas bag rolled off the bed, hit the floor, and spilled its contents. Christine opened her eyes a slit and peered into the dark. The moon dropped just enough light through the window for her to make out the shape of her aunt wrapped in the coverlet that lay on the bed. A soft breeze from the open window carried a sour smell past her nose. She rolled over, buried her nose in her pillow, and went back to sleep.

A few hours later, the smell of coffee and toast woke Christine. She rubbed the sandy sleep from her eyes and sat up. Underneath her thin pajama top, the one with pink French poodle and black Eiffel Tower patterns, she hunched her shoulders to keep warm. Rocking back and forth to wake herself up, she felt pressure in her bladder. It was too soon to put bare foot to cold floor, so she set her eyes on the face of Jesus printed on a prayer card stuck to the dresser mirror.

The card had a glow-in-the-dark cross she had wanted since she first spotted it in the gold offering plate that held Bible-themed prizes. Children who recited Bible verses from memory during children's church received awards. She liked the saying too: *Let the words of my mouth, and the meditation of my heart, be acceptable in thy sight, O LORD, my strength, and my redeemer.* She hated to memorize, but this verse had a nice rhythm. It was easy to learn.

The pressure became urgent. Christine threw off her covers and looked over to the other bed. It was made up. The neatly packed green canvas bag sat upright at the end of the bed. Christine hung her feet over the side of her bed and dangled them. Slowly she lowered one foot to the floor, then the other. She ran on tiptoes down the hall to the bathroom.

"Christine, your toast is ready. Your oatmeal will be done in a minute." Opal's voice was as clear through the wall as if she had been standing right beside the toilet. Christine knocked on the wall in response. While she sat, she leaned over and put her ear to the wall. A metal spoon circling inside an aluminum pot kept rhythm with the measured tones of conversation.

"I've ordered a taxi," she heard Leone say. "It should be here in an hour."

The stirring stopped. "But …"

"But listen, can you do me a favor? Take Christine shopping today. Buy her a dress. Tell Jane I bought the dress. I will send you the money for it."

"You can't give me the money for it now?"

"No. I didn't plan on having to take a taxi to the bus station."

"You don't have to, you know. Why do you feel you have to leave today?"

"I just do."

"I could drive you to the station."

"It's okay. I've already made arrangements."

Christine flushed, and the conversation stopped. A few moments later, she padded into the kitchen in the puffy slippers she had found under the bed. Nana would have sent her back to get them if she had shown up barefooted. Leone sat at the far end of the table, drinking coffee. Christine slid into her chair, and Nana slipped a plate of her favorite cinnamon toast in front of her. Generous sprinkles of sugar and cinnamon melted into warm butter spread on toasted white bread. Christine bent over and inhaled the sweet spiciness.

"*Mmmmmm*." She looked up at Leone. "Do you like cinnamon toast?"

"Never had it." Leone began to push herself away from the table.

"Pshaw, I made it for you all the time," Nana said.

"I don't remember."

"Aren't you going to finish your coffee?" An edge of pleading embroidered Christine's voice. "Because I have something for you." She jumped up from the table and ran into the bedroom. When she returned, Leone picked up her coffee cup and set it in the sink. Opal retrieved the cup, emptied it's cooling contents into the drain, and added it to the soapy dishwater she had prepared.

"Always making me look bad," Leone half-joked.

Christine thrust a piece of ruled paper into her aunt's hand. "Here. I wrote you a poem."

"You write poetry?"

"Some of my poetry has been published in the newspaper." Christine rocked back and forth on her feet.

"Your school newspaper?" Leone set the paper down on the table and folded her arms across her chest.

"No, the *Times*; the one that gets delivered in the afternoon. It's not as important as the one that comes in the morning." Christine sat back down at the table and shoveled a spoonful of oatmeal into her mouth.

Leone picked up the paper and looked at the poem. "Is this one of the poems that got published?"

"No. I wrote this one last night."

"The Bay City," Leone read the poem aloud. "Why did you write a poem about San Francisco for me?"

"Because you like that city, and I do too."

"This isn't bad. You should send it to the paper."

She shook her head. "No. This one is for you." She pushed her half-eaten oatmeal aside and began to trace the ivy vine pattern in the tablecloth with her finger.

"Well, I have something for you too." Leone went to the bedroom and returned with her bag and a folded sheaf of yellowed legal-sized papers held together by rusty paperclips. Opal looked over from where she was washing dishes in the sink.

"I wondered where those went. How long have you had my mother's stories?"

Leone didn't answer. She unfolded the papers and laid them on the table in front of Christine, "Look at these."

Opal wiped her hands on her apron and walked over to the table to stand behind Christine. Peering over the girl's shoulder, she clucked her tongue. "I'll be. I haven't seen those stories since we all left Oregon."

"These are stories your great-grandmother Nellie Belle wrote about her life," Leone told Christine. "You keep them, and someday when you are a famous author, you put Nellie Belle Scott's stories in one of your books."

Two short honks on a taxicab horn saved Christine from having to say anything. Leone folded Christine's poem and put it in her pocket, picked up her bag, and walked briskly to the front door. Opal followed but stopped in the kitchen doorway. Christine joined her grandmother, who drew her close. Together, they waited for Leone to say something.

Leone pulled open the door and fumbled with the latch on the screen. Just before she disappeared down the steps, she turned around and flashed a big smile, her audience smile. "Bye, you two."

Opal walked to the front doorway and looked through the screen at Leone's back. "Will we see you again?" she asked.

"Of course," came the response from the bottom of the steps.

Back in the kitchen, Christine wrestled the window up far enough to where she could stick her head out. She strained to catch a glimpse of her aunt's face as the taxi backed out of the driveway, but Leone wasn't looking their way. When the taxi turned into the street, she thought she saw a hand wave, but she couldn't be sure.

36

Last Call

Los Altos, 1962

Sometimes the telephone rang in the middle of the night. Christine would hear her mother's slippered feet shuffle down the hall and the receiver click as it was lifted from the desk phone. "Hello. Yes, what is it?" Then, long silences broken by low monotone answers. Always, her mother would be snappish the next day.

Her father put a stop to it. One night, the mattress creaked a second time in her parents' room. The floor groaned as he passed Christine's bedroom door, down the hallway to the living room. There she imagined her mother hunched over the desk telephone, wrapped in her chenille robe, shivering against the cold. Then, her father's voice on the phone, the receiver settled back onto its base, feet in the hallway, a door scrape against the frame, muffled voices, quiet.

Early in the morning, her bedroom door opened and light from the hallway illuminated the foot of her bed. She was awake anyway, staring up at the ceiling. She sat up in bed. "Was it Leone?"

Her father pulled the door half shut and sat down on the edge of her bed. "Yes."

"You didn't hang up on her, did you?"

"No."

"Well then, what did you say to her?"

He was quiet for a moment. Through the high window, the last of the moonlight transferred its reflection to her father's tired face. Even with the dark stubble of a night's beard growth and sleep-

243

mussed hair sticking out from the sides of his head, he looked like someone she could always count on to tell her the truth.

"I told her she was upsetting your mother and not to call here anymore."

"But …"

"No *but.*" He stood up and walked to the door. Christine sniffed air into her lungs and held her breath. When he reached the doorway, he turned back to face her.

"You have to understand. When Leone calls in the middle of the night like she does, it's because she's drunk. There's nothing we can do for her. It upsets your mother, and I can't have that."

Christine let out the breath she was holding and fell back on her pillow.

"Can you get back to sleep?" he asked.

"I'll try."

After he had pulled the door closed, Christine folded her hands behind her head. She tried to picture Leone at the end of the telephone line. Did she prop herself up in a barroom phone booth? Or sit on a sofa in a lonely room surrounded by empty bottles? What did she want to say at three in the morning that she could not say at any other time? To keep the peace, Christine would have to obey her father. *There is nothing we can do for her*, he had said, but it was his departing words that chilled her.

"We will speak of her no more."

EPILOGUE

*C*hristine looked out over the audience and took a centering breath before hitting the button on her remote to bring up her first slide. Each audience was different. Younger people had to be convinced that genealogical research was worth the long hours, the detours, and the dead ends they would encounter. Older people needed to be encouraged that it was not too late to tackle such a daunting project. Her job was to paint a vision of life both temporal and timeless. Hardest of all, both groups needed to learn to use their imaginations.

She always watched for the moment when the energy dropped in the room. Then she would depart from the data projected on the screen. The statistics would remain on the screen for a time, and then go dark. She would close her computer and open up her life.

"Some people live forever in the hearts of those who loved them. Others live in the imaginations of those who barely knew them. To tell a good story, you must depart from data. Recall what you learned from the cautionary tales your family told around the dinner table. Study your ancestor's photos, puzzle over scrapbook clippings. The black sheep in your family fold have stories to tell."

The inevitable question would come during Q&A. "Is the story you told in your book true?" Christine always gave the same answer, even though it rarely satisfied.

"Every family story is a fiction. Some parts are fact, but what we don't know, we make up. It's living history. As you interpret what you see and reenact what you've heard, your story gains some and loses some. That's what makes it worth revisiting."

Then she would pull an old scrapbook out of a green canvas bag, set a letterbox on the table in front of her, unfold yellowed sheets of legal paper covered with faded, typewritten copy, and tell her stories.

Author's Note

The Trials of Nellie Belle is a fictional story based on events in the lives of my great-grandmother, Nellie Belle Scott, and my aunt, Leone Barry. What I know about these events, I learned through conversation around the family dinner table, photographs, preserved writing, and research. I have used the real names of most of the historical characters, with some alterations.

Because family stories that pass down through generations are notoriously unreliable, it is safe to say that much of this story is pure conjecture. I believe the stories that Nellie wrote for her creative writing class derive from her courtroom experiences, but how much is true and how much is embellishment I have no way of knowing.

About the Author

Sydney Avey has a bachelor's degree in English from the University of California, Berkeley, and a lifetime of experience writing news for non-profits and corporations.

Other titles by Sydney Avey include *The Sheep Walker's Daughter* and *The Lyre and the Lambs*. Her poetry, short stories, and articles have appeared in *Foliate Oak*, *Forge*, *American Athenaeum*, *Unstrung*, *Blue Guitar Magazine*, *Ruminate*, and *MTL Magazine*. She has participated in the Iowa Summer Writing Festival as well as many other conferences and seminars. She is a choral singer and enjoys travel, theater, and spending time with family and friends.

Sydney and her airplane enthusiast husband divide their time between the Sierra Nevada foothills of Yosemite, California, and the Sonoran Desert in Arizona.

Follow Sydney online:
SydneyAvey@Gmail.com
www.SydneyAvey.com
Facebook.com/YosemiteSyd
Pinterest.com/yosemitesyd/
Twitter: @SydneyAvey

Resources

South County Historical Society, San Luis Obispo Counnty, CA. Copies of *Dune Forum* may be read online at: http://www.southcountyhistory.org/duneforum.htm

Linda Austin and Norm Hammond, *Images of America, Oceano*, Arcadia Publishing, Charleston, South Carolina, 2010.

Ella Thorpe Ellis, *Dune Child*, El León Literary Arts, Berkeley, California, 2011

Luther Whitman, T*he Face of the Clam*, South County Historical Society, Inc. 2010

Other Books by Sydney Avey

The Sheep Walker's Daughter pairs a colorful immigrant history of loss, survival, and tough choices with one woman's search for spiritual identity and personal fulfillment. Dee's journey will take her through the Northern and Central California valleys of the 1950s and reach across the world to the obscure Basque region of Spain. She will begin to discover who she is and why family history matters.

A Korean War widow's difficult mother dies before revealing the identity of her daughter's father and his cultural heritage. As Dee sorts through what little her mother left, she unearths puzzling clues that raise more questions: Why did Leora send money every month to the Basque Relief Agency? Why is her own daughter so secretive about her soon-to-be published book? And what does an Anglican priest know that he isn't telling? All this head-spinning breaks a long, dry period in Dee's life. She might just as well lose her job and see where the counsel of her new spiritual advisor and the attentions of an enigmatic ex-coworker lead her.

The Lyre and the Lambs explores the passions that draw people together and the faith it takes overcome trauma.

It's the '60s. Modernity and tradition clash as two newlywed couples set up house together. Dee and her daughter Valerie move with their husbands into a modern glass house Valerie built in a proudly rural Los Altos, California, neighborhood. When their young relatives start showing up and moving in, the neighbors get suspicious. Then a body is found in the backyard and the life they are trying to build comes undone.

Father Mike is back to guide Dee through a difficult time with humor and grace, even as his own life is unraveling. Now he's going to have to take some of his own advice about love.